The Vault Of Echoes

Self-Published by Rodrigo Fernandez Ayala
ISBN: 9781069140401

Cover design by Rodrigo Fernandez Ayala

First Edition: January 2025

Printed in Canada

For more information, visit www.rodrigokhervfx.com

The Vault of Echoes

Roy F. Ayala

Contents

Day Three:

The Fourth Dream

Day Four:

The First Dream

Erydis Nott opened her eyes, but she did not feel awake. Her surroundings seemed real, yet also like something out of a strange dream.

Towering white dunes enclosed her as a dark, starless night spread beyond the hazy horizon, and all around her were faint echoes of an unknown origin. It was a strange place to be in. From time to time, she was sure there were people passing closely by her, but they were nothing but ghostly shadows. They moved around her as if she was invisible.

A giggle echoed in the air. Erydis did not know where it came from, but she was sure of one thing. Someone was looking at her. She could sense it.

Erydis ignored the feeling of being observed. After all, this was a peaceful place. She felt protected here. Removed from judgment, from her disappointments, and from memories she would rather forget. It was as if this dream had been created just for her. And she welcomed it.

Erydis got up slowly and began to walk. As she dragged her boots across the sand, she saw a lone tree in the distance. Its leafless black trunk was curved towards one side, almost as if it felt tired. But what was even more curious was the clock attached to its bark; a round clock made of blue metal, with five numbers encircling its perimeter.

Suddenly, the single hand of the clock moved to the number one, and the clear note of a bell rang out clearly, startling Erydis. As she stared at the clock, she wondered what it could mean.

Clocks tell time, but this one was different—it was marking something else. Maybe something she'd been expecting. Something that could mean the beginning of her biggest challenge yet. Perhaps another chance to prove herself during the Five Festivals of the Dust, the most anticipated event in Dust City.

Day One

Chapter I

Dust City

Erydis

Erydis opened her eyes once more. A mix of emotions washed over her as she focused on the crack in her bedroom ceiling. She wished to go back to that mysterious place in her dreams to analyse the clock and its meaning. But she also felt a thrill of anticipation. That evening would kick off The Five Festivals of the Dust with the Inauguration Festival.

As usual, her bed was covered with a mound of clothes. The floor and desk overflowed with piles of notes and books amid clay jars, filled either with water or coloured dust, scattered in every corner of the room. Her room was a sanctuary, a place for her to rest after a long day of work at the market and to study the science of dust mixing.

Her dust mixing was evident from the markings on her desk; its mahogany surface covered in coloured spots. Her notes were filled with comments on ingredients and formulas, and assorted glass apparatus were strewn everywhere. And there in the middle, concealed by a cloth, was her current experiment. An experiment she would reveal to no one until it was ready.

She grabbed some of the nearest clothes from the mound on top of her, paying no particular attention as she got dressed. She walked over to the nearest jar of water and started cleaning her face with a wet rag, pushing her mess of wavy, black hair out of the way. *The dark circles under my eyes are lighter this morning*, she mused as she studied her dark eyes in the frameless mirror. That was surprising, since she had gone to bed way past midnight to finish a section of her experiment in time. She studied her clothes in the hazy reflection. She was wearing an oversized, dark violet tunic that almost looked like a dress, and her favourite purple trousers. Maybe not what an ordinary fifteen year old girl would typically wear in Dust City.

Erydis suddenly remembered the clock from her dream. The five numbers could be a reminder of the upcoming days of the festival. Each day counted if she wanted to get her experiment exactly right. She needed to hurry if she wanted to achieve her goals in time. The idea filled her with excitement, yet it was also terrifying to think she could fail somehow.

Pulling on her boots, Erydis grabbed her leather pouch and drew open the curtain covering the entrance to her home, which sat at the top of an old building only a few floors high. The rays of dawn brightened the city below her as it stirred to life. Traders and merchants had started their day earlier than usual in preparation for the festivals. The thought brought a smile to Erydis's face.

She took a deep breath of the fresh morning air and gazed at the city she knew so well. A fortress of a wall surrounded the city, enclosing buildings of many sizes among a maze of streets. In the centre was the second level, a section of the city elevated above the first by giant pillars of stone. This was also called the Palace District. In the middle of everything was a single tower with flat walls that rose higher than any other building in the city: Valerios's Tower. It had been built on the first floor in ancient times, but after several decades, the second floor was built around it because people with pockets full of money felt they were above the rest—or at least, that's how Erydis saw it.

As she climbed down the wooden ladder that led from her home to the narrow streets below, she thought about the upcoming festivities. The celebration grew larger and grander with each passing year, and she'd heard whispers that this year would be the biggest festival yet.

The Dust Ring was the biggest and busiest street in the city, forming a perfect circle on the first floor around the Tower. Erydis found the Dust Ring's energy infectious. It was filled with merchants peddling their wares, their carriages parked all over. Royal soldiers rushed around chasing pick-pockets while students and teachers hurried to the academy, idolising the dust mixers as they passed by.

Erydis entered the Sandstone Barrio, one of the five districts of the city, named for its famous sand-coloured buildings. She headed for the Dust Bazaar, and it wasn't long before she was surrounded by colourful tents covering the streets. Most of the merchants were still erecting their tents, but they were all ready for the festival season and all its jubilant customers.

Many of the wares caught Erydis's eye, but it was the dust she was the most attracted to, as well as all the ingredients needed for dust mixing. Those were the most in-demand products in the entire city and the reason she was there.

Every merchant had different strategies to attract customers. A merchant close to Erydis hawked his products loudly while a lady tried to attract customers by burning herbs, the pleasant scents wafting into the market. Another lady, who was selling dust-powered lamps, hung them in her tent, where they caught and reflected the early sunlight. Meanwhile, a young man would get up close to customers and nudge them towards his tent.

Erydis was well-known at the bazaar. Some merchants would wave at her with a smile or try to trade with her. But there were some who would look at her with distrust or even with anger. She knew why. Sometimes she was too good at bargaining and would trade the cheapest dust for more valuable products, catching the traders unawares. And there were merchants who still remembered her as a thief. At least she had stopped doing that… mostly. Sometimes she would steal small items from dealers who were rude to her.

One of the famous dust stores in the city was the Dusty Corner, where Erydis had started working when she turned over a new leaf. Usually, the tent would already be upright and ready by the time she arrived, but that day she was earlier than usual. A young worker and the owner were moving around some crates and jars, setting up for the day's business. The owner's name was Trinos Kontos. He was a man in his forties who always wore a set of expensive yellow robes and a yellow turban. Trinos had a brown beard so dense it looked like wool covering his mouth—a mouth usually turned down on account of his perpetual bad temper.

"Erydis!" Trinos yelled as he lifted a wooden pillar to prop up the tent. "What are you doing over there? Help Isaac lift the tent!"

Isaac Drokka, Trinos's right-hand helper, stared out from under his hair with his signature laid-back gaze and a smile. He waved at Erydis and went back to work. He didn't say much most of the time.

"Sorry, Trinos, I don't work today, remember?" Erydis said as she knelt down next to him and started digging around in-between some crates.

"What are you doing here then?" He turned to look at her from between his merchandise. "Get out of there! Who gave you permission to–"

"I gave her permission, dear."

A tall woman approached, placing a crate next to Erydis carefully. She wore a dress as expensive as Trinos's robes, which hugged her shapely body. Her hair was straight under a rectangular headdress, and under her sharp nose, she had thin, painted lips that formed a striking contrast to her dark-gold skin.

"Oh, did you?" Trinos's expression changed. Now he looked like a smiling child as the woman planted a small kiss on his cheek.

"Thank you for taming your beast, Kitri. He wanted me to work today!" Erydis said.

Kitri gazed at Trinos with her serene smile. He looked guilty, as if he expected a lecture.

"Erydis and I have an agreement," Kitri said. "She takes some of our dust to Kemia in exchange for mixtures that we can sell."

"Kemia?!" Trinos narrowed his eyes at Erydis. "I don't trust you and that crazy old hag. What are you up to now? If I find out you did something illegal again, I'll fire you."

Erydis took some bags of dust from the crates, slipped them into her pouch, and turned to Trinos.

"What I'm up to is a secret, Trinos. Besides, we both know that you'll never want to get rid of me! Who helped you get the best mixtures in the city? Who helped you buy those fancy robes you wear?" Erydis winked.

"You are right, but I'd better see you this early tomorrow! It's the busiest day at the bazaar, and if you're not here when it starts..."

Kitri hugged Trinos from behind, calming him successfully. Such a special couple, Erydis thought.

"We'll see you tomorrow, Erydis," Kitri said kindly. "Send my greetings to Kemia."

Erydis nodded and darted off. Despite all her trouble with Trinos, she still appreciated the couple. They had given her a job when she most needed it, and they were good to people most of the time. Not like Sikaal Fumus, the old, hairless owner of Famous Smoke Candies next door, who would yell at beggars when they got close to his store. It was for that exact reason that Erydis would steal some of his spherical candies each time she passed by—like at that exact moment.

She had promised to meet Kemia at the Geberus Dust Academy before midday. Unfortunately, she wasn't allowed to go inside anymore; not that it ever stopped her. But this meant that Erydis had to seek a less conventional route through the city's second floor.

There were two ways to get to the second floor: up the grand stairs in the Marble Barrio to the south or by taking one of the city's three funiculars, which cost a few Imperial coins per ride. Erydis decided to take the funicular closest to her at Sandstone Station–but for free.

The beige walls and ceilings of Sandstone Station were covered in beautiful carvings currently hidden by the busy rush of people trying to get in, hauling their carriages and crates behind them. At the entrance, a man with a tangled moustache and a tan uniform scrambled to collect Imperials from passengers. Soon, a funicular only slightly larger than Erydis's bedroom arrived. The machinery that moved it was powered by the combustion of dust, expelling a thick, red cloud from its chimney. Erydis saw her opportunity.

She scaled one of the station's rough pillars and slid in through a window just next to the roof of the funicular. Hiding in the red cloud, she jumped on top of the vehicle, hoping the conductor wouldn't hear the noise, and lay down. But she was not alone–some beggar children had already beaten her to the top.

"Driving up! Hold on!" barked the conductor, who apparently hadn't heard the noise above him, or he would have surely given them an earful. The funicular's wheels rotated faster and faster as it climbed on a crimson steel railing forged from red dust.

As the funicular ascended diagonally out of Sandstone Station, Erydis sat up and got settled on the top corner of the vehicle. She enjoyed the ride up every time. She could see the Sandstone Barrio moving further and further away as the sun rose above the heavily guarded fortress that protected the city from the outside world. On her right, the funicular passed the colossal pillars that supported the second floor. Under it was another section of the city, one that Erydis feared. Not because it was where the city's thieves gathered, but because of someone she desperately wanted to forget. There, under the second floor of the city, was the Hidden Barrio.

Erydis was jolted from her thoughts as the children next to her suddenly laughed together loudly. They were eating smoke candies like the ones she had in her pouch. She took one out of her pocket and studied its spherical, hollow form. The candies were meant for adults, but no adult was watching the top of the funicular. Erydis wondered why the children liked them so much. She placed the candy gingerly in her mouth and bit through it. As it broke open, a very pungent, green smoke came out through her mouth and nose. She could taste lime and honey just before she started coughing uncontrollably. This was only the third time she had tried the candy, and the results were no different.

The children next to her started laughing at her. "I don't see what's so funny," Erydis said as she breathed in deeply. They had almost arrived at the second floor of the city.

The upper floor station was getting closer, and Erydis and the beggar children prepared to jump. They leapt across just as the silver railings bordering the second floor appeared, right before the funicular entered the station. Erydis scurried away before anyone could notice her.

Something about the Palace District made Erydis feel uncomfortable. The streets were well-organised, always clean, and adorned with beautiful patterns. Every building was perfectly crafted. People with the most exclusive robes and dresses walked with wide smiles as vehicles powered by dust-combustion engines spewed amber clouds. Why weren't other neighbourhoods like this one?

Erydis ignored it all as she looked up at the gigantic tower. Regardless of how many times she saw it, it remained impressive with its dark-grey walls as thick as a big street in the city. The walls were mostly smooth and polished, with some circular windows through which multi-coloured clouds of dust escaped. The only entrance to Valerios's Tower was through the palace.

Erydis dreamed of one day working inside the Tower. Only the best dust mixers in the city had that privilege, along with the strongest soldiers protecting them. It was said that the technology inside was beyond belief. She would have given anything to go there, but all she had at this point was an incomplete experiment. Someday, she thought.

Her daydream was interrupted by soldiers marching by. They wore coats of mail under their uniform robes. Most of them held a long, curved knife and a small bow, but they would hardly ever use them. They were looking for "random" pouches in search of contraband. She knew all too well that they would always target people with the cheapest outfits, so she slipped into the crowd, slinking away with the illegal items safely hidden in her pouch.

Erydis stopped and looked around. She saw a lady in very expensive robes who was holding hands with a little boy. Erydis waited for the mother to get distracted by a handsome banker passing by next to her and gently took the boy's other hand, pretending to be the boy's sister. The boy was startled, but before he could turn back to his mother, Erydis gave him a small, blue caramel wrapped in paper. He grabbed it with a grin, placed it in his robes, and held onto Erydis's hand. She smiled, her mission accomplished. She now walked the streets without arousing the suspicion of the soldiers nearby.

But she had covered only a few steps when someone yanked at her free hand. Alarmed, she released her grip on the boy. She had been caught.

"Why are you trying to hide?" a familiar voice asked.

A slim young adult soldier was frowning at Erydis with concerned, blue eyes. He was ten years her senior, with thick, golden hair and tanned skin. He wore grey robes and a black coat of mail with the city crest on his chest: A black triangle inside a white circle–the flag of Dust City and its Tower. His expression, as always, was worried as he stroked his short beard.

"Ah, Thylac! You scared me for a moment," Erydis said, relieved, brushing dust off her baggy tunic.

"Erydis, I know you were hiding something, or you wouldn't be avoiding the soldiers like that. Is it really worth it?"

"Did you get promoted?" Erydis asked, trying to change the subject.

Thylac stared at her for a few seconds and straightened his posture, resting a hand on the handle of his elegant sword.

"I did," he said proudly. "I'm going to be part of Emperor Engyl's elite forces, starting with the Inauguration Festival."

"Oh, I'm happy for you! Searching peoples' pockets all day was worth it after all."

He stared at her in silence.

"I mean it; you finally made it," she said more sincerely.

"Well, I missed some suspicious pockets at times," he said, staring at her pouch. "But we have bigger problems than just children pickpocketing for food, I'll admit."

"Is something wrong?" Erydis asked. "I've seen a lot of activity from the army lately. Many scouting to the outside and not a word from the Emperor."

"I thought you didn't care about the Emperor's doings."

"As long as he doesn't hide behind his lies."

"Well, sometimes we don't want to spread any panic," Thylac said, tiredly rubbing his temple with his fingers. "Can you at least tell me what you have in your pouch?"

"Just some dust bags and smoke candies for Kemia. Do you want a candy? I have a red one, a green one…"

"Erydis! Those are for adults only."

"I know you like the purple ones."

"And what kind of dust do you have?"

"Blue, green, white…"

"Black?" he asked, more serious this time.

"Just a little."

"Do you ever listen to me?" Thylac gave her an exasperated look and Erydis shrugged. "Tell Kemia to buy her own candies and to stop using so much black dust for her experiments. Why are you spending so much time with her?"

"Because she's the best dust mixer I know, and even you can't deny that."

"I guess I can't, but please be careful with her." He raised an eyebrow.

Thylac was almost like a brother to Erydis, but sometimes she wished he would relax.

"Thylac, should I be worried about what the soldiers are getting up to outside the city?"

Thylac glanced around him furtively and gently pushed Erydis to a more discreet corner of the street.

"You can't tell anyone. Can you promise me that?" he asked seriously.

"I can try."

Thylac looked at her, unimpressed.

Erydis sighed. "You know I won't say anything."

"It's about the outsiders. There's been a conflict."

"Is it true? I thought the fortress had made them surrender and cross the boundary?"

"That is indeed what happened, but not long ago, we started battling them again."

"I know, but I thought they stopped coming after their last defeat?"

"That's what we thought yes, until some weeks ago, when a soldier found some of their tracks close to the fortress."

"Why would they be walking around the fortress?"

"That's what we're wondering too." Thylac stepped closer to her. "This morning, there was an explosion somewhere in the west of the city, a few kilometres from here. We sent troops to investigate."

Erydis stared at him with her mouth hanging open.

"You shouldn't worry though; we have it under control," he said.

"Worry? Are you joking? This is the most exciting thing that has happened in a while!"

"Erydis, many have been hurt in this useless war. This is not entertainment."

"I know, I'm sorry."

Of course Erydis didn't want people to get hurt, but she had to admit that news like this changed things inside the city she was so used to. Even so, it was definitely not as exciting as her dream with the clock or the possibility of one day working inside Valerios's Tower as a dust mixer.

"Very well, off you go," Thylac said. "I'll pretend I didn't see you. Just please make sure not to carry those things around here."

Erydis nodded and hurried to her next destination, the Dust Academy.

Chapter II

Jerboa Clan

Rapach

Dear Members of the Jerboa Clan,

I understand you are quite gentle people. I recognise the many dangers of these lands and acknowledge the difficult tasks that you may encounter. But if you happen to read this letter, my efforts will not be in vain.

The motive of my letter is to discuss the restless elderly man who is always walking by the bank of the polluted river. Many of us, the lucky ones, have heard the melancholy tune he plays as he searches endlessly for something next to the water. Many presume that this man has lost his sanity. Whatever he's looking for must be gone now, they say.

Nonetheless, I believe I have found what he is looking for. You see, I live next to Rabaska Lake in the southwest territory. On a day of low tide, I chanced upon this curious object, and I can only imagine that it belongs to this man. I admit it seems too ordinary to have any value, but it is also far too peculiar to be considered garbage.

I've placed it inside a package, and I'm hoping that you can deliver it to the elderly man. I believe the object has some kind of sentimental value, and I do not want to simply leave it in one of your mailboxes. I distrust those who roam these lands silently. I am sure you understand whom I refer to.

I understand that you have many other messages and packages you must deliver, possibly more urgent than this one. But if you happen to find the time, I'll be waiting at Rabaska Lake with the package and a map with the elderly man's last location. If you would consider a humble stranger's opinion, I believe the man has spent so much of his life searching for this package that it must be of significant importance.

I take this opportunity to thank you for all your valiant efforts journeying across these doomed lands and wish you luck. I know you put your lives on the line.

Sincerely,
A Friend in Red

Rapach finished reading the letter. A cerulean-blue metal cube stood in the middle of the forest, in vivid contrast against the trees with their yellow bark and red leaves. People would pass letters into the box through its narrow slot, though sometimes months would go by with only emptiness inside. That day, Rapach and his older sister Mat had found just that one letter inside a red envelope. They had to wait for permission to start their delivery.

Rapach stood up from the red grass and brushed his tunic, creating a cloud of dust around him. He was used to the dust. Since he could remember, these lands they searched had been covered in that pale-coloured filth. Trees, rocks, lakes, and even animals were victims to it. Some days, when the wind was strong, he had to use his scarf and blue goggles all day long. Fortunately, for this, his first clan mission, the winds were calm.

He had just turned fourteen, which was the age they would allow you to go on missions. He didn't know how to feel about his new journey, but his sister seemed prepared, as she always was. Mat had fulfilled over fifty missions and delivered even more letters than that. She was smart and agile, not to mention she had impeccable navigation skills. She was responsible for tracing many new paths and destinations for the Jerboa Clan.

At the moment, she was drawing the forest on her meticulously measured map. Her focused eyes were the same honey colour as Rapach's, but his skin had a darker gold tone compared to hers. Her hair was blond, dense and dry, with a band pushing it back. Rapach preferred his brown hair tied in a large bun on his head so it wouldn't get in his line of sight. Both siblings also had "dust spots" that defined them. Mat's was on her forehead. It was purple and looked like an eye with small, irregular spots around it. Rapach had a dark orange one covering his left eye and cheek, ending just shy of the corner of his mouth.

"Scars made by the dust," Mat had once told him in her serious yet optimistic tone. "The more we roam these lands, the more they grow. Always be proud of them, little brother."

He was proud of it and proud to call himself part of the Jerboa Clan, though sometimes he wondered if the sacrifice was worth it, traversing the dusty lands for days at a time, with no other clan members around for company. Still, he and Mat would wear the uniform with determination every day. Boots with thick soles, goggles with lenses made of blue glass, a caerulean scarf, a long tunic, and short trousers with a thick belt. The bright colours were often muted under the thick cover of dust.

"Mat, do you think they'll approve this mission?" Rapach asked. As he did, he noticed a yellow chameleon on a rock and started following the creature.

"From the explanation in the letter, it seems like a proper task for your first clan mission. Simple enough, yet we'll have to travel through uncharted territory. But since we haven't been finding many letters recently, every letter must be a priority right now."

Rapach lifted the chameleon up, staring at the dust spots on its belly.

"Have you seen this old man before? The one from the letter?" he asked.

"Never. Just heard the tune he plays from other people that chant it at the camps." Mat interrupted her drawing to look at him. "Rapach, leave that poor animal alone."

"He doesn't seem to mind. Aaargh!"

Rapach dropped the snapping reptile and it scurried away through a red bush.

"I hope you survive your first mission," Mat said, shaking her head with a smile as she continued tracing the map.

Suddenly, the red bush that the chameleon had escaped into rustled as if something was approaching. Rapach took a few steps back, startled.

"Calm down, Rapach. The camp is in that direction. The sounds must be from Pek," Mat said.

He stared towards the red bush and realised his sister must be right. Beams of morning light radiated from the sky behind the bush as particles of dust floated in the slow wind. Just before Rapach could take another step, a creature jumped towards him, pushing him to the ground.

He sat up to pet the creature–a large dog with dusty, orange fur and a noble face. It wore blue goggles that covered its eyes perfectly and a cloth resembling a uniform to protect his torso from the dust. Strapped to its back were two bags that fell over both its sides, and around its neck was a small, cylindrical case. The dog was Pek, one of the many provisions dogs from the Jerboa Camp that Rapach had helped train. Pek was fast, yet as silent as he could be in those lands. As a provider for the clan, Pek distributed quick messages from camp to camp and to caerulean cubes. The only trace he left was the dust he lifted with every step.

"Pek! I wasn't expecting you so soon." Rapach petted Pek happily. He took the bags from the dog's back and gave the cylindrical case to Mat. As Pek shook the dust from his fur, Rapach took three round canteens from one of the bags and poured some clean water from one of them for Pek.

After drinking, Pek lay down to rest as Rapach patted the dust out of his fur. "They've granted us permission to make this your first mission, Rapach," Mat said with a crooked smile as she took a caerulean pearl out of the case. She then took three old coins from it. "We have three days to give them a progress report or they'll declare us as lost."

Mat pulled a small roll of paper out of the case. It was not very common for one to receive such instructions before a mission. The message was written in a coded language only a navigator like herself could understand.

"It seems that the Central Camp will be moving to the northeast. They also think a dust storm might come in a few days, and it says if we are interrupted by an enemy or the miasma, we must return to the Central Camp immediately."

This last part gave Rapach the chills. The miasma was one of the main reasons he feared those lands; the territory the clan called the Miasma Realm. He'd heard many legends of the silent enemies and monstrous creatures roaming it. But how many of those stories were true?

Pek stood up and barked at Rapach, distracting him from his wandering thoughts. He stared at the dog and prepared himself just before Pek jumped onto him, starting another bout of their familiar rough play. They rolled on the ground for a little while before Mat stepped in.

"Cut it out, you two. Do you really have to do this every time you see each other?" She opened the bags Pek had brought on a patch of red grass. "Rapach, let's not lose more time. Let us begin your initiation."

Rapach nodded, taking some flat bread from one of the bags to feed Pek. As the dog devoured the bread silently, Rapach knelt in front of his sister. Many times he had dreamed of this day, yet now it somehow felt less impactful than he thought it would.

Mat stood straight and closed her eyes. Rapach, too, closed his eyes. After waiting for complete silence to fall around them, they spoke together:

"We, of the Jerboa Clan, will search these lands restlessly to find those who are forgotten. We will roam eternally to find equilibrium with land and men, with doomed creatures and what's left of the waters. We believe in the caerulean hand, given by the Witness and her words. Please, jerboas of the land, help us find the one that sees our world and guide us to our destined paths."

Mat then continued alone, "With permission of the elders, I, Mat Angarum, declare the commencement of Rapach Angarum's first task." She grabbed some dust from the ground and clapped, creating a cloud.

As Rapach stood up, Mat took some objects from one of the bags and held them out. "Brother, these are your tools for the mission. This shovel is for you to seek shelter under the ground in case of strong winds." She gave him a clean shovel as big as his forearm, which he placed on his back belt.

"This shield is to protect you in your shelter and from silent enemies." She handed him a big, round shield made of blue glass–a material the Jerboa had mastered since their arrival at the Miasma Realm.

"And take this dagger as the last resource in a fight." The dagger was small, with the blade also of blue glass.

"Use these tools to guide you through dust and evil, and may the Witness guide you on your journey."

Rapach placed the dagger on his belt and his shield on his back. He then folded the letter, returned it into the red envelope, and placed it in his dusty pouch. It all felt heavy, but he had been forewarned about this at the camps. A sense of power came to Rapach. He felt like he had grown up, as if the child's play was left behind and a new journey as a man had begun. Hopefully, this didn't mean he had to stop being himself.

Mat and Rapach had a quick meal before preparing Pek for his journey back to the camps. They then walked into the woods together.

The trees around them gradually became thinner yet taller than before. They walked on an irregular terrain which slanted downwards in parts. The grass was still crimson, but full of roots and plants Rapach had never seen before. This territory, which Mat had been tracing parts of for days, was completely new to him.

"There's a river to the south of the caerulean cube. The lake must be further to the west from there," she said, without needing to consult the map.

"I don't remember seeing trees this tall or grass like this before. Have you named this place yet? Mother told me the elders gave you permission to do so, is that right?" Rapach asked in awe.

"Yes. It was difficult until I saw a big colony of jerboas close to here. I've decided to call the area the Jerboa Grasswoods."

"Makes sense, I suppose," Rapach said, not convinced that the name was entirely creative. "Are you sure there's a lake there? We don't really know if it's Rabaska Lake, do we?"

"I thought you trusted my skills blindly, brother. I'm quite convinced. The terrain slants in that direction, and it's the closest lake to the mailbox. If it's not the lake we're looking for, we'll just follow the river from there. Many times lakes are connected to one another that way."

They kept on walking silently, leaving footprints in patches of dust in the grass. Every so often they would clean dust from their faces with their scarves. Rapach kept getting distracted from the road ahead, looking at the new flora around him. Fruit with dust spots, flowers with intense colours, mushrooms of different forms. At times he saw animals, like antelopes with red tails and yellow spots on their brown fur, that watched them curiously, yet strangely, they didn't seem frightened of the newcomers.

Mat suddenly stretched out her arm, stopping Rapach in his tracks. She observed something in the distance silently. Rapach squinted to see what she was looking at.

That was not dust floating around the trees. The way it moved and its dense texture meant that they had encountered exactly what Rapach feared: the purple mist, which had taken many victims in these lands.

"Miasma," he muttered, almost breathless.

"I wasn't expecting it here," Mat said, slowly studying the terrain around them.

"Is it safe to be here?" Rapach asked.

"Yes, it's not too dense and seems to be floating around in small clouds. But we need help to walk through it."

"You mean..."

"Brother, it looks like you'll finally get your jerboa guide," Mat said with a crooked smile.

Chapter III

The Inauguration Festival

Erydis

Erydis stood at the edge of the second floor of Dust City, looking down at the northern district below her. Better known as the Emerald Barrio, the buildings were constructed from light-green bricks, not emerald bricks like most visitors to the city expected. The barrio housed two prominent locations: the food market next to the Dust Ring and Geberus Dust Academy.

Erydis always felt her insides twist whenever she stepped into the prestigious school, unable to deny the beauty of the building. Inside its four walls were spacious hallways, a central garden, and classrooms where students mixed dust with the same tools used by the best dust mixers of the Tower. Erydis knew every corner of the building well.

In each corner of the academy were four small towers, no taller than ten floors each. One of those towers always had a pillar of colourful smoke coming out of its chimney. It had a single window that usually remained shut.

Erydis leaned on the railing bordering the second floor of the city, waiting for her opportunity. She bided her time until some soldiers had passed behind her and moved away. Then she grabbed some small stones from the floor and cautiously pelted them at the closed window of the tower. After a few strikes, the window opened.

She grabbed a wooden plank hidden between two narrow buildings next to her, placed it firmly across the railings, and lay down flat on top of it. She started crawling towards the window, balancing on the plank as she edged closer, trying to ignore the tremendous distance between her and the very solid floor of the Emerald Barrio underneath.

Erydis climbed into the room and placed the plank next to the window, careful not to knock into anything around her. She was in a dark chamber with a high roof, illuminated by the light coming from a big chimney. A few stone pots sat over its powerful flames, and dust lamps hung over its sides. Cabinets with categorised materials for mixing lined the walls, along with a jar taller than Erydis that contained white dust. In the middle of the room was a square red metal table, where someone sat deftly working with mixing tools.

"I've brought you the dust you wanted, Kemia," Erydis said.

"There," Kemia said, pointing towards a corner of the table as she analysed a substance in a glass against the light.

A dust lamp illuminated her long-sleeved dress and a seasoned apron covered in burns. Kemia's black, frizzy hair was pulled into a tight bun, revealing a few streaks of silver. Her stare, intense underneath her thick eyebrows, was focused on the mixture in front of her. Erydis saw dedication, intelligence, and fury in her black eyes as Kemia worked ceaselessly.

"I also brought you some smoke candies."

Kemia raised a free hand and Erydis gave her a red candy, which she popped in her mouth. As a crimson cloud came out of Kemia's nose and mouth, Erydis marvelled at the way she worked. It was almost as if she had someone dictating instructions and measurements inside her head. She hardly made annotations, mixing many things at the same time, not wasting a single second. Erydis was overcome with admiration.

Kemia raised her hand again, and Erydis gave her a green smoke candy.

"I cough every time I eat one of those," Erydis said as she studied the cabinets against the walls. There were always new things to see.

"Don't eat my candies, or you'll have to search for another way in here," Kemia said, an olive cloud gathering around her as she ground up some dust-infused herbs.

"But you know they won't let me in through the main entrance since the incident!"

"Well, that's what happens when you burn an entire classroom trying to make ointment for burns," Kemia said, laughing between her teeth.

"I wasn't trying to make an ointment for burns! You know very well it was stupid Tulia who spread that rumor."

"What were you trying to do again?"

"It was a mixture to create rapid combustion to power up the experiment I'm working on, but I had the wrong measurements."

"The only way a flame could heat like that is by using black dust. That's the real reason the headmaster expelled you. If you're going to use such unstable dust, you have to be extremely careful. That's why its use is illegal outside Valerios's Tower."

"I know. That's why I need advice for a small chamber that could contain the heat," Erydis said.

"So you're planning to use black dust again?" Kemia asked as she heated a mixture over the chimney flames.

"Well, you use it all the time, I don't see why I wouldn't."

"Did you bring some for me?" Kemia asked calmly.

"Yes. I had to search through the Hidden Barrio, but I found this strange man who gave me some of it." Erydis took out a pouch filled with black dust. "I made sure it's not forged."

"Good." Kemia hid the pouch under the table.

"I thought all mixers who work or worked at the Tower could use it anytime."

"Not all." Kemia went quiet as she mixed a bubbling, black liquid over the flames.

"The man also gave me this blue amber necklace," Erydis said as she took the unpolished amber hanging from her neck out from under her tunic. It was quite big, almost the size of her palm, and had rounded corners crafted with a bronze ring on top that held a simple string.

"Blue amber? Never heard of such a thing, but amber doesn't usually work well for mixing dust."

Erydis nodded. "It looks nice, though. I just wish it weren't so opaque."

"Have you been working on your experiment?" Kemia continued, neglecting to compliment Erydis's new jewellery. She didn't care much for that sort of thing.

"Yes, I have, but I can barely make it before Festival Closure. I need four more things before it's ready."

"What are they ?" Kemia asked with a rare hint of interest.

"A thick glass sphere, small heat-resistant gears, elite mixers' dust from Valerios's Tower, and the Emperor's sceptre."

Kemia stared at her, sceptical.

"The first two are expensive, but you can obtain them. But elite mixers' dust from the Tower? The Emperor's sceptre? Getting expelled affected you more than I thought."

"Well, without those, I won't be able to finish my experiment."

Kemia turned back to her mixtures, thoughtful.

"You can ask my students in the Machina classes for the gears, and I have a glass sphere in that cabinet. See if that's what you need." She pointed to a cabinet close to the door. "But I have no idea how you can get the last two. Maybe you can ask your friend Thylac for help, but I don't think he'll agree. What's this experiment about?"

"Tell me what you are researching, and I'll tell you every detail of my experiment," Erydis challenged.

"Clever attempt but unsuccessful," Kemia said with a patient smile.

"This is the only way I'll be able to work at the Tower. If my experiment wins the Festival Closure contest, I have another chance."

"You'll be competing against the best students from the academy, you know? Not to mention all those who also want to work at the Tower. Do not take this lightly."

"I won't lose. I'll become a mixer, just you wait," Erydis said confidently.

Kemia wiped her hands on her apron and sat down close to Erydis.

"Don't be so arrogant before you see the results of your experiment, Erydis. Now, the Inauguration Festival will start in a few hours, so if you want to learn how to build a small heating chamber strong enough to support those flames you almost burned that classroom down with, you'll have to listen to every word. I won't repeat myself, and you'll have to stand next to me as I try to finish a mixture. Understood?"

"It's a deal. Will you be going to the Inauguration Festival?" Erydis asked, taking out a small notebook from her pouch.

"And why would I do such a thing?" Kemia stood up and took some blue flowers from a pot on top of the cabinet. They were of an intense blue, from the roots to the stem.

"Oh, I'll be needing some of those, too!"

"Blue flowers? For your experiment? Hmm, you're in luck. I won't be using all of them." Kemia stared at the flower. "I still can't figure out what your experiment is."

"I guess you'll just have to be patient," Erydis said with a radiant smile.

After an intense lesson with Kemia, Erydis walked towards the south of the Palace District. She was trying to memorise some of the techniques she had just learned, but she felt like she needed a break. Placing her notebook back into her pouch, Erydis glanced up at a clock on a fancy building. Like every other clock in the city, this one had twenty-four numbers and a single hand. It would soon point to twenty, and the Inauguration Festival would begin.

Erydis took long strides through the crowd, recalling the clock from her dream. Five numbers. It had to be a reminder that this was her last opportunity to work at the Tower. Fortunately, she needed only three more items to finish her experiment. Unfortunately, it seemed impossible to get two of them. To get the sceptre or dust she needed, she would have to enter the palace. But only selected merchants, dust mixers, the strongest soldiers, and royalty were allowed inside.

The palace was located in the south of the Palace District. The only entrance to Valerios's Tower was through the palace. Early every morning, the best dust mixers would enter through the palace doors and walk through the gardens and into the Tower. Erydis imagined herself taking that stroll as she passed next to the heavily guarded palace. The palace was a tall, white building with intricate gold patterns adorning its walls, windows, and doors. On its pillars were carvings of old emperors staring down at the streets, and the city's flag waved above the heavy doors at its entrance. It was the most complex structure in Dust City aside from the Tower.

Right behind the palace rose the grand marble stairs. As wide as the Dust Ring, it consisted of multiple steps on each landing that connected the first floor of the city to the second. Flanking the stairs were buildings of alabaster, and at the bottom lay the marble plaza next to the gigantic stone doors of the city. The citizens called this southern district section of the city the Marble Barrio.

A large, round platform had been built in the plaza to accommodate the hundreds of people who gathered to watch the festival every year. Others, like Erydis, sat on the stairs to observe the spectacle. The lucky ones who lived in the Marble Barrio could watch the event from their windows.

As Erydis found a good spot with a great view of the stage, a group of boys and girls in dirty clothes who were sitting near her started laughing loudly. They called themselves the Gecko Gang. Their leader was a ginger boy with a serious face who was a few years older than Erydis. His name was Cuiha.

"Good seats, Nott," he said without looking at Erydis. "Did you hear we're getting a new presenter this year? Seems they finally found someone better than that annoying lady from the last festival."

"Oh, I'm glad. She was such a Palace District snob," Erydis said, smiling.

"I remember a certain someone who once lived there as well."

"It wasn't for long, Cuiha," Erydis said, trying to forget. "I was at the Hidden Barrio for a lot longer."

"Some miss you there. You should visit us more often."

"Spit it out, Cuiha, what do you need?"

"Some dust marbles. Not your special ones, just normal ones," he admitted with no trace of shame.

Erydis counted out a few marbles of various colours from her pouch and gave them to Cuiha.

"Thank you, Nott. The Gecko Gang is in your debt once more."

Suddenly, a blast of powerful music shushed everyone. There were trumpet players standing on top of the buildings around the plaza. As people listened, anticipating what was to come next, twilight slowly spread through the sky. After a long, high note, dancers dressed as animals and musicians playing string instruments emerged from the buildings and surrounded the stage, dancing and moving joyfully.

In the middle of the stage was a young man playing an accordion with pipes. As he compressed the instrument, clouds of dust escaped from it.

"That's Isaac! He works with me at Dusty Corner," Erydis said, recognising his lazy smile instantly.

After a few seconds of ominous notes, another man stepped onto the stage. He was thin, with sand-coloured skin and messy, brown hair down to his shoulders. He wore a slightly yellowed mask with small holes over the eyes and a mocking smile. He extended his hands to the crowd, and everyone cheered vigorously.

"People from every corner of this astounding city! I have the pleasure of being your presenter on this beautiful night. The night we celebrate the Five Festivals of the Dust!"

Everyone, including Erydis, applauded. The presenter was much more enthusiastic than the previous year's lady. She wondered what his name was.

"Before I have the pleasure of performing today, I would like to welcome some people we all know well because they hold the heart of this kingdom. With us, the three Masters of the Dust Disciplines!"

People cheered as three people came out of the building, guarded closely by several soldiers. They headed for their royal seats right next to the stage, which were also well protected. Erydis noticed that Thylac was among the guards.

"First, I'd like you to cheer for the Master of Vita. Thanks to him, our cattle and plants will always be bountiful enough to feed our children and to create the most efficient medicines. Please give your applause to Lord Aerzzo Chimara!"

Everyone clapped as a shy man with dark red hair and a big moustache waved to the crowd.

"Second, the extraordinary man who gave us the funiculars and other dust-combusted vehicles, not to mention all the machinery powering the city. Master of Machina, Lord Herra Gull!"

A tall man with a frizzy, silver beard and square glasses stood up to wave at the people. He had smart, brown eyes and wore ruby robes. He smiled kindly under his white turban, tipping the cane he held in his hand.

"And finally, the lady who protects us from the outsiders. One of the smartest people in history, Master of Arma and recent Master of Alchemia. The mother of the Bomba Branch, Lady Lyudmila Dametot!"

A woman with a silver braid down her back and an expressionless face stood up, holding her hands in front of her. She was quite attractive, causing the men around her to clap even more enthusiastically. Erydis did not applaud.

"I thought Kemia was the Master of Alchemia," Cuiha said.

"Not anymore. I believe Kemia decided to quit," Erydis said, wondering why someone would ever quit working at the Tower.

"Our Masters of the main Dust Disciplines are here tonight because a wise man has selected them to be the mixers who will guide us towards advancements and new technology. A wise man with the blood of the finder of these lands. The heir of Great Orn Ryk, our Emperor Engyl Ryk!"

"Here we go," Erydis said as everyone stood up to take a bow. She also got up but did not bow, and neither did the Gecko Gang.

The Emperor wore long black-and-white robes, a tall headdress, and a golden mask displaying a neutral expression. The mask, like many in the city, had been passed on to him from generation to generation.

He also held a familiar relic as he walked—a golden sceptre. Clouds of shining gold dust trailed out from its top. Erydis knew that the gold dust was really worthless. But she had her eyes on the sceptre for her experiment.

The Emperor reached his seat, which was elevated above the rest, and turned to face the crowd. He took his mask off, revealing a man with small eyes, a hooked nose, and a smile that was somehow charming.

"Today we are gathered here to celebrate the fuel of the city," he said. "That element that keeps us fed and well protected." His voice was powerful and deep. "This celebration is for you, people of Dust City, as a reminder of your dedication and effort to keep the harmony inside our fortress. Like every other year, the top five students of the Geberus Dust Academy will join the Tower as dust mixers, and a contest will be held at the Closure Festival to choose one more person privileged to work with them. Best of luck to the participants. Now, as night falls our city, I declare the commencement of the Inauguration Festival!"

As people cheered, the lights on the stage dimmed and the presenter came back holding a dust lamp.

"Dust," the presenter began in a mysterious tone as Isaac played a tune on his accordion, "used by all in Dust City, it has shaped our homes, our daily lives, our strength. In its honour, we celebrate the Five Festivals of the Dust."

"Today we celebrate the Inauguration Festival to remember our history and the history of dust."

Dancers wearing animal masks and beautiful dresses moved slowly up to the stage. Isaac placed a simple dog mask on his face and continued playing.

"The second festival is the Festival of the People, so wear your masks from your ancestors and show your family pride! Or buy a fancy new one from the bazaar."

The presenter shrugged in a frivolous manner, drawing chuckles from some in the audience. Then he and the dancers grabbed dust marbles from their pockets and threw them onto the floor. The marbles exploded in small clouds of various colours that dissolved into the night.

"The third festival will be the Festival of Many Dusts, a day we show off our discoveries of dust mixing. It may be better known to many of you as the day you eat for three from the food market."

Erydis grinned at that. It was true, all people did during that Festival was throw dust marbles on the floor and eat seasonal food like it was their last meal.

The dancers left the stage and the presenter raised his hands to the crowd. People looked confused—until he made a swift movement with his right hand, and a mask appeared in his hand. He placed it over the mask he was already wearing to reveal a replicated paper version of the Emperor's mask. Erydis laughed loudly at this, as did the majority of the audience. The Masters and the Emperor, however, did not, although Herra Gull seemed to be hiding a smile behind his hand.

"With the fourth festival, we celebrate those who hold our city together," the presenter said. Dust mixers, bankers, soldiers, and royalty. We call this the Festival of the Palace, a party we people from lower barrios are not invited to." The crowd erupted with laughter. The presenter tore his paper mask and bowed to the unamused Emperor. "I apologise; just having a laugh, sir." He turned back to the people.

"And on the last day, at the Closure Festival, we celebrate the Tower and those who will be granted the opportunity to work in its new chambers. Best of luck to all of you." The presenter paused and the crowd hushed in anticipation of the next segment.

"We come to celebrate the dust, but what exactly is it? Many of your young ones might ask, and it is wise to recall its origins on this day. Let me tell you a story.

"Many centuries ago, people from the lost villages gathered in search of better lands. They started from the south and searched the entire realm. A great man, Orn Ryk, found what he later called the Mist Grounds, a land where a shining mist covered the skies. Many were convinced that mist was dangerous, but Orn was sure that the mist had a sacred power within it. After a few years of experimentation, he created dust, a white essence that could enhance every element it was mixed with. And with the dust they forged stronger and more resistant metals, created powerful medicines, and made food taste exquisite.

"Orn discovered the main colours of the dust, which we still use today." Performers arranged jars of dust on the stage next to large cloth-covered objects. A large jar with white dust was placed in the middle.

"White dust, the main dust used to create the others," the presenter said as he picked up a handful of the white dust and poured it back into the jar. "We call it virgin dust, since it forms the base of many other dusts."

He then approached a jar with caerulean dust and uncovered the object next to it, revealing a cabinet filled with small flasks containing many mixtures.

"Blue dust, to cure the deadliest illness." The presenter grabbed a flask and showed it to the crowd. He set it down again and moved on to the next jar containing crimson dust. He removed the cloth from the next object with a flourish, revealing red swords, arrows, and shields eerily reflecting the light from the dust lamps onstage.

"Red dust, to forge the strongest weapons and the funicular railings."

He walked to the next jar; inside it was dust of an emerald-green colour. Under the cloth was a square vehicle with large, metallic wheels and a chimney. It was a rare sight in the city, and some people in the crowd leaned in to get a better look. A driver powered the engine and green clouds came out of the vehicle's chimney.

"We use green dust for fuel, dust lamps, and, of course, to clean our toilets."

People laughed as the presenter moved on to the next jar, which held dust of a canary-yellow sheen. Performers revealed a table with steaming food and plates of spices in bright hues.

"Yellow dust is famous for the delicious food of the city. It enhances flavours and makes food last longer. But it is also used for medicines in certain mixtures."

"Even more types of dust were discovered after Finder Orn died, but their use is allowed only inside the Tower itself." The presenter paused, signalling a close to the end of his spiel.

"Before I take my leave, let me remind you all of Valerios's Tower's function. It was built in the old city of the Mist Grounds by the villagers, as planned by Orn himself. After the Finder's death, a fortress was raised to protect the Tower and the people from the nasty outsiders and their beasts, the djinnis, which are now extinct. The Mist Grounds then became Dust City. The leader of the outsiders was Vakandi, a repugnant man who wanted to take the power of dust to doom these lands.

"We all know how the Tower works. It pulls water from the underground river and mixes it with mist. The mist and water mixture is then condensed in a chamber with powerful flames, resulting in the white dust that we know so well.

"But I'll tell you something none of you know." The crowd fell silent. Many already knew the history and dust very well, so any new information was welcomed with attention. "After the dust is created, another type of dust is released: grey dust, or useless dust as you know it. And where does this dust go to, you wonder? Into the underground river to outside the city."

Something strange was happening. The Emperor rose from his seat, and soldiers were approaching the stage. The crowd murmured in confusion.

"That river eventually emerges from the earth and flows into a river, which runs next to areas filled with people. Many have died drinking its water, and it has slowly made many innocent people sick.

"These people known as the outsiders, or as I prefer to call them, the Vakandi Clan, came to us in peace in search of a solution. But that man, Engyl Ryk, has decided to silence us with a war we cannot win." The presenter pointed to the Emperor. The energy of the crowd intensified as people grew more confused.

"But now, dear Engyl, we are here, inside your city, walking your streets as you enjoy our suffering."

Soldiers tried to run up the stage, but they were stopped by some masked performers. What was happening? Erydis could not tear her eyes away.

"People of Dust City!" the presenter continued. We come in peace and we need your support. We ask for your help to find a solution to this problem. If you believe Engyl is wrong to silence us and you want to join our humble cause, paint a purple dot on your masks tomorrow at the Festival of the People, and we'll know you want to help."

The presenter removed his smiling mask to reveal a tanned man with a wide smile and green eyes. He had a weird mark on the left side of his mouth.

"People of Dust City, the Vakandi Clan is in your home." He started laughing uncontrollably before Thylac reached him and knocked him to the floor.

People rose and mumbled to one another as the light came on in the buildings and on the streets.

Erydis stayed seated for a few seconds, not really believing what she had just heard.

This will be interesting, she thought, a smile spreading across her face slowly.

Chapter IV

Benu

Rapach

Rapach and Mat had reached flat terrain in the newly named Jerboa Grasswoods. As the name suggested, jerboas were an important symbol of protection to the Jerboa Clan. They cherished these animals more than anything, and those tasked with walking through the unknown lands were required to carry a jerboa as a loyal guide.

"Mat, why didn't you bring Yumka on this mission?" Rapach asked.

"The poor creature had such a hard time when I was investigating these lands," Mat answered. "Almost got eaten by a snake. And, well, you need a jerboa for yourself, so I felt that bringing Yumka would be cheating on your first mission."

"Oh, I suppose she has lots of experience," Rapach said, hoping to find a jerboa as loyal as Yumka.

They walked for almost an hour, trying to find the telltale holes in the ground made by jerboa. They were surrounded by trees with dense, orange leaves, making the dust less thick than it usually was in other places. Round, yellow fruit with red spikes hung from some of the branches. Rapach grabbed a fruit carefully and opened it to reveal its sweet and creamy orange interior.

"I don't see any trace of jerboas, Mat," he said as he devoured a chunk of the fruit.

"Maybe if you stop getting distracted, you might spot some." She pointed ahead to a series of jerboa holes in the dust-covered grass. Rapach hadn't noticed them under the cover of the shade.

"Do you think there are any jerboas right now?" he asked hopefully.

"That's for you to discover." Mat smiled, nodding towards the ground.

Rapach carefully handed her the spiky fruit and grabbed his small shovel. Mat looked confused, but before she could say something, Rapach sprinted towards the holes. He started shoveling the soil around one of the larger holes as fast as he could.

"Rapach!" Mat called out, but Rapach was too excited to notice.

Something moved in the soil. Rapach stopped shovelling as he saw a small rodent the size of his palm leap from the hole.

It was definitely a jerboa. The small, grey creature had a plump body with long hind legs for jumping high and very short forelegs. This species of jerboa was unfamiliar to Rapach. Its ears were longer and pointier than what he had seen before, and it had a tuft of thick, dense hair at the end of its long tail. Its raven eyes sparkled in the light.

Rapach stared at it for a few seconds, stepping back in anticipation. Then, in one swift move, he lunged forward to capture the jerboa, but it leapt over his head to escape.

Suddenly, the earth started moving under Rapach. After a fraction of a second, jerboas of all imaginable colours started jumping out of their holes and scampering off in different directions.

Rapach targeted a small one. He ran after it as the animal jumped onto a dust patch, kicking up small clouds of dust. Rapach managed to corner the jerboa against the roots of a tree and got close to the trembling creature. He leaped towards it and finally grabbed hold of the jerboa.

"Rapach!" Mat strutted towards him.

"I captured one!" Rapach exclaimed. But his sister slapped his hands, making him drop the jerboa, which escaped speedily into a bush.

"You're supposed to tame the jerboa, not frighten it to death!" Mat chastised him.

"Well, yeah, but don't I need to catch and then feed it to tame it?"

"No. It's more like an invitation. You have to approach slowly and be respectful of the animal; offer some food. If it accepts, it might be tameable." She looked around. "Now all the jerboas are gone. It might be difficult to find them again. Try not to be too hasty next time, little brother."

Rapach stared at the ground, embarrassed. He knew he was impatient, and he'd tried hard to change that at the camps. But on this first mission, he wanted to get through all his tasks quickly and show Mat how brave he was.

A rustling noise close by broke the silence. Mat and Rapach looked around but saw nothing.

"I thought I heard something," Mat said quietly.

The rustling started up again, louder this time. Rapach turned towards the bush the sound was originating from.

A tinny jerboa sprang into the air. It stared at the siblings mid-jump and landed in a bush of blue flowers, where it stopped.

"There, Mat," Rapach said, walking slowly to not scare the jerboa off.

He approached the flowers carefully, but before he reached the bush, the jerboa cautiously crawled out from under it. It wasn't as pretty as other jerboas. It was tiny. Way smaller than the other jerboas Rapach had seen. It also had a torn ear and bald patches on its pale, blue fur, but its tail swished from side to side playfully. Its fearless, sharp blue eyes stared at Rapach as if it had been expecting him.

"Sister, look!" Rapach said, dropping down to get a closer look at the jerboa.

"It's a female," Mat said. "Seems hurt and skinny. It might also be difficult for you to find it from a distance since it's so small, but who am I to judge?" She grabbed a ball from her pouch and gave it to Rapach. "Take this kibble. I made it with fruits and insects; a recipe from Mama. Offer it to the jerboa and see what happens."

Rapach placed the kibble on his palm and approached the jerboa. The animal stared at the snack and jumped onto Rapach's palm to eat.

"Look at this, Mat," Rapach said, smiling. After the jerboa had eaten, it jumped onto the top of Rapach's head, where it stood quietly.

"Interesting..." Mat said, "not even Yumka was this trusting when I found him." She took a closer look at the jerboa, which seemed a bit more sceptical of her. "This one seems to have taken an instant liking to you. I wonder why."

"Now I need to think of a name for it, don't I?"

"Yes. Be wise, as many in the clan will remember that name as if it were yours," Mat advised, studying their surroundings. "We should go back to that place with the miasma. I can show you the searching technique there."

They made their way back to the slanted terrain where they had first encountered the small clouds of miasma among the trees. It seemed the winds had not dragged it away. It was as terrifying as Rapach remembered—silent, yet a single breath of it would turn you into one of them. The Silent People.

"How do you know when it's not dangerous to walk in a place with miasma?" he asked.

"You should know this already," Mat said. "If you can see through it, it's probably dispersed enough for you to pass through it unharmed. If it's dense enough to block your view, you should stay away. And if the wind is strong, stay away from any trace of it." Mat frowned with concern. "I need you to listen well to my instructions for the next part, Rapach. A small mistake could have great repercussions. Did you bring your slingshot from the camps?"

Rapach moved to get his pouch slowly, worried the jerboa might fall off, but it was balancing very well on his head. Rapach opened his pouch. Nestled inside it was a slingshot with a wooden handle he had carved to be as smooth as possible.

"Here it is."

"Very well. If we encounter small clouds of miasma, we'll need to find a safe path around or under it. Unfortunately, it is quite difficult for us humans to find these safe paths. But rodents, especially the jerboas of these lands, have a sixth sense to avoid the most dangerous parts of miasma. And as you know, animals are not affected by it. Only humans are. That's why the jerboas are essential to us."

"Yes, I remember Papa advising us to 'always follow the jerboa if you get surrounded by miasma'," Rapach said, imitating the slow tone of their father. Mat chuckled and nodded.

"Exactly. You'll need to spend some time training your jerboa. You have to teach it to be your guide. Now, grab a kibble and shoot it as far as you can, in the direction you want to go. If there's a safe path through the miasma, the jerboa will run along it. Cover your mouth with a scarf and your eyes with goggles, and follow it. Repeat this until there's no more miasma around you or until there's an obstruction. Ready?"

Rapach nodded, trying to memorise every step. He grabbed a piece of kibble and let the jerboa smell it before placing it in his slingshot. He stretched the leather sling as far back as possible, and just like he practised back at the camps, released it towards the east, where he wanted to explore. The kibble flew forward with a sharp whistle.

The jerboa jumped from Rapach's head and ran towards the food in zigzag movements. Rapach and Mat quickly covered themselves in scarves and goggles and made a beeline for it.

"Stay as low as you can," Mat said, running faster than him.

They passed floating clouds of miasma as they ran. Rapach felt trapped. Many of their clan had breathed in the doomed substance and walked into the woods to become Silent People. He shook his head, trying to ease his mind, but his hands were trembling. Mat, on the contrary, seemed confident in the jerboa's steps. She had always been this brave, possibly more than Rapach would ever be.

The jerboa waited for them as it ate the kibble. The miasma around them was still as dense as before, but it wasn't overwhelming.

"Again, Mat?" Rapach asked.

"Yes, try to shoot as far as you can," Mat said, handing him another piece of kibble.

Rapach shot higher this time, and the jerboa took off.

They followed it into an even more slanted terrain, covered with denser trees than before. It was difficult to follow the jerboa through so many obstacles. There were almost no animals around, and the silence was eerie. After a minute, the jerboa suddenly stopped in front of a smooth wall, seeming lost. "What is it, jerboa?" Rapach asked, getting closer to the wall.

"Rapach, stop!" Mat yelled from a few metres behind him.

Rapach froze with a horrified realization. How could he have been so stupid? It wasn't a wall. He knew it, yet this was something he'd never encountered before.

It was miasma; so dense it was impossible to see through even though Rapach was merely centimetres away. He tried to step back, but his feet were frozen in place. Mat pulled him back sharply.

"How is it possible?" she asked, scared. "I thought these lands were not as doomed."

"Sister, what do we do?" Rapach was frightened. "Do we cancel the mission?"

Mat studied the terrain.

"Let's get out of here first. We don't want any winds to reach us while we're next to the miasma." She gave some kibbles to Rapach. "Let your jerboa guide us back to a more level area."

As they made their way out, Rapach glanced back at the dense miasma. The fear he'd seen in his people was not due to rumours. He thought of those in the clan surrounded by a wall of miasma like that one and how hopeless they must have felt.

They soon reached an area with no miasma, just small patches of dust. As they ate some fruit for dinner, Mat thought deeply, frowning as she stared at the ground.

"With this much miasma, it will be difficult to reach Rabaska Lake. And we do not know whether there will be Silent People waiting for us on the other side of the miasma. It's common for them to hide next to spots where the miasma is dense like what we saw, but they also ambush people in places far beyond it."

"I hope we don't have to cancel my first mission," Rapach said. He would feel like a failure if they did.

"Let me see the letter again," Mat said thoughtfully. Rapach gave her the letter.

She scanned it several times, slowly.

"This message is strange. It sounds urgent, yet we don't really know if what we'll obtain is worth it. But I believe it's our mission to find out. Let's wait for morning. If the miasma disperses, we might find a route to go through or around it."

They stood up and started to dig two deep, circular holes that they measured out with the length of their shields. Outside the camps, this was their only shelter from the dust and the miasma.

Once they were done digging, Mat waved goodnight and climbed inside her hole, pulling her shield down over her as cover. Rapach got into his hole along with his new companion. He also placed his shield above him to serve as a roof while he rested. The blue glass of his shield cast a blue light into their shelter as the purple moon, its true whiteness concealed by dust, shone brightly above them.

The jerboa settled on Rapach's hand, and he looked into its eyes.

"Thank you for today. I hope tomorrow you can help us more on this mission."

The jerboa looked at him, curiously sniffing with its twitching nose.

"Oh, I almost forgot that I have to give you a name!" Rapach said. "I was thinking on our way here, and I've decided to call you Benu." The jerboa hopped onto his palm. "I hope that means you like it. It doesn't really mean anything, like most names, but I like the sound of it. It's soothing, almost like the songs back at the Central Camp."

Benu looked at Rapach calmly and then jumped onto his head, where he pushed aside some hair and settled into a little nest.

"Rest well, Benu. We have a big day tomorrow. I hope I can fulfill my first mission for the clan." Rapach thought about the dense miasma, hoping to not have his recurring nightmare that night.

He closed his eyes, trying to forget the terrifying tales of his clan members falling victim to the Silent People.

THE SECOND DREAM

ERYDIS OPENED HER EYES. AGAIN, SHE DID NOT FEEL AWAKE. She was back in that place with the starless skies, yet it felt different this time. There were jars of coloured dust arranged on the white dunes, and a few trees of unusual hues. In the centre of the line of trees, of course, was the black tree with the clock.

Still holding one of the blue flowers she borrowed from Kemia, Erydis realised she had fallen asleep with it as she worked on her experiment.

She took a deep breath. The wind felt crisp and cold, even though she knew it could not be real. She smiled, suddenly feeling that protected sensation she felt in the first dream, as the familiar, distant sounds bounced away into the emptiness. But tonight she could also hear a sharper noise, much closer than the others.

She followed the noise towards the exhausted tree, and with every step, she could hear an echo. A haunting tune of five simple notes, lacking joy or words, coming from a young voice. Even though Erydis lacked musical skills, she felt the melody, full of tranquility and sadness. Those five repeated notes were better than the clamour of instruments at the Inauguration Festival had been; at least for her.

As she got close to the decrepit black tree, the song became clearer and clearer, and Erydis saw the unknown singer. It was a boy singing with no words, who seemed just as old as her. But he was unlike any of the people she was used to seeing in Dust City. He wore clothes covered in dust, and his dirty grey hair was pulled back. The weirdest thing about him was some kind of spot above his left eye, a slightly orange patch that contrasted with his golden, dark skin.

The strange boy continued whistling as he stared thoughtfully at the white dunes. He was clutching a red envelope as if his life depended on it. Erydis observed him curiously, intently listening to those five notes. But suddenly, the tune went silent.

In one swift movement, the boy jumped to his feet and stared at Erydis with a combination of fear and aggression.

"Who are you?" he asked through gritted teeth.

Erydis was surprised by his melodic accent. She sensed no malice behind his amber eyes.

"Erydis Nott. What's your name?" She extended her hand to greet him. The boy stepped back. "Don't be afraid, I won't hurt you," she said with a smile.

"I am not afraid," the boy replied in the same serious tone.

"No? Then why aren't you telling me your name?" The boy fixed his eyes on hers. Erydis walked around him in a circle, her hands behind her back. "I've never seen someone like you," she said. "No one in the city dresses the way you do or even speaks with the same accent. I know dreams are weird at times, but I've never dreamed of someone so different. You're as unique as this entire place I keep coming back to, dream boy."

"Dream boy? You're the one in my dream!" he said as he tried and failed to hide the red envelope in his trousers. "I suppose if I'm dreaming, it doesn't really matter if you know my name. Call me Rapach."

Erydis approached the boy again but stayed a step away.

"Welcome to my dream, Rapach." The boy blushed. "What's in that envelope?"

"It's confidential," Rapach said, tucking it under his tunic.

"Confidential?" Erydis laughed loudly. "You sound just like my friend Thylac! Let me see what's inside!" She tried to reach for the envelope, but Rapach jumped to the side skillfully. Erydis grinned. "That song. I've never heard a tune that beautiful. I never thought I could dream something like that. Did you create it?"

"No." Rapach stared at the ground, thoughtful again.

"Who, then?" Erydis asked, more serious this time. She wanted to keep the conversation going.

Rapach looked at her doubtfully, but after taking a deep breath he answered. "There's an elderly man who walks beside the silver river. Many people know of him, but no one has seen him in years. I need to know where he is. Have you heard of him?" Rapach asked, hopeful.

"River? So you're from outside the fortress."

Rapach looked confused.

"So who's that man?" Erydis prodded.

"I've never seen him, but I know of people who have crossed paths with him," Rapach said. "It's said that he has been searching day and night for something by the river for many years. He sometimes helps people in his path, but then he continues on searching. Every evening, if the Silent People are far and there's no miasma, he plays that song to the night. There's always debate on whether he sings or plays some sort of wind instrument. And many remember those notes." Rapach looked into Erydis' eyes. "But it's been a few years since anyone has seen him."

"No one knows what he's searching for?" She noticed Rapach instinctively place his hand on the red envelope. "Is that what the envelope is for?"

Rapach seemed impressed by her intuition.

"Where exactly are you from, Rapach?" Erydis asked more gently.

"That's confidential, too. And even if you try to find me, you wouldn't want to go there."

"Where?"

"The Miasma Realm."

"Miasma?"

"You've never heard of miasma? This dream is too weird."

"It is," Erydis agreed, rubbing her head in confusion.

"The miasma is a purple cloud that has doomed many villages, cursing any human who breathes it in. Those people then become whom we call the Silent People or the hypnotised. It's as if the once living person fades and a soulless being takes their place. Many people from my clan have fallen victim to it. We all fear the miasma."

Rapach was clenching his fists, trying to hide how they were shaking. Then he noticed Erydis's blue flower. "That flower. I saw it close to me, right before I fell asleep."

"This flower?" she asked, surprised. "It's rare to find them in nature, but

I've heard there are places outside my city where they grow in clusters." Erydis thought for a moment. "I have an idea. Tell me more about this letter and where you come from, and I'll tell you how to walk through this miasma without being affected."

"That's impossible."

Erydis smiled confidently. "It is not."

Rapach looked at her with doubt. "I suppose this is just a dream, but tell me how the flower helps first, and I'll tell you everything you want to know."

Erydis lifted the flower and nodded.

"Many years ago," she began, "someone in my city discovered that this peculiar flower has many healing properties including the ability to heal respiratory illnesses. It's especially good at preventing harm from toxic scents. For the effect to last about a week, you'll need to infuse the flower with diluted dust from the Tower and…" She stopped. Rapach seemed completely lost.

"Infusing diluted dusts?" He asked.

"Hmm. It seems you don't really know what dust mixing is. You're definitely from outside of the city. Look, to breathe through the miasma and hopefully not be affected by it, you'll have to place the whole flower in your mouth, including the stem and leaves. Chew it and keep it in your mouth until it exudes a scent. Breathe in as much of the scent as possible, and the effect should last about five to ten minutes. It's not long, but it's the best I can think of for your situation, without any dust around."

"So I won't be hypnotised?" Rapach asked.

"That's right. In theory, nothing you breathe in would affect you if you have this flower's scent inside your system. Though, I've never heard of this miasma before." Erydis got close to Rapach and pointed at his chest. "Now it's your turn!"

Rapach frowned.

"It is complicated to explain."

"Try."

He took a deep breath.

"Very well. I come from a camp that is constantly moving. We are called the Jerboa Clan." Rapach stood proudly.

"Why are you constantly moving?" Erydis asked, curious.

"We hide from the hypnotised and we help people in need all through the Miasma Realm. But no one knows much about our enemy." Rapach went silent for a moment, his eyes darting as he thought. "We search for messages passed around and try to connect lost people with one another across this doomed land of miasma and dust. This is my first mission. I have to find the elderly man who wrote the song I was whistling." He paused and a look of determination came into his eyes. "I have to deliver a package to him, and to do that I need to get to a place called Rabaska Lake."

"What package?" Erydis asked.

"The package is from someone I've never met. My sister is with me as my guide, but we still don't know what's inside the package."

"Miasma and dust? Rabaska Lake?" Erydis tried to make sense out of his story.

But her thoughts were interrupted by the sound of a bell. It chimed twice, and the hand of the clock on the tree moved to the number two.

"I believe it's time for me to wake up, Rapach. I hope to see you in my next dream," Erydis said, smiling gently and closing her eyes.

Day Two

Chapter V

Monkey Mask

Erydis

A glint of bright daylight struck Erydis's eyes. She awoke at her desk, her head lying flat on the table, surrounded by a mess of notes and dust mixtures. She had fallen asleep while trying to finish a portion of her experiment, but it was far from complete.

Staring at the blue flower still in her hand, Erydis remembered her dream and the boy, Rapach. A boy so different from anyone in Dust City. But she knew well enough that it was all just a dream, albeit a peculiar one.

She stood up, cracking her stiff neck, and turned to the window. The sight of the clock on a building close by made her realise she had to hurry. After changing her clothes and washing up as quickly as she could, she headed out and ran towards the market. It was the busiest day of the year, and it was only just beginning.

As she walked through the Dust Ring, a crowd was starting to gather, all heading in the direction of the market. Some opportunists were running to be the first at the festival, but many others were deliberating on the surprising events that had happened at the Inauguration Festival.

"I took the children as far away from the Tower as I could," a heavily made-up lady said in a scandalised tone. "I fear that's where they'll attack first."

"They say they come in peace, but I'm sure they say that so we'll let our guard down," a big man replied.

Others seemed to be on the side of the invaders.

"I've heard Engyl Ryk keeps many secrets from his people, so it was not a surprise to me to hear the Vakandi man's words yesterday. I'm sure they're fighting for a living, so I'll paint the purple dots on my mask tonight!" a young man declared.

"Shh. Keep it quiet! We don't want to get arrested before buying our masks, do we?" whispered his friend with a timid expression.

Erydis was mostly siding in favour of the outsiders. They seemed to be taking desperate measures. If they were violent, they would have attacked the city already, but things were running like any other day. Most people seemed excited for the day to come. Some were already wearing their masks from the previous festival or masks they inherited from their families. Erydis had one before, but like many others in the city, it was stolen.

She entered the market along with the throngs of people waiting for the tents to open. After squeezing through the crowd, she finally reached Dusty Corner. The entrance was covered with a curtain, and people were standing in front of it waiting for the shop to open. They knew that the little shop had the best masks in the city as well as top-quality dust mixtures for any occasion—all thanks to Kemia's contributions.

A man with a sheep mask peered out from inside the tent.

"Erydis! I'm so glad you're here!" Trinos said overeagerly from behind his mask. Erydis grinned as she realised that he was clearly faking his enthusiasm. "Please come inside!" he said.

Erydis pushed through the people, went inside the tent, and closed the curtain behind her.

"You'll be at the used clothes and masks stall today," Trinos said, back to his usual grumpy self.

"Good morning!" Kitri smiled from behind them as she placed a yellow carpet on the floor. She was wearing a long green dress that flowed delicately over her slim figure.

"It looks like you're ready for the opening," Erydis said as she carefully took some old masks from a crate and placed them on the tables. "Will you be dancing today?"

"I will. Isaac brought his flute to play for the clients, so I can't wait to show them my new moves," she said with a smile. Dancing was serious talk for her, and a great tactic to attract more passersby.

After a few more minutes of setting up, Dusty Corner was ready to greet its customers. Green, yellow, and dark-red tapestries covered the floors. Curtains with intricate patterns hung from the walls. Like on any other day, there were several tables and stands in the middle of the shop displaying dust they were allowed to sell—blue, green, red, and yellow. In the middle of each table was a big jar with white dust. They also sold cloth bags for carrying dust, plants and flowers for common infusions, and some mixtures of dust provided by Kemia. For this occasion, she had prepared a mixture of red dust and other metals that were perfect for forging, some mixtures for spicing up food, and also medicines to cure nausea or pain. There were also jars of paint customers could use to decorate their masks.

On the day of the Festival of the People, it was tradition for Dusty Corner to also display new masks and allow customers to sell or exchange their old masks for ones of equal or lower value. A myriad of animal masks hung from the walls. Some others were inspired by djinnis, displaying unique patterns and unnatural creatures. It was said that the djinnis were like many animals fused into one. The most expensive masks were displayed on a golden framed table in a corner, where Trinos could keep an eye on it.

Erydis was in one of the opposite corners of the store as always. Trinos placed her there because she was good at bargaining and at catching those who tried to haggle. People would often try asking for less than half the price of a mask's true worth, but Erydis knew the true value of the masks well. In another section of the store, Isaac was preparing to play the flute under his dog djinni mask.

"Take your positions, everyone. We're about to open," Trinos said with excitement as he picked up a box from under a table. "Kitri, I finally found it! The man wouldn't sell it easily, but after some negotiating, I finally got it!"

He opened the box to reveal a shiny elephant mask with a joyful expression and elegant shape. That must have cost him so many Imperials, Erydis thought.

Kitri stared at him in disbelief. "My little lamb, you shouldn't have," she said, admiring its craftsmanship. She kissed Trinos appreciatively and placed the mask on her face. Then she walked to the side of the room and struck a pose in anticipation of her dance. "Erydis, dear, open the shop."

Erydis slid the entrance curtains open, provoking gasps of excitement from the crowd. People of all ages entered with smiles, admiring all the objects around them. Some had brought masks to sell or exchange, and children ran towards the most expensive masks, amazed. Trinos watched them, trying to hide his discontent in front of their parents. He was very careful to catch any sign of theft in the store. On the other side of the store, Kitri danced with slow movements, pausing every time she struck a new pose, accompanied by Isaac on the flute. Many admired her dance more than the masks, and she always got applause from the people who walked by her performance.

Busy with the crowd at her stand, Erydis smiled confidently with every deal. What worked the best for selling masks, she had figured out, was to give them a back story. She would use old legends of djinnis in the time of the Mist Grounds, but if a customer seemed naive enough, she would even invent a new story. She sometimes felt bad for abusing her knowledge of masks and myths, but Trinos paid her fairly to do so.

Erydis was, however, careful of annoying mask collectors. They were knowledgeable about the real value of the masks and didn't offer much profit for an exchange. She once crossed paths with a master collector wearing a mask made of flint, who knew his masks better than anyone she'd met. The safest thing to do then was to sell the masks as fast as she could so that other people didn't listen in on those bargains.

After buying masks, many of the customers would walk towards the paint jars and brushes to decorate their new masks or revive their old ones. Erydis observed that certain people were putting dots on the masks they just bought, meaning that what the presenter said the previous day had made an impact. Erydis wondered if she should do the same, but she didn't know which side to be on. Should she believe the Vakandi outsiders or her Emperor?

By the time the sun was setting, most of the stands in the shop had been emptied out. Trinos carefully counted the Imperials they'd made from the day's work as Kitri and Isaac took a break from their performance. Dusty Corner's clients were thinning out after word spread that all the new masks had been sold out.

Erydis started to rearrange her table of used masks, thinking about the boy from her dream. Rapach and his song. She tried to whistle it, but she was not very musical. She was sure she had the first two notes right, but she couldn't remember the other three. So she tried again and again, hoping to get it right.

As she approached another table with a handful of masks, she noticed a suspicious-looking boy on the other side. He was staring at her as he walked haphazardly through the shop in patched clothes, trying to hide his face under a scarf.

Erydis slammed her palm down on the table.

"Can I help you?" she asked coldly. The boy stared at her with big green eyes, a slight smile resting between his puffy cheeks. He seemed not to care that Erydis had caught him, his expression naive yet confident.

"Do you need a mask? You have to pay for it, you know?" she prompted. The boy stared back without a word. After a few seconds, he whistled the two notes Erydis had been sure of before. "What? Are you trying to imitate me? I guess thieves are running out of ideas these days." The boy continued staring, still whistling those two notes. Erydis walked towards him, annoyed, and she realised the boy was about a couple of years younger than her. She crouched down to his level. "Aren't you listening? What in the name of dust do you want? If you're trying to steal something, the man there with the sheep mask will kick you out."

But the boy only continued staring at her with those bright eyes and infuriating smile. He then produced a note from under his tunic and held it out to Erydis.

"*Hello, friend. You might have noticed that I am not answering your questions with my voice. I am mute, but with your patience, I can speak with my written words better than most.*"

Erydis felt a weight on her chest.

"I'm sorry, all right?" She scratched her head. "But next time, start by giving people the card first." The boy nodded. Erydis thought for a minute. "You know, your face reminds me of a mask I have around here."

She opened a trunk under the table and started rummaging through it, then pulled out an old mask of a monkey with a comical expression similar to the boy's.

"Have you heard of the legend of the monkey djinni mask?" The boy widened his smile and shook his head. "Well, you're in luck. We're not too busy at the moment, so I can share this tale." Erydis smiled as Isaac approached them. He'd heard her and started to play a tune in the background.

"Before the Tower ever existed in this city, before the city was built to its fullest extent, and during the battles for the Mist Grounds, many roamed these lands in search of more mist to create dust.

"But many got lost in those lands full of monstrous djinni. Lost soldiers, wives, and even children like you. Legend says when many cried for their lost ones, the one who knew the lands well went to them.

"With a torch in his hand and a long cape, a valiant man wearing a monkey djinni mask marched through the lands, rescuing hundreds of lost children and adults. After many years, the man left the lands, but the people would always remember him as a hero.

"Nevertheless…" Erydis raised the mask in her hand. "Someone left us his mask here at Dusty Corner, and now it is yours."

The boy gasped slightly and carefully took the mask with both hands as Isaac went back to his corner to rest. Erydis could see that the boy really believed her story. Of course, it wasn't the hero's mask. But the legend she'd narrated was indeed true.

The boy approached a mirror and placed the mask on his face.

"I'm glad you like it," Erydis said.

The boy grabbed a charcoal stick and wrote something on the table. Erydis anxiously glanced at Trinos, but he was busy helping a customer. He would be angry if he caught the boy, so Erydis said nothing as she read silently.

What's your name, friendly girl? No one has ever given me a mask.

"My name is Erydis Nott. Let me write it down somewhere. Oh, I have an idea. Give me your mask for a second."

She grabbed a knife and carved her name on the back of the monkey djinni mask.

"E...ry...dis Nott. Here you go," she said, handing the mask back to the boy. "Remember my name! One day I'll become a famous dust mixer at the Tower!"

The boy put the mask on again and wrote something else on the table.

May I buy more masks now?

"Oh, well. I really can't give you a discount if you want more, you'll have to buy it with real mon—"

The boy took something else from his tunic and placed it on the table in one movement. *Are those Imperials?* Erydis wondered. No, it seemed even more valuable.

"Azure gold? How do you have something like this with you?" The boy took another fistful of gold from his tunic and placed it on the table. "You know this is more valuable than all the masks here, don't you?" Erydis asked. "Do you want to buy them all?" The boy nodded.

Such a sale would make Trinos and Kitri very happy, and Erydis realised she could use her share of the money to buy some dust for her experiment. She placed the masks carefully into two large cloth bags. She wondered why the boy would want such old and used masks, with that kind of money. Maybe her tale about the monkey djinni mask had been too convincing.

After placing the last mask in the bag, she tied it shut and handed it over to the boy.

"I don't really understand why you need so many masks, but I admit your visit has been special. It was nice to meet you," she said.

The boy bowed, placing a hand over his heart. Erydis had never seen a gesture like that. She also noticed that his scarf had moved, revealing a purple mark on his neck. "What's your name, boy?"

The boy put the monkey djinni mask on again and placed a flat, red coin on the table in front of Erydis. There was no inscription on the coin. Before Erydis could ask the boy what it was, the boy left as fast as he could carrying both bags.

She had never seen someone handing over azure gold like that just to buy some old masks. The whole thing was strange, but she sat down to count the money she'd received.

"Erydis!" Trinos approached her, taking off his sheep mask to reveal his grumpy expression. "What happened to all the used masks? And who wrote all this on my table?!"

Erydis stared back at him with a cunning smile and slid the azure gold gently in front of her. Trinos stared at it, his mouth wide open. "Is that..."

"Time to discuss a raise, don't you agree?"

Trinos guffawed, jumping and dancing awkwardly. He petted Erydis roughly on her head.

"Isaac, play a tune! Kitri, come see what Erydis has got for us."

Kitri raised her brows in elegant surprise.

"Erydis, you're remarkable! We have to celebrate! Isaac, close the shop. Let's go to the food bazaar and have dinner. It's on us!"

"Closing early? You must have had a successful day," Thylac said, entering the shop in his Imperial black-and-white robes. He looked around the store with a smile on his face.

"What a magnificent surprise," Kitri said, giving Thylac a hug. "It's been so long since we last saw you here at the shop."

"I know. So many memories of this place." Thylac gazed at the stands with the last of the new masks. "I remember when I was your age, Erydis. I would come to see the new masks, pushing my friends away to choose the best one."

"Was Trinos always this grumpy?" Erydis asked with a laugh, making Trinos frown.

"And what can we do for you today?" Trinos asked, stepping in front of Erydis.

"We were ordered by the Emperor to remove the paints from all the mask shops," Thylac answered.

"Because of what happened yesterday?" Erydis asked.

Thylac nodded.

"Some people have followed the instructions of the Vakandi man from the festival and have painted purple dots on their masks. We've been asking people to remove those masks all morning, since outsiders could be hiding under them. To make matters worse, the same Vakandi man escaped from prison this morning."

Thylac's eyes darted towards Erydis, who was frowning. The talk of prison had jogged her memory of someone who got incarcerated.

"Have you found any Vakandi?" asked Trinos, raising an eyebrow. "The faster they get out of here, the less I'll have to worry for my business."

"None, I'm afraid," Thylac said. "If they're really inside the city, then they must be hiding well. The Emperor has even decided to close Valerios's Tower until the festival ends. All the mixers inside will have to spend the night there."

"Poor people, the Vakandi. First a war against the Emperor, now they're in fear for their lives," Kitri sighed, a hand over her mouth.

"Well, they're savages. They're the ones coming to destroy our civilization," Trinos said.

"I'm afraid Trinos is right. We don't know their intentions, so be on the lookout, but don't panic. We're trying to keep everything under control," Thylac explained.

"Looks like Engyl is far from having actual control," Erydis said.

"Erydis, please do not take their side. I don't want to see you with a mask with any sign of purple dots," Thylac said sternly.

"Well, without a mask that'll be difficult," she retorted.

Thylac suddenly smiled.

"Erydis, remember when you started working at Dusty Corner?"

"She was the same annoying brat she is now," said Trinos, clearing the table with the paints.

"And she was just what this business needed," Kitri added with a gentle smile.

"Of course I remember," Erydis said. "You introduced me to Kitri and Sheep beard. Thanks to you, I managed to get enough money to study at the Geberus Dust Academy."

"Just to get expelled from it," Trinos whispered. Kitri glared at him and he shrugged.

"And you remember the mask you bought with your first Imperials?" Thylac prodded.

"The lost djinni mask!" Erydis smiled. "My favourite legend of the Mist Grounds times. Unfortunately someone stole it."

"Which legend is that?" Isaac drawled from his corner. He loved it when Erydis narrated legends.

"The story of a lost girl who flew from her village into the far southern forest. It is said that the girl found a djinni during her travels, the only djinni smarter than a human. Its wisdom was such that it could borrow magic from the spirits to use as its own. It passed that knowledge to the lost girl, who is said to still live isolated from any civilisation. That djinni the girl saw was called the Lost Djinni."

"Such nonsense…" murmured Trinos.

"But a few years ago, someone stole the mask from me at the Hidden Barrio," Erydis said sadly.

Thylac opened his elegant pouch and took out a grim violet mask with big round eyes. It had tall rabbit-like ears at the top and a small, flat bird beak which pointed to the ground. Most people thought it was too scary, but it reminded Erydis of all the myths from the outside lands.

"The lost djinni mask!" Erydis grabbed the mask, seeing her name carved on its back. "You shouldn't have." She hugged Thylac gratefully. "Thank you, really. How did you find this?"

"I got this mask from a thief we caught a while back. I want you to wear it at the parade tonight—without purple dots."

"I will," Erydis said with an earnest smile.

"I should be going now, there's too much work to do today. Doesn't seem like I'll be able to celebrate any of the Festivals of Dust this year. Oh,

I almost forgot." Thylac's tone turned more serious. "Have you seen a boy with a purple scar on his neck? A witness said he was present at the time the Vakandi man escaped from prison. We think the boy is one of them."

Erydis remembered the mute boy. She thought he might have had some weird intentions, but she didn't think he would be one of the outsiders. He hadn't seemed malicious. "Never seen him before," she lied.

Chapter VI

Purple Breath

Rapach

Someone rapped on Rapach's shield twice, rousing him from his sleep.

"I made breakfast, brother. I woke up earlier than I wanted to," Mat said, her voice sounding muffled through the thick blue glass of the shield.

As Rapach tried to focus his vision, Benu was jumping with excitement right next to him. All Rapach could think of was the dream of the girl he just had. "Erydis…" he whispered. All the explanations she'd given him felt too complex for it to just have been a dream.

Rapach placed the eager jerboa on his head and pushed the handle of the shield up to move it away from the hole. Outside, Mat was cutting some fruit. She handed some pieces to Rapach and also gave him a flat piece of bread from the pouch that Pek had brought them.

Rapach patted his clothes to remove the grey dust from the ground he had slept on and shovelled the food into his mouth.

"I also cut some fruit for the jerboa," Mat said. "They use the water in the fruit for nutrition." She was now analysing her map and making the occasional note.

"I've decided to name her Benu," Rapach said, sitting down next to his sister.

"Benu? I've never heard such a name before."

"I know, but I like the sound of it," he replied shyly.

"Benu it is, then." Mat took a bite of an orange fruit. "I miss the thick stews at the camp. Sadly, making a fire could alert the enemy to our position." She stared at the sky pensively. There were no traces of blue, just a screen of coloured dust and a red sun that radiated a distant warmth they could barely feel. "I miss Central Camp," she said. "Our parents, Zelle, Yumka, the dances, all of it. Life was so much better before we arrived in these lands. Remember when we came down the Khana Mountains to the east? Maybe you were too little. You were born just before we reached the Miasma Realm. Before we found that purple thing and all those who hid under it. It feels like a distant dream now."

"A dream..." That reminded Rapach. "Mat, what did the ancient people say about dreams back at Central Camp?"

"I'm not sure," she answered. "Mama said we dream about the thoughts the Witness whispers in our heads. But Papa and I think it's just a recollection of things we've seen or thought about during the day. And we try to make sense of it when we wake up, even though it's tough to, since we forget the details. Why? Are you having vivid dreams or nightmares that interrupt your sleep?"

Rapach shook his head. "I'm not sure. I don't think so. It was all too real and yet very strange. For one thing, I actually remember all the details. There was a desert with white sand and a black tree with some sort of device to tell time. And a girl with no trace of dust spots on her skin. She told me that to avoid falling victim to the miasma, I should chew on a blue flower, like the ones from the bush Benu was hiding in, and breathe in deeply."

"Don't you even think about trying that," Mat said, pointing at him with a piece of bread. "You just saw the flower and it was memorable enough for you to dream about." She stood up, grabbing a handkerchief from her tunic, lifted it, and let it fall to the ground. "It seems there's slightly more wind today, but it's not dangerously strong. Gather your things. Hopefully the miasma has dispersed a little."

Mat started packing up but left the fruit skins for the wild animals. Rapach started to help her but couldn't help noticing some blue flowers under a tree nearby.

"What if it was true?" he wondered as he inched towards them. But Mat's words rang in his ears. She was right about the flower, he reasoned. Maybe he'd dreamed about it because it was quite unique. But he couldn't get his mind off the girl. Erydis…she felt too real and too different to be just a memory of someone from the camps.

He glanced towards his sister, who was busy filling the holes they'd slept in with dirt and levelling them out. What if, for once, Mat was wrong? He quickly sneaked over to the flowers, ripped them from the soil in one swift move, and hid them in his pouch. He felt somehow stupid for doing it.

Once the camp was packed up, Mat and Rapach walked back the same path they took the previous day. They followed in Benu's steps, Rapach shooting kibbles in quick succession. He noticed that the jerboa seemed to have more confidence around them and was jumping with more spirit than before. Sometimes she even waited for them, so they were never too far behind her.

"She might not be faster than Yumka, but your jerboa seems quite loyal to you so far," Mat commented with a crooked smile.

They made their way back through the same slanted forest terrain they had left the day before, and it wasn't long before they saw small clouds of miasma again. Rapach shot kibbles to the south-west, and Benu leaped forward to chase each well-earned snack.

But soon Benu started looking lost. The jerboa couldn't find a way through the miasma as it slowly enveloped them, becoming thicker and thicker.

"It doesn't seem as dense as yesterday, but I can see the wind moving the miasma towards us." Mat signaled at Rapach to be careful. "Rapach, shoot another kibble a little more towards the south, hopefully there's a gap through there."

Rapach nodded as his knees trembled in fear of the horrific miasma around them. He shot a kibble as far as he could. Benu studied the terrain for a while and then jumped after it.

"I think Benu has found a way around it," Mat said, following the jerboa.

The terrain seemed steeper than it had the day before, and the miasma seemed to get thicker and closer with each step. Benu stopped for a kibble and then jumped onto Rapach's head.

"I guess Benu can't find a way around it after all," Mat said, taking out her map. "Rabaska Lake is not too far from here. Unfortunately, the miasma is too dense."

"We can try waiting a few hours," Rapach suggested, desperate to succeed on his first mission.

"I have instructions to head back if we run into dense miasma, and I don't think it'll move anytime soon. I'm sorry, Rapach. We'll find another mission for you."

"But, Mat!"

"Rapach!" Mat sounded exasperated. "I know this is your first mission and I really wanted it to go well. But I don't want you to turn into one of them. I won't risk our lives for this mission. The miasma is getting closer to us, we have to go."

Rapach went quiet. He accepted Mat's decision even as he felt a stubborn determination to complete his task. He kept walking, staring down at the ground. He'd been so excited about the contents of the package awaiting them at Rabaska Lake.

Suddenly, he bumped into his sister's back. Rapach looked up, confused. Mat was trembling in a way he had never seen before. Something was not right.

"A Purple Breather," Mat said in a strange tone.

Rapach peered ahead to see what she was looking at. In the distance was a dark figure in a black cloak that dragged on the ground. A hood covered the back of the figure's head and a striking mask covered its face. The mask was pearly white with two large, dark circles for eyes and a rectangular hole for a mouth. Metallic tubes snaked around its sides. The figure had its gaze fixed on the ground, and it was standing eerily still.

Then the figure inhaled deeply and exhaled with a frightening, blowing sound. A silent cloud of miasma emerged from the slit over its mouth. Rapach realised then why they were called Purple Breathers. They were

Silent People who would go to places without miasma, filling the air with the doomed clouds, turning the innocent into one of them.

"What do we do, Mat? What do we do?" Rapach whispered in fear.

"We must wait for him to move." Mat stood frozen in place. "I don't think it has seen us."

"But the miasma around us; it's getting closer!"

Mat was breathing rapidly, her eyes darting from side to side, searching for an escape. The wind was picking up speed, bringing the miasma closer and closer. Every possible escape route seemed to be blocked. The Purple Breather started moving towards them, apparently not aware of the siblings' presence. It moved slowly over the ground, almost hovering, spreading more miasma as it exhaled. Benu seemed scared too, and was clinging on to Rapach's head and quivering.

Rapach closed his eyes tightly, trying to think. A memory flashed into his mind of a girl with a blue flower.

There was no other choice. He took the blue flowers from his pouch.

"Mat," he said, forcing one of the flowers into her hand. "I'm going to start chewing and breathe in. I'll run to Rabaska Lake, and if you don't hear my voice right after, then know that I've become a Silent One."

"Don't you dare," Mat said, grabbing his arm. "It was just a dream."

"Do we have a choice? Please do the same. The effect will last only five minutes. Every moment counts, Mat."

He broke free from his sister's grip and ran in the opposite direction towards the dense wall of purple clouds. He placed a whole flower into his mouth and chewed quickly. As he got closer to the miasma, he felt a sweet scent emanating from his mouth and trailing into his nose.

Rapach jumped onto the steep terrain, drawing a deep, sharp breath. The flower's scent felt fresh in his chest. Suddenly he fell and rolled onto the ground, hitting some bushes. As he recovered, he could see only purple. He tried holding his breath, afraid he would transform, but then he could not wait any longer.

He took a deep breath of the warm miasma, thinking what a fool he was to have believed a dumb dream.

But when Rapach opened his eyes, he felt no different. Nothing had changed. He moved the same as always, with unclouded sight, unlike what he thought Silent People would go through. It had worked. The flower had worked, and he was safe.

"MAAAAAAAT!" He shouted into the miasma, as loudly as he could. "DO AS I SAID! SEE YOU AT RABASKA LAKE!"

He would have waited for his sister, but he had only minutes left before the flower's effect would wear off. He ran as fast as he could, making sure Benu was still on his head. Luckily, the miasma only affected humans.

The miasma was thinning out as he ran. After one final stride, he emerged from it. He ran a bit more, just to be safe, then tripped over a rock and tumbled to the ground again. Rapach groaned and raised his head to look at his surroundings. There it was. A glimmering lake with white water. Rabaska Lake.

He heard steps behind him and turned, alert.

"Never…" said Mat, panting as she spat the blue flower to the ground, "... scare me like that again."

Rapach stood up with a smile.

Thank you, Erydis, he thought as he hugged his sister.

Chapter VII

Night Parade

Erydis

Erydis walked to the food market with Kitri, Trinos, and Isaac. The market was conveniently located within the Emerald Barrio. The tables outside each tarp-covered building accommodated numerous people concocting recipes for their businesses. The waiters were always in friendly competition with one another, luring customers to their stalls while street musicians played songs for a coin. But the lack of people on the streets suggested that they were saving their Imperials for the next day, when unique dishes would be cooked for the Festival of Many Dusts.

Trinos and Kitri ordered an overwhelming amount of food and drinks for all of them.

"Good work, everyone. Well-deserved feast for the first day of the festival," Trinos said with a smile as he took a sip of his blue anise liquor and poured some for Kitri. "And such a breathtaking dance, darling."

Kitri raised her dainty glass to clink Trinos's.

"It was a wonderful start to the day," she replied, taking a sip. "With today's gains, we might be able to afford that small house in the Palace Barrio, and it's thanks to you both."

Isaac lifted his glass in silent agreement. He took a bite of a large, sweet-smelling turkey leg.

Erydis was focused on her own meal, which wasn't as fancy as the other plates. She had ordered a thick, yellow soup with rice and steamed, spice-infused vegetables.

"Are you sure you don't want anything else, love?" Kitri asked, smiling. "Gullkorn is too common for a celebratory meal, don't you agree?"

"Well, it's nostalgic for me," Erydis answered. "Reminds me of when I was younger. My mum used to cook this for me when she worked here, at the market."

"I remember the good Aris and her comfort soups," Isaac drawled. "She would come up with such delicious, yellow dust mixtures and infusions."

"Yes, I remember you coming often with different girls," Erydis teased. "My mum advised you each time not to break anyone's heart."

"And I would tell her that the one with multiple cracks in the heart is me. That's why I took the path of music," he retorted, taking a big sip of his emerald wine.

"I wish I had met her," Kitri said. "I bet there is so much of her in you."

Erydis smiled brightly. She missed her mother, but she knew that she would have loved every one she knew, even Trinos.

She lifted her bowl to take a big slurp of the soup. "I can't stay for long, I'm afraid. I have to go and see Kemia."

Kitri nodded. "Say hello to her for us. See you tomorrow, Erydis."

Erydis took off to the Geberus Dust Academy. This time, she didn't have to go all the way to the second floor of the city to enter Kemia's Tower. During the celebration of the Festival of the People, citizens from Dust City were allowed inside the academy to see the students' dust-mixing presentations. Erydis entered through the main doors, which were adorned with tiles in different shades of green.

A rush of memories overwhelmed her as she took a moment to look around. She remembered being a part of this place's fabric well. The garden in the open centre of the building was flourishing. Some masked students sat about on a patch of grass next to a statue of a bearded man wearing a turban and full robes. He was Geberus Lyceum, the creator of the Geberus Dust Academy. The current headmaster, Jabir Lyceum, was his descendant, and many students joked that he was identical to his ancestor.

Erydis walked through the gardens and entered one of the hallways. As she walked along, she peered into the different classrooms. She remembered running there on her first day as a student, going from classroom to classroom to see what her older classmates were mixing. But today, students were showing off their mixtures in the hallway. Erydis thought they were interesting but lacked potential to win the contest on the festival's last day. The contest attracted people of advanced skill, and Erydis was determined to be one of them.

She headed to a classroom of seventh grade Alchemia students, where Kemia would likely be giving her lecture.

"Seems like everything is ready, Tulia," said a boy as Erydis entered the classroom of stone walls.

A crowd was observing an experiment in the middle of the room. Erydis squeezed through to get a closer look. A girl with curly, red hair and blue robes was working on a machine in the shape of a cat. Her tools and machinery looked quite expensive, and the joints on the legs looked quite similar to that of a real cat.

"This is my feline machine," the girl announced, facing the crowd and batting her light-blue eyes charmingly. The girl was Tulia. She was a few years older than Erydis and someone she truly despised. "I've mixed Machina with Vita to create a replica of a dust-operated feline that should be able to walk and jump like a true cat! And maybe someday, even think like an animal," Tulia said.

Behind her, Kori Pegasos, a boy with thick brown hair started applauding.

"I just need to add some of this dust mixture to make it work." Tulia poured a thick green liquid into an opening in the silver machine. Erydis covered her face instinctively.

A cloud of green dust appeared through a tiny chimney on the mechanical cat's head. After a second, the cat took several graceful steps and the crowd started to applaud. But just as they did, grey smoke started leaking from the cat's mouth and it exploded, bits of the expensive creation sent flying around the room. A few gears hit Erydis lightly on her tunic.

"But...why?!" Tulia was dismayed. "Kori, what did you do?"

"I simply tightened a loose piece! It should have worked, I'm sorry." Kori hung his head, looking clearly upset.

"The machine works fine," Erydis said, stepping forward. "It's the dust mixture you used that's not working. The consistency is too thick. I understand if you wanted a potent combustion, but you would have better results with a lighter mixture."

Tulia stared at her coldly.

"Haven't seen you here since you were dismissed for incinerating that classroom with your failed burn ointment," she said.

The other students snickered at Tulia's comment.

"Hi, Erydis!" Kori said with his naive but gentle smile. "What are you doing here?"

"I was looking for Kemia. I thought she would be here."

"Why do you keep trying to talk to her?" Tulia asked arrogantly. "Does she pity you? I don't understand why she still talks to you after you burnt down a classroom and stole from other students. You still owe me the dust you stole from the Tower! My father had brought them just for me."

"We agreed that I'd help you with Alchemia only if you gave me some of that dust, remember?" Erydis answered calmly. "Besides, Kemia trusts my skills enough to help me win the contest."

"Hah! You win the contest? What makes you think you're on my level? You're just a beggar from the Hidden Barrio. I'm Tulia Chimara, daughter of the Master of Vita! And will you seek help from your father?" She placed a hand to her mouth in mock surprise. "Oh no...but your father is just a disgusting prisoner, isn't he?"

Students stared at one another silently, waiting for Erydis's response. She could feel her blood rushing to her head as she clenched her hands into tight fists.

Erydis crouched, holding her head with one hand and reaching to the floor with the other. She started shaking, fake crying.

"Erydis, she didn't mean it," Kori said.

"Of course I did! She'll never reach any heights. Ever." Tulia flashed a victorious smile.

"This girl…" Erydis stood up, full of energy. "This street rat will work beside the best mixers at the Tower while you ask your father how to fix your flashy pyrotechnics."

Tulia stared at her angrily, but then Kori stepped in-between the girls.

"I'm sure you'll both go far. You both are very skilled. Erydis, you can find Kemia in the library."

Erydis nodded and left the classroom as Tulia stared unforgivingly at Kori. She wiped her tearless face as she walked away, unclenched a fist, and looked at the expensive heat resistant gears from Tulia's feline machine in her hand. She grinned and went on her way.

The library was in one of the towers of the academy. Walking towards the stairs, Erydis noticed that some of the older students were wearing masks with purple dots. Some had multiple large dots, while others had painted just a few discrete ones. If they were to get caught by a guard, they would surely get in trouble.

Erydis walked through an arched entrance on the second floor and into the academy's distinguished library. The library contained row upon row of shelves full of books, but in the centre was an open space with several tables arranged neatly. A spiral staircase rose to the third floor. Erydis had never seen the third floor before, so she decided to climb up and explore it.

As she was exploring, she caught a glimpse of Kemia behind some tall shelves, surrounded by a pile of books.

"You finally found me," Kemia said without looking up from her thick book.

"This place has really changed." Erydis looked around. "I have to admit that I miss it."

"Did you manage to get the dust from Valerios's Tower? The dust you needed for your experiment?" Kemia asked, curious.

"No, but I did arrange for some expensive pieces of machinery from

Tulia."

"Knowing how you and that bratty girl get along, I assume you stole them." Erydis simply grinned in response. Kemia raised an eyebrow. "Well done."

"You worked with her father at the Tower, didn't you?" Erydis asked.

"Aerzzo? Yes, that cowardly man. No wonder Tulia is spoilt. The man is afraid of not giving in to her every demand. Can't deny his talent for Vita, however."

The loud chatter of a group of masked students from another table interrupted their conversation, making Kemia stare for a second before going back to her work.

"First graders; so much energy," she said.

"Won't you teach them who they're sitting next to?" Erydis asked with a mischievous smile.

Kemia winked and stood up, looking at the students authoritatively. She walked slowly over to them, and one by one they noticed her presence.

"Is this how you study in a library?" Kemia asked with her powerful voice. "Take off your masks; there's no parade inside the academy." The kids hastily obeyed without question. "I see you're studying the new book by Liudmila Dametot. *Basics of Alchemia and Arma: A Double-Edged Sword.* It's too basic, even for first graders. If you want to learn more about Alchemia, try *Diaries of the First Alchemia Masters.*"

"Thank you, Lady Zosimos," the children said.

Kemia walked back to the table, where Erydis was watching the entire situation.

"That innocent face of terror. Priceless!" Kemia said with a smile. "Even you made that face the first time we met, Erydis."

"No, I did not!"

"I caught you working with black dust and you begged me not to expel you." Kemia laughed quietly at the memory.

"Too bad it wasn't you who caught me when that classroom started burning," Erydis murmured, looking down.

Kemia went quiet and looked down at her book.

"Erydis, you need to spend more time with this experiment of yours," she said. You still can work at the Tower, if that's what you really desire."

Erydis looked at her. Kemia was right—she could still do it if things went according to plan.

"Kemia, I need some books."

"To research what?"

"The extraction of white dust from coloured dust...and one about dreams."

"Extraction of white dust? Not an easy read, but the book *From Mist to Coloured Dust* is one I constantly go back to. Be sure to look for the advanced edition of it. But dreams? I wouldn't think that's something you would like to read about."

"The thing is, I had a dream about a boy," Erydis said.

"A boy?"

"But I've never seen this boy before! He was hiding from something, and he was singing this song I can't shake off. And I have no talent for music, so I never dream about it. That boy; his name was Rapach. I've never seen someone like him. He was dirty, covered with grey dust, and he had some kind of mark over his left eye."

Kemia glanced at her, thoughtful.

"You mean like this?" Kemia lifted her sleeve. She had several black and red dots on the skin around her right wrist.

"Yes! Why do you have those?"

"Because I've been exposed to the dust too long," she said thoughtfully before standing up and stacking the books in front of her. "Erydis, if you have more dreams like this, let me know. Now, I have to continue my mixing."

Kemia walked out of the library. The first graders froze as she passed by.

Erydis walked back through the academy gardens after checking out a book about dreams, though she had struggled to find many with promising titles. Kemia's reaction towards her dream surprised her, as did her abrupt exit. She also wondered how Kemia had the same dust marks on her wrist that Rapach had. Would the same happen to her some day?

As she was about to leave the academy, she noticed someone looking at her from next to the statue of Geberus. It was a boy with a monkey mask.

"You!" she called out. "What are you doing here?"

The boy waved and started walking towards the exit, looking back at her several times. Did he want her to follow him? She tracked him as he walked through the garden and into the streets, where citizens were preparing for the evening's Festival of the People parade.

The masked boy took a turn into an alley and waited for Erydis to catch up a little before he carried on. He walked around the back of the funicular station at the Emerald Barrio. Erydis noticed some guards looking for people with purple dots on their masks, asking them to remove their masks so they could ask them questions about their intentions. The boy in the monkey mask seemed to be avoiding the soldiers. Of course he was—he knew they were searching for him. Were the rumours true? Did he help that man escape from prison?

The boy suddenly sped up, squeezing through the crowd on the busy street. Erydis took a deep breath and followed him. He was walking briskly towards the Dust Ring, where people were gathering for the parade. In the middle of the street, musicians were playing the festival's traditional jolly tune. Performers took to the streets to dance with dust lamps hanging from chains. The lamps created a path of coloured clouds. Erydis was always fascinated by them. And she wasn't alone—the boy stopped for a moment to watch the performers before continuing to walk purposefully again.

Just like in previous years, people were dancing and singing in the Dust Ring, wearing their masks. But that year, there was also a large vehicle with enormous wheels slowly roaming the streets. It almost looked like a wagon from the funicular, with three levels occupied by people waving Dust City's flags through the windows. It was made of crimson steel, and yellow smoke spat from its chimney. The masked conductors inside the vehicle waved at the crowd to get on top of it. Excited passersby climbed up its sides and found seats, as did the masked boy. He gestured for her to follow. Erydis had to push a few people aside to get onto the vehicle. She settled into a seat on the uncovered top deck of the vehicle with a dozen other people and the boy in the monkey mask.

"Where are you taking me?" Erydis asked. The boy pointed at her mask resting on her back, and then touched his. "You want me to wear it?" The boy nodded. Erydis hesitated, wondering if this was all a trap. But she pushed aside her doubts and put on her lost djinni mask. The boy jumped off the vehicle, joining a group of decorated performers who were marching and singing with dust lamps creating coloured clouds. Erydis jumped off the vehicle too and followed the boy towards another alley. There was only one place he could be going... The Hidden Barrio, a place where all her fears resided. Not because of who lived there, but because of memories she wished didn't exist.

The streets were tight, dirty, and dark under the second floor of the city. There weren't many dust lamps to light the street at night, and during the day, the sun was blocked by the shadow cast by the Palace District. But people in the barrio didn't care, just like Erydis didn't when she lived there.

The boy sprinted along, taking many turns. Erydis almost lost him. She started running after him, and after a sharp turn to the left, she caught sight of him entering a two-storey house. With windows sealed behind bricks and cracks on its walls, there was no sign of any light or life coming from the house.

Erydis walked to the red metal door and tried to push it open unsuccessfully. She started knocking. A wrinkled hand extended from a round opening in the middle of the door, palm open as if asking for something. Erydis stared at it in confusion, but she eventually realised what she needed to do.

She pulled out the red coin the boy had given her that morning and pressed it into the open palm. The hand closed on the coin quickly, and after a few seconds, the door opened slightly. Erydis pushed it slowly and entered.

She could barely see in front of her as she closed the door behind her. Whispers surrounded her in the darkness. Then the boy in the monkey mask lit a dust lamp, casting just enough light to illuminate the space around them and reveal people behind many different masks staring at her. They grew quiet as she followed the boy with the monkey mask through them. Erydis noticed that some of them were wearing purple dots on their masks, but not all.

The boy led Erydis into a small room and closed the door behind them. He removed a tapestry on the floor, revealing a wooden trapdoor. He opened it. Erydis saw a ladder leading down into a room with warm but dim light.

"What are you hiding here?" she asked as the boy climbed down the ladder. He said nothing, and Erydis followed.

They walked through the dark hallway until they reached a room with brick walls. The walls were covered in tapestries, and there were pillows scattered all over the floor. Sitting in a chair made of pillows was the same man who had announced the Vakandi's arrival at the Inauguration Festival. He wore the same wide grin under his staring green eyes.

"Welcome, Erydis," he said with the same enthusiasm he had at the festival, but in a slightly different accent.

"You're that man who got out of prison."

"Yes, thanks to my fellow Vakandi Clan members," he said proudly.

"Who are you?"

"Ah...forgive me." He stood up. His clothes were colourful but shredded in many parts. "Behind the monkey mask is my little brother, Eko. He drank from the polluted river several years ago and unfortunately lost his voice, but not his enthusiasm. And I am Ferus, leader of the Vakandi Clan, owner of the mocking mask and permanent visitor of your city. We, the Vakandi, have had enough of fighting, and we've decided to do things peacefully from now on. We are the clan of trickery, and we just want to survive."

The brothers bowed, their right hands over their hearts.

"We are recruiting people who believe in our cause, and we think you might be a fitting member."

"But I'm not wearing a purple dot on my mask," Erydis said, confused. "I thought you were reaching out to whomever had them."

"Well, the purple dots have two purposes," Ferus said, holding a finger up, "one, to measure how much support we have inside the city, which seems to be a decent amount. That's also the reason I announced our arrival, you see? And two, the Emperor will be searching for us behind the masks with purple dots, which means he won't have time to search the rest.

That way, we can walk this city with normal masks without problems, recruiting people for our cause."

Erydis couldn't believe it. It was such a simple yet effective plan. "So your plan is to invade the city?"

Ferus stared at her, still smiling widely.

"As I said at the Initiation, we just want to be heard. But the Emperor has no desire to listen to us. He prefers to kill us instead of finding a solution. And of course we can't allow it. Invade the city?" He laughed. "Perhaps, but it's more important to us to take over the source of the problem."

"Valerios's Tower," Erydis realised out loud, and Ferus nodded. "Is it really affecting your clan that much?"

"Terribly. Our city, Sorrow City, has been a victim of that grey dust discarded into the river. We could not handle all the fights against you 'dusters'. So, we came a long way from our homes and into yours."

"Sorrow City? I've never heard of it."

"Of course you haven't. Your Emperor tries to hide everything related to us. Our city is in the far south of these lands. If you follow the polluted river until it's divided by three different-coloured rocks, take two left turns and one right, you'll reach our home. Of course, right now it's deserted since we're all here."

Erydis took a moment to think. She knew almost nothing of the lands outside of the city.

"But why are you telling me this? How did you know my name?" she asked.

"Well, Erydis Nott, we've seen you and heard of you. We know you know the city and how to handle it. You know the streets and the people well. We are very interested in having you on our side," Ferus explained.

"But I don't know how to get inside the Tower. What help do you need from me?"

"We need a diversion as we enter the Tower. Perhaps you can help us by creating a distraction."

"And why would I help you?" Erydis asked. She understood their cause, but she didn't see why she should help them.

Eko tugged at his brother's torn tunic and gestured with his hands.

"Ah, very observant of you, Eko. Erydis, if you help us get inside the Tower, we'll let you go with us. I hear you want some dust from the Tower?"

Eko smiled at Erydis.

"So you were listening to my conversation with Kemia in the library?" Eko only stared at her with his piercing eyes. "Even if I help you," Erydis said, "how in the world will you enter the Tower? The only entrance is through the palace, exactly where all the royal quarters are. Not to mention some of the elite soldiers who protect the Tower. I don't want to help you if you plan on hurting innocent people."

"You have my word that no one will die," Ferus assured her. "We want you dusters to join us, not hate us. As for the Tower, you're right. Many soldiers defend the entrance, but inside the Tower, their numbers thin out. They are strong soldiers, but are not as many as our people. No, my comrade, we won't be using the main entrance."

Erydis frowned. "Another entrance."

"Less conventional, but yes. You see, the walls of the Tower are made of a strong mix of dust, steel, and rocks. It's impenetrable. But under the Tower, where the mist comes out, it is just rock—easy to drill through. Whoever built it did not count on people entering from under it."

"A tunnel," Erydis said, her eyes wide.

"Eko, if you would do the honours."

Eko walked towards a tapestry on the wall behind them and pulled it down.

There, in an almost perfect circle, was a tunnel.

"Tomorrow, after your distraction, we'll enter the Tower. What do you say?" Ferus extended his hand.

Erydis couldn't believe it. She felt a pressure on her chest, but she immediately shook his hand.

"For the dust," she said, thinking of her experiment.

Chapter VIII

Lion Mask

Rapach

The siblings faced the opaque white expanse of Rabaska Lake. The water emitted an eerie glow. Many ominous stories were told about people drinking its polluted water and dying. But there was a beauty about the place. The lake was surrounded by crimson trees shrouded in clouds of miasma. Daylight illuminated specks of dust in the still air. Surrounded by the peaceful silence, Rapach breathed deeply. "Mat, I'm sorry for leaving you behind. I just acted without thinking."

"You saved us both. That's all that matters." Mat patted Rapach's back. "I have no idea how you could have possibly dreamed of something like that. Maybe it was just a coincidence, but it seems so extraordinary."

She surveyed the lake in front of them. "Now we have no other choice but to continue on our mission. Our way back to the camps could be dangerous, with the miasma and the Purple Breathers that are probably hiding within it. I see a brick road to the south. It seems like it hasn't been used recently, but it should lead us to Rabaska City." Rapach nodded.

As they walked by the lake, Rapach thought of Erydis. She had to be real. He had so many questions about her. Was she trustworthy? It was difficult for him to be certain of anyone outside his clan. But even as his head swam with more questions, he hoped to dream of her again and maybe find the answers.

The brick road curved around the side of the lake and led them to a red wooden bridge across a river. On the other side, a couple of triangular flags on wooden poles marked the entrance to Rabaska City.

"I don't see anyone on this path. Do you think the city is deserted, sister?" Rapach asked.

"It seems so. We should be careful; there might be Silent People there. Keep your eyes open for any clue of this 'friend' dressed in red. The faster we find that package, the better."

They crossed over the curved bridge into Rabaska City, staring at the compact houses that lined the streets. Each house was elevated a few inches off the ground by wooden pillars. They followed a traditional architectural style—diamond-shaped windows and arched roofs. Rapach noticed that nature had taken over these buildings. Most of the walls were covered in yellow leaves, and patches of crimson grass stuck out from cracks in the road. Like everything else, most of the city was covered in the annoying grey dust.

"Look at this place," said Mat, staring at a house next to them. "I wonder if our clan had houses like this before we came to the Miasma Realm. Wouldn't it be nice to settle down in a place like this?"

"You could live here," said Rapach, pushing the door open, "there's no one inside."

"Rapach! What are you doing? I told you we need to be careful."

Rapach shrugged.

"Always check the windows before entering a building," Mat said. "We need to make sure we're not seen."

"But it's empty! Come on in!" Rapach barged into the house. The inside was littered with broken furniture, and wooden cooking utensils lay on the floor.

Mat followed, rubbing her forehead.

"Rapach, come here," she said calmly, grabbing his shoulder. "I know your curiosity takes over your sense of responsibility. But in these lands, outside the camps, you have to be careful of the dangers it might hold. I know you want to absorb every new place you see, but we have a mission. You have to pay attention so that after this mission, you won't need me to direct your every step."

"I'm sorry, Mat. It's just that travelling to new places like this makes me want to explore every corner."

"I know, Rapach. Hopefully one day, with the help of the Witness, we'll have all the time in the world to do that. But for now, focus."

Rapach nodded. "I'll try." He watched Benu sniff at a wooden spoon.

The Witness was a higher spirit they believed in, yet Rapach would sometimes wonder why it had never come to help them in that doomed land.

The brick road continued past several wooden canoes that lay half-sunk beside the lake. A short distance up the road, on higher ground, stood a building that was larger than all the other houses.

"Let's get up to that building, Rapach," Mat said. "It'll be easier for us to search the entire city from there. Remember, keep a lookout for the 'friend' in red."

They passed abandoned carts and makeshift tools, strewn about the streets as sure signs of the people who had once lived there.

"What happened here?" Rapach wondered out loud.

"I don't know. Maybe the villagers ran from the Silent People and abandoned the place, like what happened to many other smaller villages. Hopefully none of those who escaped is the stranger we're looking for."

Benu jumped through the city skilfully, guiding the siblings. They climbed a wide set of stairs to reach the large building, where they stopped to look around. The building had a tower on each side, each topped with red triangular flags. Its wide ground floor had been taken over by the roots of crimson trees. Weeds were growing through the cracks in its yellow walls, and the whole place was shrouded in a coat of dust. Some blue-furred monkeys sat watching them from the top of each tower, keeping quiet and apparently not minding the strangers too much.

"It seems like a temple of sorts," Mat observed.

"Should we search inside?"

"Yes, but we should climb up to where those roots are by the upper window. It wouldn't be safe to enter through the main gate."

They climbed up the roots gingerly as some monkeys got closer to observe them. As they got higher, Rapach realised a layer of fog had started to cover the top of the lake.

They entered the building through the diamond window carefully, avoiding the broken shards of glass within its frame, stepping into an inner balcony that took up the entire floor. They hid behind some crates as Benu kept watch calmly from Rapach's head. Then the siblings slowly approached the edge of the balcony to look down at the floor beneath them. They seemed to be in a space where people used to gather; many benches were arranged facing a small clearing in the middle of the room.

"Should we try to—" Rapach started, but his sister covered his mouth, watching the first floor intently.

A few Purple Breathers appeared below them.

"That's a lot of Silent People in one place," Mat whispered.

A man without a mask stood still in the centre of the room. It seemed like they were all waiting for someone.

All of a sudden, a stranger entered from another room. He didn't walk in that smooth, jarring way the others did. This person actually walked normally. He wore a yellow cape and an orange and purple suit. He held one of those pearl-like masks the Silent People wore, and wore a mask himself.

But his mask was different. The stranger wore a scary lion mask with big round eyes with minuscule eyeholes to see through. It was orange and purple with a pattern of black dots and brown fur that fell to its sides.

The stranger in the lion mask approached the still man in the centre. He placed the Silent People mask on the man and secured it behind his head with three individual belts. Then he draped a black robe around the man's shoulders and turned to face the others. Pointing at the door, he uttered a string of strange words to his followers.

The Purple Breathers left the room. The man in the lion mask remained inside. Once the others were gone, the man took a red envelope from his robe. He stared at it for a moment before leaving the building too.

Mat gave a quiet gasp, a hand over her mouth.

"Have you heard of them wearing animal masks before?" Rapach asked.

"Never." Mat was thoughtful for a moment. "Never seen someone giving them orders either. He must be some sort of leader to them. I think he's trying to find something, along with the rest of the Silent People."

"Do you think they're looking for the package?"

"Possibly." Mat tightened her lips. "The lion-masked stranger was holding a red envelope. The friend in red must have left many letters in our clan's mailboxes throughout the lands. He must have taken it from one of the mailboxes we lost in the miasma."

"Sister, then whatever's in that package must be important, don't you think?"

Mat nodded. "If their leader wants that package, we have to find it before they do. We don't know what might happen if they beat us to it."

"What do we do now?" Rapach asked.

"Our best bet is to inspect the surroundings from up here and see if we can find that 'friend in red'. I'll look through the south and west windows. You take the other two."

Rapach nodded and skulked to the east side of the inner balcony, trying not to make a sound. Through the window, he could see the white lake with many destroyed canoes along its edge. A broken dock floated in pieces, and on one of them, he spotted a glimpse of something red.

"Sister," Rapach whispered, "I see something red there, on the broken dock, but I'm not sure what it is. It doesn't look like a person."

"It's the only red thing I've seen in Rabaska City," Mat contemplated, nodding slowly. "Good job, Rapach. It might lead us somewhere. We have to be careful though… it seems like the Purple Breathers have started spreading miasma."

Rapach saw a small cloud of miasma floating above the lake.

The siblings followed Benu out of the city towards the lake. The jerboa weaved and jumped through the bushes, trying to stay away from the Silent People. When they reached the broken dock, they cautiously stepped onto the unstable wooden planks. A piece broke under Rapach's feet, and he jumped away onto another piece just in time. And there, on a steady plank in front of them, was what they had seen from the temple's window.

It was a red glove. Quite clean, even with the very thin layer of dust that covered it. All the fingers on the glove were folded down, except for the index finger and thumb.

"It seems like it's pointing towards that big rock in the middle of the lake," Rapach said. "Maybe we should go there."

"That sounds like a terrible idea."

"It's a lead, isn't it? Plus, I bet the Silent People wouldn't go there."

Mat stared at him. "Today you've made some pretty lucky decisions. Maybe too lucky. Very well. Let's get a canoe to take us there."

They searched the area for a canoe that wasn't in too bad of a condition. Rapach found one, but it sank as soon as he pushed it into the lake.

"Over there!" Mat pointed to a yellow canoe that was badly scratched. Rapach stared at her. "What? As long as it floats." Mat continued the search, this time for an oar. Rapach shook his head, feeling uncertain, but they had no other choice.

Miraculously, the canoe didn't sink. They floated silently in the water, the only sound coming from Mat's rowing. Although they were worried that a Silent One would see them, the fog around the lake seemed to be on their side.

"Imagine what this place must have been like before it was destroyed," Mat said with a smile. "People probably danced by the lake and fished every night. I wonder if the monkeys were used to people passing by."

Rapach smiled back. He wondered if they would one day live in a place like that, without having to worry about the Silent People.

These lands were broken. Doomed and unsalvageable. But at least they had survived this far, which was reason enough for him to smile again.

"We're almost there," Mat said.

As they approached the rock, they saw a boot on top of it. There were taut ropes wrapped all around the rock, each leading underwater.

"What now?" Mat asked, confused.

"I think I know what to do," Rapach said. "If we follow one of the ropes, it might lead us to the package!"

"But which rope? There must be at least ten ropes extending in different directions here."

"We follow the one the boot is pointing at, I suppose."

Mat smiled and patted her brother on the shoulder. She looked at Benu, still perched on Rapach's head.

"Proud of this little one, Benu. You are lucky to be his helper."

Benu leapt up and down a few times and stood up on her hind legs, looking around.

Rapach grabbed the rope the boot was pointing to and pulled on it. The rope tensed as he did—it was tethered to something in the distance. The boat moved in that direction as he kept on pulling the rope, gaining speed. Rapach noticed a serious look on his sister's face. She seemed full of doubt yet anxious to get to her destination. There was a tone of wonderment in the silent lake. What would they find at the end of the rope, behind the white fog?

After a few minutes, Rapach noticed a silhouette in the distance. "I see something."

"Me, too," Mat said. "It's another rock, but there seems to be a canoe anchored next to it."

She was right. The canoe was falling apart and there was a small red flag on it.

"I can't believe the Silent People didn't notice this before. If they destroyed this city, then whoever arranged all this had to have been here only recently," Mat concluded as they reached the canoe.

Rapach jumped onto the other canoe and searched under the red flag.

"See something, brother?"

"There's this hat." He passed a poorly knitted red hat to Mat. It had some small stones and dry leaves stuck to it.

Then Rapach saw something next to his feet in the canoe. "Sister! Here it is! The package!"

He grabbed the square package, which was slightly bigger than his hands.

It had another red envelope attached to it and it was labeled, "To the Jerboa Clan."

Rapach opened the envelope. Inside it was a letter and a map. He handed them to Mat.

"I'll take the map," Mat said. "But since it's your mission, you should be the one to read the letter. But do not open the package. Remember, we aren't allowed to, or else the trust in our clan will be lost."

Rapach nodded and started reading the letter.

Dear Members of the Jerboa Clan

I know what you're thinking. All this mystery to get a package to an oblivious old man? I unfortunately cannot share more in this letter. But I believe the item inside this package could be of great aid to its recipient.

Did you find my puzzle amusing? I sincerely did not have much time to plan it, but it was enough for the package to arrive safely in your hands.

Well, let's get back to the point.

The old man whom you shall take the package to is in a city far to the east. They call it Sorrow City. A rather depressing name, if you ask me.

I've included a map in the envelope to help you find this place. Do not let those that roam silently find this map. I must reiterate the importance of giving the old man what's inside the package.

Honestly, I don't think our paths will ever cross again. I have to run from the hypnotised, who return again to this city which once lived peacefully.

I wish you luck, my friends, for you will encounter a dangerous path ahead that I could not follow. But with caution and plenty of speed, you should be able to rest easy at the end of this journey.

Sincerely,
A Friend in Red

P.S. If you are in need of new clothes, please take what I have left behind.

"Didn't have much time to plan it? It seems pretty elaborate to me," Mat said. "Also, the map is very well traced. Looks like we just have to follow the white river for a while."

"Does this mean we can continue on my mission?" Rapach asked, putting on a red cape he found in another section of the canoe.

"Definitely. Whoever wrote this letter knew what he was talking about." Mat pulled the red hat onto her head. "Let's row to the bridge we saw earlier. From there we can follow the river to our destination, I believe."

The fog was dense, but as they rowed they could see how it had mixed with the miasma in some parts of the city. The lake was quiet, as usual, and they could see the bridge in the distance.

"After passing under the bridge, we row until nightfall. We will camp near the river," Mat said. "This reminds me of my first mission." She turned around to look at Rapach. "You still don't remember what happened, do you?"

Rapach shook his head.

"Maybe it is better that way. Although it was difficult and there was so much at stake, I managed to get through it. No… *we* managed to get through it. Little brother, this mission might be of bigger importance than we thought, and it will be difficult. But this time, I will be there to help you."

Mat patted Rapach on the shoulder. He nodded at her. Then something behind his sister drew his attention. He looked towards the bridge and was shocked to see someone on top of it, staring right at them.

It was the man in the lion mask, and he was about to jump down into their canoe.

Rapach tried to stop the canoe, but it was too late.

Mat jumped skillfully up towards the man, toppling him back onto the bridge. Rapach, paralysed with fear, watched as a group of Silent People approached Mat and grabbed her hands.

"GET OUT OF HERE, RA—" she screamed.

The man in the lion mask grabbed Mat by the jaw as a cloud of miasma started filtering out of his sleeve.

"NO!" Rapach yelled as he saw his sister lose strength.

It was too late to jump up, the current was too strong and pushed the boat forwards. The canoe hit a rock, sending Rapach tumbling, and his head hit a corner of the boat.

His vision went black.

The Third Dream

Rapach woke up, his heart racing. He was back in the dream he had the previous night. Wrecked canoes were scattered across the infinite white dunes extending in front of him. Around him were buildings similar to those in Rabaska City, but they seemed to be made of stone instead of wood. Now the shadows that passed around him were plenty, dancing to distant sounds. And in the centre of everything stood the old tree with the clock on its bark, this time with its hand on the number two.

But Rapach did not care about that. He didn't want to be stuck in this strange dream. He had to go back and save Mat. He couldn't accept that she could have turned into…

"No, I need to go back. I NEED TO GO BACK!"

He shut his eyes tightly, trying in vain to erase the dream. But still he remained there. He started pacing frantically, desperately trying to think.

"What are you—"

It was the voice of that girl, Erydis. He ignored her.

"I don't have time for this. I have to wake up! WAKE UP!" he screamed into nothingness.

Smack!

Erydis slapped Rapach on the cheek.

"What's your problem?" he asked, stunned.

"I thought that might wake you up."

"Well, it didn't exactly work!"

"But at least you got a grip on yourself, didn't you?" Rapach looked down, unable to decide if he was angry or sad.

"What happened?" Erydis asked. "Why are you trying to go back?"

"It's my sister," he started, shaking his head to hide his tears. "She was taken by the Silent People."

"The who?"

"They are the ones spreading the miasma. They wear masks and breathe out that damn curse." He noticed Erydis was hiding something behind her back, but he didn't care. "Whoever breathes in the miasma becomes one of them. Some people also call them the hypnotized."

"A miasma that hypnotises..." Erydis mused.

"And now they have my... my..."

"What do you have inside your pouch?" Erydis asked, trying to distract him from his loss. "You're holding it really tightly. Did you find the package for this old man you were talking about?"

Rapach was surprised by her intuition. He nodded.

"I still don't know how much I can trust you. But you helped me..."

"You can trust me, dream boy," Erydis said.

After hesitating slightly, Rapach pulled out the square red package.

"This is my mission," he said. "We went to this lake and after solving some strange puzzles, we found the package. But as we were trying to go to our next destination, my sister Mat was taken by a stranger wearing a lion mask." Rapach shut his eyes tight. "He was terrifying. I lost my balance and hit my head, and the next thing I knew, I was in this dream place. Now I have to help my sister and find this old man. My mission is more important than we ever imagined. I need to go back."

"What's your next destination?" Erydis asked.

"I don't know exactly where it is," Rapach answered. "My sister has the map. But the letter I found said its name is Sorrow City."

"That place! I know where it is."

"What? How?"

"I just met someone from there! He told me that to reach it, you must follow the polluted river. The path will fork three times where three rocks with different colours are stacked. You have to follow the left river at the first two, and turn right at the final fork."

"Twice to the left and once right," repeated Rapach. Erydis nodded.

"I still don't know who you are, Erydis," Rapach said. "But you helped my sister and me. The flower, it worked exactly as you said it would. We managed to walk through the miasma without being hypnotised. How did you know so much?"

"Well, it takes practice, dream boy." She smiled. "And like the great Kemia said, you need the deepest understanding of dust."

"Dust? You mean that substance that covers everything?"

Erydis looked confused. "What do you mean, everything?"

"Plants, entire lakes, even animals and our clothes." Rapach patted his shoulder, causing some grey dust to fall from his tunic.

"That dust is grey, it's useless," Erydis said. "Probably worked before with other mixtures."

"Used dust?" Rapach asked. Erydis nodded thoughtfully. "So you use the dust?"

"Yes, that's what my city is famous for. Don't you use the dust?"

"No. I mean we, the Jerboa Clan, discovered that if we combine the dust with soil, we can create a strong blue glass. It became our signature material for constructing weapons."

"Well, that's just the very basics of dust mixing," Erydis said. "Where I'm from, we use it constantly in our daily lives. Cooking, forging, machinery, medicine, even music! For many of us, our ambition is to work with the best dust mixers at our Tower. One day I'll be a part of them. You see, dream boy, I hope to become the best dust mixer there is. And I'll impress the whole city with the experiment I'm working on."

Rapach was confused. A city where they mix dust? It sounded so foreign.

"So you use the dust for most things?" he asked.

"Everything we can get a hold of," she answered. "The dust is incredibly powerful. You have no idea of its capabilities, dream boy."

"Powerful enough to create a weapon?" Rapach asked. "A weapon like the miasma?!" The thought of it was making him angrier and angrier.

"No, not like that," Erydis protested.

Rapach then remembered his sister, breathing in the purple curse. He clenched his fist.

"What if you're one of them?" he asked. "What if you're part of the Silent People and the man in the lion mask?" Erydis opened her mouth to defend herself but he cut her off. "I saw you hiding something. Show it to me."

"You're talking nonsense, dream boy."

Rapach leapt quickly, grabbing at what was behind Erydis's back. It was a mask of a weird creature with long ears and a bird's beak.

"That's just my lost djinni ma—" she tried to explain, but Rapach interrupted her.

"You're one of them!" He threw the mask down. "You must have created the miasma to take over the lands. You and the stranger in the mask and the Silent People! Where is my sister?! WHERE IS MAT?!"

Erydis backed away, afraid of his explosive reaction. Rapach pulled out his dagger, but just before he could attack Erydis, a bell chimed thrice. The single hand of the clock creaked slowly and pointed at the number three.

Day Three

CHAPTER IX

SPECIAL MARBLES

Erydis

ERYDIS LIFTED HER HEAD FROM HER DESK, her heart hammering against her chest. She'd almost been stabbed by that boy Rapach, but a part of her desperately wanted to go back to the dream and try to fix the misunderstanding. She wasn't part of any Silent People nor did she know anyone who wore a lion mask, even though she was familiar with many other masks.

She had fallen asleep while working through most of the night. Flasks with dust mixtures and infusions surrounded her, but none of them would work for her experiment without dust from the Tower.

Erydis stood up, her eyes still trying to adjust to the morning sun. She went to the jar of water on her dresser and cleaned her face. When she raised her face to the mirror, she jumped as she saw a silhouette appear in the entrance behind her.

Eko stared at her with a wide smile, his monkey mask on top of his head.

"Don't you know how to knock? You scared me!" Erydis said. Eko ignored her as he walked around her room, observing her belongings. He stopped in front of a jar holding white dust and wrote on the table with his charcoal pencil.

"*This place is a mess?*" Erydis read. She rolled her eyes and turned back to the dresser to splash water on her face, watching Eko in the mirror. "I'm a very busy person, you know? Between working hours for my boss and trying to finish my experiment before the Closure Festival, it's really difficult to—" She had lost sight of the boy.

She turned around, catching Eko trying to arrange some books on the floor and onto a bookcase. Then he picked up her clothes from the floor and placed them on a chair. "Hey! Stay away from my stuff!" Erydis said.

Eko dropped the tunics in his hand and started writing on the wall.

I was trying to help.

"Well, thank you, but I like my organised mess." Eko looked at the desk, where Erydis's experiment was buried under a blanket. He lifted the blanket and had a quick look into the shadows before Erydis pulled it back down. "Don't you dare look at my experiment. It's not ready yet. It still needs dust from the Tower and the Emperor's sceptre."

Eko wrote on the wall again.

Then let's be on our way. If you want dust from the Tower, we'll need a distraction.

"I know…I know…" she said.

Erydis walked to her desk and pulled opened a drawer filled with multicoloured marbles stamped with the letter "E". She placed them all in a small sack and into her pouch.

The city was still waking up. There were a few people at the Dust Ring, preparing for a busy Festival of Many Dusts. It would start at midday, when citizens went to the feast at the food market.

Eko ran behind Erydis, wearing his monkey djinni mask. He caught up with her and tugged at her tunic.

"We're going to the Marble Barrio, where the grand marble stairs are. The Gecko Gang owes me some favours," Erydis said as she slipped on her lost djinni mask with a grin.

It wasn't long before they reached the Marble Barrio. They climbed up the great stairs and made their way through some side streets where the wind blew heavily. After a few sharp turns, they reached a darker area of the barrio. A few children watched the newcomers from under reptilian masks. Most of their masks looked old and dirty, but their leader wore a more polished one that was the same colour as his red hair.

"Cuiha, look who's here!" shouted a short boy from under an angry-looking gecko mask.

"Long time no see," a girl in a blue gecko mask said.

"What brings you here, Nott?" Cuiha asked in a serious tone.

"Did you use the dust marbles I gave you?" Erydis asked.

"Yes, we managed to steal some food from some snob at the food market," Cuiha answered.

"Well, now I need you to repay the favour. I need your gang to help my monkey friend and I distract some guards."

"Easy job. Stealing some smoke candies again?"

Erydis shook her head.

"I'm talking about something more ambitious," she said, taking out her sack full of marbles and showing it to the gang. They all leapt back in surprise, except Eko, who just looked confused.

"Are these the same marbles that almost got you expelled from the academy?" Cuiha asked.

"Those are legendary," the girl in the blue mask said.

"That's right," Erydis said. "And I need you all to help me start celebrating the Festival of Many Dusts a little earlier this year."

The Gecko Gang members exchanged glances and stared at the marbles as if they were precious treasure.

"Eko, do you know what a dust marble is?" Erydis asked. Eko shook his head.

"We use many at today's festival, as we did in other years," a short boy said.

"You crack it against the floor and a colourful cloud comes out," the girl in the blue mask explained. She slipped a blue marble from her pocket and threw it on the floor. It broke, releasing a small blue cloud, which dissolved in a few seconds.

"But Erydis's special marbles are different," Cuiha said. "The reason they became illegal is because they can fill an entire building. One day, the Dust Academy almost looked like it was on fire with yellow smoke going right up to the top! And word got around that it was Erydis who created the dust marble responsible for that."

"It's amazing what black dust can do if you use it wisely," Erydis said. "Alright, time for the plan. We're separating into four groups. Four of you will go to the Emerald Barrio and drop these marbles at the food market and the academy. You four will drop these at the Dust Bazaar." She gave three special marbles to Cuiha.

"I'll crack this one on Sikaal Fumus's tent," Cuiha said, admiring one of the red marbles.

"The rest will throw theirs here on the marble stairs. Be creative." The Gecko Gang nodded and dispersed.

"Eko, you stay with me," Erydis instructed. "We'll go to the Sapphire Barrio. I have three marbles to use and two more for backup. Are you ready?"

Eko nodded excitedly under his monkey mask.

They walked to the Sapphire Barrio, which was located on the west side of the city's first floor. As they walked, the buildings grew sparser and transitioned from marble to a bright hue of blue. As they walked through the Dust Ring, they could see fields of dust-infused crops all around them. There were fields of many colours, from red wheat to blue corn, as well as all kinds of animals crammed together. Erydis barely ever set foot in the Sapphire Barrio, but the fields had nothing to do with it.

In the distance, right by the city wall, was a prison made of dark stone. Erydis feared that place. Not because she was afraid to end up there, but because a person she never wanted to see was trapped inside. A person she tried hard to forget.

Eko pulled on Erydis's tunic, distracting her from her thoughts. He shrugged.

"We're going to a farm right next to the prison," Erydis told him. "The man who owns it kicks poor children when they get close to him, calling them thieves. He also treats his cattle horribly. Today he'll celebrate the Festival of Many Dusts like no one else in the barrio."

They approached a field with crimson fruit and yellow leaves. There was a hint of sweetness in the air. Eko grabbed a fruit but before he could eat it, Erydis pulled him down to hide behind a bush as a pair of soldiers walked past.

"They've left," Erydis whispered, taking a peek. "So we're going to that hut, in the middle of the field." She pointed to a blue brick hut that had a grey cloud coming out of its chimney. "They have a grinder for the crop, and it could be a good target. It's also close to the prison."

She stared at the dark building silently. Memories from her past rushed through her head, burdening her. She stared at the ground, trying to comfort herself. Her dad was still in the prison, and he would not hurt anyone ever again.

Eko seemed to notice Erydis's change in attitude. He took his mask off and patted her gently on the back.

"Sorry, I got distracted," she said, smiling at him. "I want to target that hut because it's also close to the prison, so the guards might think the prisoners are trying to escape and we won't be detected."

They carefully approached the blue hut. Suddenly, they heard footsteps coming from the path that lead to the prison. A group of soldiers were escorting prisoners linked by chains. Eko went still.

"Are those Vakandi?" Erydis asked. Eko nodded. "I'm sorry, Eko, we should move on. There are too many guards here."

Eko nodded slowly. When they arrived at the blue hut, they pushed their backs flat against its brick wall. They could hear someone inside having a conversation. Erydis peered into the hut through the window.

A soldier in blue robes was interrogating a bearded man as he ransacked the hut. Erydis waited for a good opportunity to open the window.

"Hopefully they're not hiding among the crops," the soldier barked threateningly.

"I assure you, good man, that my hut is empty of that scum."

"You'd be surprised at how they sneak into the smallest places to hide, like rats. We found two Vakandi children in the next field, hiding inside a barrel full of water."

"Have you captured many?"

"Not yet, only the ones being marched to the prison right now."

"So what's the outsiders' destiny? How many years will they spend in the rotter?"

"Emperor Engyl is quite angry with this unexpected mess, so I'm sure he'll make an example of them."

Erydis felt bad for Eko.

"It will be fine, Eko," she whispered. "We just need to—" In a quick movement, Eko opened Erydis's pouch, grabbing three special marbles. He darted away into the crops. Erydis realised what he was about to do and groaned. He was going to attempt to rescue the prisoners. She needed to hurry if she was going to make it in time to help him.

She quietly climbed inside the hut while the soldier was searching through some barrels. In the middle of the room was a red metal grinder powered by dust. It was turned on, its powerful saws rotating wildly.

Erydis edged closer to the grinder, and after placing a yellow marble on top of it, she jumped back out through the window as fast as she could.

Behind her, an explosion went off with a deafening sound. The blue hut was instantly consumed by a burst of yellow clouds that spiralled up into the sky. She heard the men inside running to the door, coughing and yelling in shock.

Erydis ran towards the path leading to the prison, trying to stay hidden amongst the crops as much as she could. She approached the group of soldiers and the captured Vakandi, who were watching the uproar in alarm.

"What in the name of dust is happening here?" cried a soldier in red robes and a red turban. "Come with me. You three, stay."

As they moved towards the hut to investigate, Erydis noticed someone approaching them from behind. It was Eko under his monkey mask. What was he thinking?

Eko grabbed a marble and threw it to the ground, covering the group under a gigantic red cloud. Erydis froze, unsure of what to do, listening to the commotion inside the cloud.

Suddenly, Eko and two other Vakandi ran out from the cloud, covered in red dust. Erydis joined them.

"Let's go back to the hideout," she instructed. She couldn't believe Eko's crazy plan had actually worked.

"May we accompany you?" a Vakandi woman asked, running next to them to keep up.

"Yes, but we should hurry! What happened to the rest of the captured Vakandi?! Did they manage to escape?"

Two more explosions of green and red clouds covered the area behind them.

"Eko left them some of those dust marble things. They sure are powerful," the woman said.

"Smart." Erydis smiled.

As they ran towards the Hidden Barrio, pillars of clouds rose all over the other barrios while people watched, intrigued.

Chapter X

Machina Master

Erydis

Inside the hideout, masked people had begun the descent to the trap door and into the dugout tunnel that led to the Tower. Erydis, Eko, and the rescued Vakandi followed the rest into the darkness, where the only noise was the shuffling of footsteps. Not a single person whispered as the light on the other side became brighter and brighter.

Erydis's heart was racing with every step. She had dreamed of one day being inside the Tower, even though this wasn't how she had imagined it. Becoming a mixer was the future she saw for herself after many hopeless days. It meant discovery, progress, and finding the answer to the questions she had wondered about all her life.

But now, she didn't know what was going to become of the Tower if the Vakandi were to invade it. Yet she was determined not to let that deter her from her goal—to get hold of the dust she needed from the Tower for her experiment.

They reached the end of the tunnel, which opened into an underground cave. Dust lamps emitting blue light hung from the humid, rocky walls, and stalactites covered the ceiling. Erydis heard the echoes of an argument coming from a mob of people a short distance away.

A group of soldiers surrounded a hostile, older soldier who seemed to be attacking the others with his sword. He had a scar on his cheek and a well-trimmed white beard, and was decked out in white-and-gold robes. This confused Erydis.

"Enjoying the show?" A voice said behind Erydis. It was Ferus under his mocking mask.

"Why is he attacking his fellow soldiers?" Erydis asked.

"Look again," Ferus said. Erydis looked at the soldiers' faces. They smiled, and she saw they had dust marks on their skin. "Those are Vakandi, dressed as soldiers to trespass and knock out our enemies. And that's the last guard we needed to capture. The old man has some skills. Almost killed two of my men with a single swing." He chuckled as if it was all in good jest.

"I believe he must be an elite soldier. Usually, they're the ones wearing robes in those colours. It takes years to rise to his status," Erydis said, thinking of Thylac's ambitions to reach that level.

"I see. Well, he definitely knows his moves. We need the key he's holding, so I should negotiate with him," Ferus said. She noticed he had no blade with him.

"Wait. None of you are using weapons?" Erydis asked.

He shook his head. "You dusters are always relying on your violence. There are smarter ways, you know. We the Vakandi have learned how to be silent and agile rather than using brute force." He walked into the commotion with a smile on his face.

Ferus approached the muscular soldier as the latter positioned himself, ready to strike.

"Sir, I'm sorry for the inconvenience, but we will be needing that key you hold."

"You'll need to kill me first," the guard said as he sprinted towards Ferus, who didn't flinch.

The elite soldier slashed his sword horizontally, but Ferus crouched just in time to dodge it. He stepped back slightly, dodging another attempt from the soldier. Erydis watched, impressed yet concerned for Ferus. No one else seemed to want to interfere.

"We won't be killing anyone during our invasion, so I ask you to stop," Ferus said.

"After you've killed so many of ours in battle?" the soldier asked.

"After the Emperor tried to annihilate our families, we had to do something, naturally. Do you even know why you were killing Vakandi after Vakandi?"

"Because you're trying to invade Dust City!" The soldier lunged his blade forward again but failed to connect.

"Follow me, please," Ferus said, walking deeper into the cave. The rest of the Vakandi accompanied him. After a moment of hesitation, the elite soldier followed the crowd with his curved sword at the ready, trailed by Eko and a puzzled Erydis.

As they walked, the sound of rushing water grew steadily louder. The group approached an underground river with crystal clear water running into the dark.

"Lost djinni girl, come here," Ferus said, gesturing to Erydis, who was still wearing her mask. "Such a clean river, isn't it?"

"This is the river that is used for our water source and to create dust at the Tower!" As Erydis said this, she noticed a gigantic pipe siphoning off some of the river's water further downstream.

"That's right. Come with me, Eko and Erydis. You too, soldier." Ferus led them to follow the current. He unhooked a dust lamp from the cave's wall to light their path.

"You'd better not push me into the river, outsider," warned the soldier, less wary now, but still holding his blade. The air grew mustier the further they walked. They entered a secondary cave and Ferus stopped.

"Gentlemen and lady, I present to you, the lie." He pointed towards the ceiling.

Hidden in-between the stalactites, a dense grey liquid dripped steadily from the pipes into the river where it mixed with the current, changing the colour of the water to an unnatural white.

Ferus and Eko stared grimly as Erydis and the soldier watched in horror.

"I have heard rumours about such a pipe in this part of the cavern, but

Engyl said even he was prohibited from approaching it. I didn't know what to make of his words back then," the soldier said, his expression stricken.

"So it is true," Erydis said. That grey dust was useless; worse than filth. Yet, every day it was thrown into the river as if it would spontaneously disappear.

Ferus continued in a somber tone. "This underground river spreads out all across the land, eventually emerging in the form of springs. Your Emperor knows this, and so did the Finder. And yet they never stopped, even after the Vakandi told him."

The elite soldier looked on with horror as the grey liquid poured into the river.

"If you don't believe me, just look at the neck of my little brother." Ferus looked at Eko, who removed his scarf to show the purple scar on his neck. "He has never hurt a soul. Yet when he innocently drank from the polluted river, he lost his voice."

The soldier looked at Eko empathetically. He shook his head, furious.

"I became a soldier to protect the innocent. And this is what I was really defending in those wars?" he said with palpable fury. "I thought your words at the Inauguration Festival were just outsiders' trickery. But I was wrong."

There was a heavy silence as the four of them watched the river. Eko was proof that this polluted, dangerous river was consuming the lands and everyone who relied on it. And if Rapach was anywhere close to the Vakandi's Sorrow City, Erydis realised, he was also in danger.

"Very well," the soldier said, sheathing his blade. He unhooked a silver key from his belt and handed it to Ferus. "This does not mean I'll join your side, outsider. But I do not feel the need to fight you. I understand you've suffered enough."

"We Vakandi search for joy in sorrow, sir. So we will never suffer. But we will fight for our future, and our future will not forget your kindness to us." Ferus bowed with a hand over his heart. Eko imitated his brother, making Erydis smile. This was a hopeful mission for them after all, and she was glad to help them.

"Let me show you something else, lost djinni girl," Ferus said.

Ferus then led them to a colossal part of the cavern, its walls covered in lanterns.

"This was once the Mist Grounds," Ferus said as everyone watched, amazed.

A continuous mist of sparkling particles floated up from a gigantic hole in the ground to a network of blue-gold pipes on the ceiling. The thin silver mist reflected the light of the dust lamps around it. Such an incredible sight, Erydis thought. She had heard stories about this mist's beauty, and there she was, standing in front of it. The mist that created the dust.

"Magnificent, isn't it," Ferus said. "The cause of many disasters."

"And improvements," Erydis added.

"Like weapons?" Ferus asked, laughing.

"Well, I suppose." Erydis blushed. "But if used wisely, it can create more than destroy."

"That's curious. That's exactly what the Vakandi told the Founder before he started the djinni wars. But let's leave the history lessons for later. Follow me."

They walked towards the center of the cavern, where shallow steps led up to a cylindrical chamber. Above the cold, curved metallic door, a mass of crimson pipes converged upwards into the ceiling.

Ferus grabbed the silver key and turned it in the door's keyhole. Erydis felt a rumbling vibration under her feet. A brief silence followed before the metallic doors opened to reveal a chamber large enough to fit the majority of the group.

"This must be the elevation chamber," Erydis said, marveling at the technology. "I read about it in a Machina book!"

"It is," Ferus said. "This chamber goes through all the five floors of the Tower, my Vakandi friends. You see these?" He pointed to five keyholes in the wall. "One for each floor. The silver key our generous friend gave us will take us through the first three. The Mist Grounds, where we are, then the mixing chambers, and then the Finder's chamber. I'm still waiting for someone to bring us the keys to the top floors—the dust chamber, and finally, the dust machine chamber. We will meet them at the Finder's chamber on the third floor."

Ferus ushered the group to enter the chamber. He turned the silver key in the keyhole second from the bottom, triggering the doors to close. The chamber vibrated as it ascended to the next floor. Erydis had imagined this chamber ride all her life. She'd even asked Kemia to describe it to her, but her teacher had refused every time, saying that Erydis would experience it herself when she became a dust-mixer.

"The mixing chambers," Ferus announced as the chamber slowed down. "Everyone, get ready to capture the soldiers in there. Be silent, be fast. Keep an eye on any mixer who tries anything suspicious. And, as always, have fun." Ferus chuckled under his mocking mask.

The chamber staggered to a halt and the doors opened. Before anyone could do something to stop the invasion, the Vakandi silently infiltrated the chamber in their soldier disguises. They soon had all the soldiers on the floor and ordered the mixers to gather.

Erydis looked around, fascinated by the large circular room with the elevation chamber in its centre. This was every mixer's paradise—full of jars with different types of dust and infusions. The Vakandi went through the four doors that led from the chamber to search for more mixers.

After a few minutes, all the soldiers were captured and gathered to sit down on the floor in the main chamber. Some looked scared, some angry—but surprisingly, a few of them seemed fine with the Vakandi being there.

"Thank you, everyone, for cooperating," Ferus addressed them. "My name is Ferus and we are about to invade your Tower. But do not worry! Food and drinks will be provided to all of you." Ferus made it sound like the invasion was a celebration. "Now, since we have some time to spare as I wait for my Vakandi friends to retrieve the remaining keys, can someone here guide us around your precious Tower?"

A man with a white turban and crimson robes stood up, and Erydis gasped as she recognised him.

"Well, well… the Master of Machina himself. A pleasure, Master," Ferus said.

"That's Herra Gull!" Erydis whispered excitedly to Eko. She couldn't believe that she was seeing him up close.

"I'll provide you with the answers you need," Herra Gull said in a powerful voice. He walked towards them slowly, leaning on his cane, bearing a confident yet gentle smile. "I just ask that you not bring my fellow mixers any trouble."

"Do not worry, my good sir. We won't, as long as they behave."

"I believe they will." Herra Gull scanned the crowd with a smile. "Very well, what would you like to know about the Tower?"

Herra Gull seemed too trusting in Erydis's opinion. But he seemed aware of his situation, and if she was in his shoes, she would have behaved the same.

"That's a good question. Lost djinni, something you want to ask?"

"Well, where do I begin?" Erydis said from under her mask. "I've heard there are four different chambers on this floor, one for every discipline of the dust. Is that true?"

"It is," Herra answered. "Each door leads to a chamber where a main discipline is researched."

"The first chamber, through that door," Said Herra, pointing with his crane. "is dedicated to Alchemia. The door next to it leads to the chamber dedicated to my discipline of focus, Machina. Then there's the Vita chamber, and finally, Arma." Herra pointed at each of the four doors as he mentioned the corresponding discipline.

"Can we see them?" Erydis asked eagerly.

"As I said, we do have some time to spare," Ferus said. "Please, Vakandi brothers, stay vigilant." Herra led them to the first open door. The wall next to it bore a blue sign with gold lettering: *Alchemia Chamber.*

Erydis gasped as she entered the room. Flasks covered most of the tables. There were several furnaces with gigantic pots—larger than any she had seen before— over them; red hot from the flames below. Bookcases in every corner held hundreds of volumes of all disciplines, along with stands filled with dust-infused plants and jars of coloured dust. Magnifying lenses hung from one wall, and a large dust lamp on the ceiling illuminated the whole room. Clouds of every imaginable colour spilled out of the windows.

Alchemia was Erydis's favourite discipline, and this chamber was a mixing paradise.

"This is where dust mixers investigate the essence of the dust," Herra said with a gentle smile. "Alchemia is separated into three sub-disciplines—"

"Coloura, Herba, and Obscura, my favourite," Erydis blurted out.

"You seem to know it well," Herra observed, curious. "Coloura investigates every mix possible that can be made with the dust. Herba investigates the art of dust infusion, distillation, and decomposition. And Obscura investigates the black dust, usually found in nature, close to the mist. But ever since Liudmila Dametot became Master of Alchemia, she has moved all the black dust from this room to investigate its potential use for weaponry in the Arma chamber."

"Kemia must have been a better Alchemia Master," Erydis said.

"So you know Kemia?" Herra asked.

Erydis froze, feeling foolish. She'd wanted to keep her identity hidden.

"It's fine, I won't say a thing," Herra said. "Besides, Kemia is an old, good friend, and a talented one at that." Herra walked to a table covered in many scorch marks. "She used to work here. No one dared to mix the black dust before her because of its unstable properties. But she knew that with more research, it could benefit every discipline. And that's when she created the sub-disciplines of Obscura."

"What?" Erydis was impressed. "She created the Obscura discipline?"

"She did. Unfortunately, some of her discoveries were exploited for other purposes."

"Is that why she no longer works at the Tower?"

"When she noticed how her research was being used for destruction instead of aid, it was all too late." Herra looked down. "But maybe she's the one who should tell you more about it. Are you a student from the Dust Academy?"

"Yes." Erydis took her mask off. There was no point in hiding her identity anymore. "I mean, I was, before I got expelled."

"So you're Erydis," Herra said with a knowing look.

"How do you know that?"

"Like I said, Kemia is a good friend. I believe she's talked about you a few times."

"A few times, huh?" Erydis grinned. It was not common for Kemia to talk about her students, especially not to the Master of Machina.

"Sorry to interrupt, but we should continue our tour," Ferus said, taking his mask off as well. "We have a few minutes, not weeks."

Herra laughed. "Very well, follow me. Pardon my partiality, but the next chamber is my favourite."

As they followed him, Erydis thought about all the things she still didn't know about Kemia. It was no secret that Kemia kept her cards close to the chest, but Erydis wanted to know so much more about her, her past, and why she had left the incredible Tower.

They walked to the next room, the Machina chamber. Numerous metallic beasts and an incredible amount of tools of all sizes were spread around the room. There were large vehicles, like the one she had seen at the parade, and machines that puffed out clouds of coloured dust. Erydis had never seen anything like it. The beautiful roof and walls of the chamber were adorned with ornaments of red iron, which shone from the reflection of all the dust lamps.

Erydis was almost as impressed with this chamber as she had been with the previous one—Machina was a close runner-up for her favourite discipline after Alchemia.

"This is the chamber I lead," Herra said, smiling with a twinkle in his eyes. "The roof was designed by the pioneer of Machina, Valerios Kythera. He also planned the function of the whole Tower. Therefore the name Valerios's Tower. Such an incredible man he was."

"It is impressive, I must admit," Ferus said. "I understand the Machina discipline is separated into two sub-disciplines?"

"Yes!" Erydis said, eager to answer. "Fabrica studies the functionality of any type of machinery, and Terra studies terrain vehicles, like the ones in the second floor of the city!"

"Well, yes, those are the ones known to people outside the Tower, but there's one more new discipline that I'm working on," Herra said. "And I'm getting closer every day."

"A new Machina sub-discipline?" Erydis asked, her eyes wide. "Is it a new type of machine that you're working on? Can we see it?"

"Follow me, please." Herra smiled, matching her excitement.

They followed Herra along a narrow path in-between mysterious machinery. Erydis analysed them as best she could for her experiment, which would require some Fabrica studies, and caught up to the group.

"Valerios was a great man," Herra explained brightly. "He was already building machines before the discovery of the Mist Grounds. After discovering the use of dust in machines, his creations became outstanding. One of his most important inventions was the dust machine at the top of the Tower."

"I heard he left Dust City in his older years," Erydis said.

"He did. It is said that far away he created other magnificent things, even a castle. But the rumour I like the most is that he created a machine that could fly further than the highest clouds. It was this that inspired me to build this new machine."

Herra stopped in front of a circular machine that was no bigger than Erydis. There were some rotating blades below it and a miniscule chimney in the middle.

Herra grabbed a small bottle containing green liquid close to the machine and poured the content into its chimney.

"Many have told me that trying to build a machine that could soar into the skies was a fool's errand," he said. "But impossible? I think not."

Herra cranked a handle on the side of the machine and stepped back.

The blades below the machine started rotating faster and faster, until they became just a blur to the eye. A strong draft pushed them back, but a fascinated Erydis stood her ground. The machine was rising, floating in the air steadily.

"What you see is the beginning of an era of soaring into the skies! The Aera discipline," Herra said proudly.

The machine slowly descended, landing softly, and the blades came to a stop.

"Unfortunately, I'll have to wait to finish this creation. Engyl seems to want to focus on Arma inventions for now."

"What a shame. I have a friend who would love to see a flying machine," Erydis said. "He's part of the royal guard."

"Thylac, yes," Herra said, surprising Erydis. "A good lad. We talk often as I walk at the palace gardens on my way to the Tower."

"So dear Engyl seems to care only for destruction," Ferus mused. "We've seen some of this destructive machinery in battle, so I fear to see the Arma chamber. But I want to see what your Emperor plans to use against us Vakandi."

"I feared such a thing, but if you insist," Herra said, gesturing to the next chamber.

The Arma chamber was by far the most complex. Stand after stand held swords of all shapes, as well as bows, arrows, and hammers. Heavy tools shone with the light coming from the molten metals simmering in a gigantic stone bowl. From there, the liquid metal flowed like streams towards different forging stations. The chamber also contained many vehicles of war. Erydis feared to find out what they could do.

Eko and Ferus walked together, quietly looking at all the terrible weapons used against their clans. Some stands held stacks of multicoloured stone spheres.

"As sharp as those swords are forged," Ferus said in a serious tone, "what pierces us the most is the destructive explosions of those cursed things." He looked at the stone spheres with unease.

"Some are convinced war means progress and gain," Herra said. "I believe that mentality should cease. But I have to admit that from time to time, there are some creations I welcome."

They walked to a corner of the chamber where a crimson, diamond object lay on top of a pedestal. Around it were arranged bottles of diverse consistencies and colours.

"This is a morph blade," Herra said, lifting the crimson diamond that was a bit larger than his hand. "This is marvellous work. This instrument could give a normal man the power of a veteran warrior."

He picked up a bottle containing a purple liquid.

"This is a mix made with a type of dust from the Tower. Purple dust, capable of modifying and adapting cognitive behaviour." Eko and Ferus stared at the bottle in confusion. Erydis was simply curious. She had never seen that colour of dust before. Herra took a sip from the bottle and then exchanged it for a flask that contained a silver liquid. "This is a mix of another dust from the Tower, platinum dust. It is extremely rare, capable of manipulating metals. The morph blade is made with it as well. Now, observe what two powerful combinations are capable of. This must be our most remarkable experiment."

Herra extended the morph blade and poured some of the silver mixture onto it. He closed his eyes. Suddenly, the blade vanished into specs of dust. Then, slowly, the dust accumulated in Herra's hand again, solidifying into the shape of a small sword with a sharp metallic sound.

"Incredible," Erydis said with a wide smile.

"This would be catastrophic in battle." Ferus frowned.

"The morph blade can transform into any kind of hard object, making it durable and convenient for a soldier." Herra closed his eyes again and the sword morphed into a circular shield, then into a helmet, and then an axe. Finally, it resumed its original diamond shape. "It's still in the experimentation stage, but apart from battle, imagine a society with these all around. It would be an unstoppable force."

"It seems we've arrived just in time to stop this horrible experiment," Ferus said.

"Don't underestimate the Emperor's army," Herra warned. "Many of them will not stop a war against you, even though they try to do things peacefully."

"And I believe you're underestimating our intentions. We will invade this city and fix it. We won't let Engyl rule us," Ferus said. Erydis had to smile at his pride.

The last chamber on the floor was the Vita chamber. This room was darker than the others, and there were noises coming from the shadows.

"Many people find this chamber quite unsettling, so please be warned," Herra said.

As their eyes adjusted to the dim light, Erydis started to distinguish what was inside the room. Animal skeletons hung from the ceiling, and glass jars filled with organs lined the tables. Around the room, there were several cages with live animals inside them—rodents, birds, and insects. The air was heavy and gloomy, and every creature seemed to be immersed in it. Eko was looking at the floor, as if avoiding eye contact with the poor creatures.

Vita was Erydis's least favourite discipline, but she understood its importance.

"Here in the Vita chamber, mixers research the dust and its effects on people and animals," Herra said. "Mostly for medical purposes. The only sub-discipline is Animalia."

"Something tells me it's not only for medical purposes," Ferus said seriously. "You dusters will never understand."

Suddenly, they heard a racket close by. They turned to see a jar broken next to a stand, and hiding behind it, a man with green robes and a large red mustache.

"I suggest you come out before I come and get you," Ferus said.

"Aerzzo Chimara?" Erydis realised she'd seen him before. It was Tulia's father.

"You're that girl who keeps getting my dear Tulia into trouble, aren't you?" He had a high, shaky voice.

"Master of Vita!" Ferus laughed. "You've certainly hid very well, but now I must ask you to join the rest of the group."

"Please, I don't want any trouble," Aerzzo said in a high, frightened voice. "Please don't get me involved."

Ferus approached Aerzzo, who started shaking uncontrollably.

"I've seen this look before. You're scared of me not because I'm invading your precious chamber, but because you've never been this close to a Vakandi."

"Please don't kill us all," Aerzzo pleaded, ignoring Ferus's words.

"Let's make a deal. You show us something interesting in this chamber, and we'll leave you be."

Aerzzo opened his mouth as if trying to protest. But then he slowly nodded and walked towards a glass cage on a table.

"Maybe you'll appreciate this experiment, outsider."

They looked into the cage, which was full of insects. But there was something different about them. These insects had weird colours and patterns on their bodies. Some were red with blue dots, others looked like emerald spiders with tails. "Is this a mutation experiment?" Erydis asked. She had never encountered such creatures.

"Not quite. These insects are faster and stronger than normal ones. Their survival instincts are better than ordinary spiders."

"These are creatures created by natural dust in the air," Herra added.

"Are these..." Erydis trailed off, shocked. This was impossible.

"That's right, girl. These are the same beasts that once roamed the land before the creation of the Tower. The same creatures that inspire us to wear masks during our celebrations," Aerzzo said with wide eyes. "These are human-engineered djinni. This is the sub-discipline I created, Dijenia!"

"The djinni once fought along the Vakandi," Ferus said. "It is said that they're extinct, but now it seems you're bringing them back."

"Not as long as you, outsiders, are here," Aerzzo said quietly.

"What?" asked Ferus, trying to intimidate him, although Erydis could see a glint of mischief in his eyes.

"Nothing, please don't hurt me!" Aerzzo cried.

The group went back to the central chamber, where the Vakandi stood waiting vigilantly, watching their prisoners. Ferus pushed Aerzzo to sit down with the prisoners and turned to face everyone.

"We have looked at some of the mixers' experiments," he said. "I will not pretend that they are all horrible discoveries, but indeed, most of them are focused on the art of killing, on the so-called Arma discipline. I shall continue exploring this Tower as I wait for our other group to arrive. I ask you, my fellow Vakandi, to respect the dusters—but never take your eyes off them. Herra, sir, I ask you to accompany us to the next floor."

Herra bowed and walked into the elevation chamber.

"You as well, lost djinni girl," Ferus said to Erydis. "I believe what you're looking for is two floors up, in the dust chamber."

Erydis nodded. She walked inside along with Eko. Ferus inserted a key into the keyhole in the middle.

"We'll be waiting for some soldiers on the next floor, the Finder's chamber. They have the key that will lead us to the next floor. That's where you can get your reward, Erydis."

Eko gestured to Ferus.

"What about your reward, Eko?" Ferus laughed heartily. "Isn't your reward following in the steps of your dear, big brother?"

Eko shook his head, smiling.

Chapter XI

Two Tales

Erydis

The doors of the elevation chamber opened once more. This time, the group stepped into a gigantic chamber with a high ceiling. A colossal red iron door stood at the other end, covered in complex patterns and chains.

"Seems like we might have to wait for my fellow Vakandi to bring the key to the next two floors above us," Ferus said, contemplating the new chamber.

"No soldiers?" Erydis asked.

"No. They all think we'll arrive from the palace, so they'll be protecting the outside."

"Are those the doors to the palace gardens?" Erydis asked.

"Indeed," Herra answered. "Every day, mixers and soldiers arrive at the palace through the gardens and into this chamber to start our work. Only select merchants are allowed to enter every morning, for an hour. This is the only passage in and out of the Tower."

"So the merchants supply dust to the Dust Bazaar?" Ferus asked.

"Yes. The dust is created or collected in its various colours in the chamber above us. Then it gets transported through the pipes down to this floor. ”

Erydis looked up. A maze of pipes snaked into several gigantic jars in the room.

“Red dust for forging, green for fuel and other daily uses, blue for medicine, yellow for spices, and white to make everything else,” Ferus explained to Eko.

“I don’t see any dust from the Tower,” Erydis said with a frown. Those five types of dust were easy to find at the bazaar, but the dust exclusive to the Tower was what she needed.

“Mixers need a special permit to get them from the dust chamber,” Herra said. “Only Liudmila has the key to reach that floor.”

“Let the Vakandi worry about getting that,” Ferus said, examining the rest of the chamber. He stopped next to four big murals on a wall. Each was painted in muted colours.

Eko gestured to Ferus.

“Yes, brother, this is a mural about the creation of Dust City,” Ferus said, studying the first painting.

“I’ve seen some of these paintings replicated in our books at the academy,” Erydis said, approaching the first mural. There was an inscription below it in blue gold, which she read out loud. “*The Founder walks through the shadows and savage djinni to uncover the origins of the puzzling mist in the air.*”

The painting depicted two men. One wore the Finder’s golden mask while the other was unmasked. The latter, smaller man stared at the Finder with an ugly, envious expression. Djinni of monstrous shapes surrounded the men, and a shroud of silver cloud represented the mist around them.

“This mural represents the clan of the Finder, Orn Ryk, and the outsider Vakandi searching for the origin of the mist,” Herra said, gazing at the mural he probably saw every day. “Back then, the mist spread everywhere across the lands, and djinnis created by the natural dust in the air would hunt innocent people. It is said that the Vakandi were jealous of the leadership of the Finder, Orn, ever since those days.”

They walked to the next mural. In this painting, the Finder was holding a pile of white dust as mist drifted out of a crater in the ground. This time, the Vakandi figure was looking at Orn with fury.

"The Finder encounters the mist. After one hundred and thirty-two days, he creates white dust with the mist and finds its power. They call the land the Mist Grounds."

"This is what the city looked like before the Tower was built; a gigantic hole in the ground. It is said Vakandi saw the dust and wanted it for himself," Herra said. They moved on to the next mural.

"Jealousy overcomes the outsider, who attempts to invade the Mist Grounds. But the great Finder builds a fortress to protect the mist."

This painting showed the outsider within a circle representing the fortress. Outside of it was the Vakandi and the djinni, looking towards Orn with fury.

"It is said that the Vakandi somehow managed to control the djinnis and used them to attack the Finder," Herra said. "But Orn had the dust and the power to stop the Vakandi from invading the Mist Grounds," Herra said. They all turned their attention to the last mural.

"Before his last breath, the Finder attains peace. He ends the djinnis' existence, making the Vakandi surrender, and builds this magnificent Tower."

In the painting, the Finder lay peacefully on a pedestal below the Tower as people cried around him.

"He killed the djinni and finished building the Tower before he died. He really was an extraordinary man," Herra said with admiration.

Ferus burst into laughter. Everyone stared at him, perplexed, except Eko.

"So this is the heroic tale you dusters tell about your dear Finder, Orn," Ferus said in a mocking tone. "Let me tell you the other version. The Vakandi's tale."

"There were many masked kings back then," he began. "Most of them wanted to spend their time alone and never wandered, except three kings—Orn, Vakandi, and the Forgotten.

"The three masked kings wanted to discover what the mist in the air was, since it was affecting their lands. After travelling for years through the djinni lands, they found the origin of the mist coming from the crater. They founded a large city there and called it the Mist Grounds.

"One day, the three masked kings discovered the dust and what they could do with it. It would enhance metals and flavours and heal sickness.

But with such power in everyone's hands, there were also dangers."

"There was an argument between the kings. Orn Ryk said they should use the dust to its full potential, but Vakandi knew it should be researched first before offering it to the people, since they knew powerful weapons could be made with it. The Forgotten king said it was wiser to leave the Dust alone, but both Orn and Vakandi believed that would lead to someone else using it against them. They could not come to an agreement."

"One day after the argument, Ryk decided not to listen to the other leaders. He convinced the people of the Mist Grounds to attack Vakandi and his people and push them out of the city. Vakandi found out about this plot and asked for help from the Forgotten king. But the Forgotten king ignored King Vakandi's plea and his people, and disappeared on his blind spiritual search.

"After successfully winning the battle, Orn renamed the Mist Grounds as Dust City. Vakandi tried many times to claim his land back. The legends even say that the djinni helped him during the battle. But Orn had the dust and with it, an aggressive defense. Vakandi never succeeded in returning to the Mist Grounds.

"Then the Tower was created and with it a danger that we, the Vakandi, did not know about. With the battle lost, the clan decided to go back to their old lands and named it Sorrow City. Vakandi fell ill. Some say he was driven crazy by his failures, yet in the end he found his peace. And everything was well.

"But then, the pollution from the Tower finally reached Sorrow City. We tried reasoning with your new Emperor, Engyl. But instead of fixing the problem, he decided to attack us. We fled Sorrow City to return here, where we rightfully belong, to take back the Mist Grounds."

Everyone was silent, trying to comprehend Ferus's tale. Finally, Herra broke the silence. "I never wanted to accept that Orn was an evil man, but this seems quite horrifying."

"It's a matter of perspective. Each tale has its own truths and lies," Erydis reasoned.

"Vakandi was a good man, and we will not accept the way you dusters speak of him," Ferus said in all seriousness. "Orn may have been a brilliant man, but he was a horrible human for treating our people this way. And his heir, Engyl, is no different."

"Wait," Erydis said to Ferus. "If you're Vakandi's leader, are you Vakandi's heir?"

"Me? No, not me. I am no leader either, but I will always remember his sorrow. It is precious to us."

Erydis thought about the two tales. She still considered Orn a genius for discovering how to use the dust. But Vakandi sounded like a miserable man if everything he went through was indeed true. A man with the poorest luck. A man filled with sorrow.

"There's something I don't understand. Why do you honour sorrow so much?" she asked.

"In his last days, Vakandi told his people to never be a victim of sadness but to smile through sorrowful times. And we have respected his words to this day. We will treasure being content, even with Engyl trying his hardest to push us down," Ferus said as he and Eko bowed with their hands over their hearts. Erydis understood them more now. Their noble intentions and their sense of justice. It warmed her heart, but she didn't know why. Perhaps she had never truly felt a sense of justice before, and now she had a glimpse of it.

Her thoughts were interrupted by the hiss of the elevation chamber arriving from below. The doors opened, and Ferus smiled widely.

"You're finally here," Ferus said as Erydis turned to look at the newcomers.

There were five masked people standing in front of them. Their masks looked average, except for one. The man on the far right wore a mask that seemed familiar, as if someone had described it to her before. It had round eyes with tiny eyeholes, and thick brown fur framed the mask. There was something fearsome about it.

"The man in the lion mask," Erydis whispered, thinking of the fear she had seen on Rapach's face. A cold chill washed over her.

Chapter XII

Djinni

Rapach

Rapach heard a dog barking nearby. Then, a drooling tongue vigorously licked his face.

He opened his eyes. He was lying on reddish soil. Everything was a blur at first, but he slowly started to make out some shapes—the curve of the polluted river next to a large tree with a knot of roots. Then he felt the side of his head hurting. He groaned and sat up, reaching for his throbbing temple. Pek, the provider dog, was trying to lick his face.

"Oi, Pek! Is he awake?" The voice sounded familiar. Rapach saw a man approaching.

"Danaa, is that you?" Rapach asked, trying to grasp what was happening.

Danaa sported a tangled black beard and his face was furrowed with concern, like it always was. Rapach and most of the Jerboa Clan knew of Danaa's bravery, which was also evident from the scar on his temple. A brown jerboa trailed him, not far behind.

"Boy, ya scared me there for a moment. Thought we lost ya for good. Such a miracle you didn't fall from that canoe before Pek found ya," he said in his raspy voice. "Wait, boy, where is ya sister?"

Rapach's tears filled his eyes as he remembered what happened. "Mat has been hypnotised," he said sadly, wishing it wasn't true. "She's a Silent One now."

"Mat? For the Witness's sake, I've never met someone braver. She will be remembered. I'm sorry for your loss," Danaa said.

Rapach remained silent. Surely this couldn't be the end of Mat. It couldn't.

He felt something move under his tunic. Benu peeked out from underneath it and stared at him.

"Benu, I'm glad you're safe." He lifted the jerboa to rest on his head. Then he suddenly remembered something. "I saw their leader, Danaa."

"They have a leader? I've never heard of such a person. Most people who encountered them said they worked on their own, approaching people silently to hypnotise them, unnoticed."

"No. I could tell this man was not one of them," Rapach said, remembering. " They obeyed him, even though he spoke no words. He was wearing a very distinct lion mask." Rapach reached for the pouch he was still wearing on his waist. "I'm sure he was looking for this package." He showed the red package to Danaa, who examined it closely.

"Who's this for?"

"The elderly man, the one who walks next to the river at night."

"The one who sings that one song?" Danaa asked. "So, someone finally found what he was looking for. What could be so important?"

They looked at the package but knew they could not open it. Only the owner was allowed to.

"So, where do we find him?" Danaa asked.

"There was a map, but Mat had it," Rapach said, panicking with this realization. "They have the map! I have to get to the elderly man at Sorrow City before they do! Danaa, you must know where this Sorrow City is, don't you?"

"Sorry boy…never heard of it."

Rapach pulled at his hair in frustration.

"I have to go there before it's too late," Rapach said, thinking of the stranger in the lion mask taking his sister.

"But they have the map. How will we get to such a place?"

Rapach stood up, deep in thought. He turned to face the white river. Its current ran at a high speed, deep into the forest. Downstream, Rapach noticed the river forking, wedged by three stacked rocks. They each had a different hue and shade.

"Erydis," Rapach whispered. These were the rocks Erydis had described in his dream. He was not sure if he could trust her entirely, but such a coincidence could not be overlooked. If there was a chance to find Sorrow City, even if it was slim, he had to try.

"What, boy?" Danaa asked.

"Danaa, listen carefully," Rapach instructed. "I need you to send a message to the clan. Whatever is going on, the elderly man must have the answers. I need to go to Sorrow City before the man in the lion mask finds him." Rapach pointed at the river. "Danaa, you see those three rocks, between the two streams of the river?" Danaa nodded, still confused.

"Follow the river to the left. Make another left at the next bend and then once more to the right. Sorrow City must be somewhere there."

"Wait. Kid, how do ya know all that? You should come with us."

"No, please, Danaa. You and Pek have to inform the clan of the importance of finding this man."

"Understood, boy. I trust ya. Leave it to me." Danaa bowed.

Rapach started sprinting along the river. "Benu! I need you to lead the way! Can you do that?"

Benu jumped swiftly off Rapach's head and darted forward decisively. Rapach snapped on his blue goggles and placed his scarf over his mouth as he ran. The river grew faster with the land's descent, and a strong wind hit his face, fiercer than the day before. A dust storm was coming.

As Rapach followed the smart jerboa, who seemed to intuitively understand the path Rapach needed to take, he saw a patch of blue flowers.

"Benu, wait! I'll need some of these in case we encounter miasma." Rapach grabbed a handful of flowers and placed them in his pouch.

Erydis had been right all along. She was real, this confirmed it. She was probably not even too far from him right now, since she'd heard someone at her home talking about Sorrow City.

Rapach followed Erydis's instructions and had only one more turn to take. He crossed the river, jumping from one rock to the next, careful not to fall into the dangerous white water. As he reached the other side and made a right, a cloud of miasma blocked his path.

"Benu, get in my pouch," he said. "If Erydis was right, Sorrow City must be right behind this miasma." Benu blinked and climbed into Rapach's pouch. Rapach placed a blue flower in his mouth, breathing in its sweet scent as he chewed on it.

Then he ran through the miasma, feeling surer about his direction than before. He was determined to face whatever was in that city. More Silent People or Purple Breathers? Their leader, the man in the lion mask? Surely not. He had travelled down that river in the canoe for a long time, unconscious. He had to be closer than they were.

But what if they had faster ways to travel? It didn't matter, he reasoned. He had a mission, and he was going to deliver that package one way or another. That elderly man...people said he was crazy. But maybe he knew things that no one else did.

The miasma thinned out steadily until the air around Rapach cleared again. The river forked into two waterfalls falling down a cliff a few steps away. Rapach crossed a small bridge before the river's fork and came to a path.

He walked through numerous small arches of old and broken wood marking the way. They were adorned with flags of assorted colours flapping rhythmically in the wind. Rapach checked for more miasma and walked down the path. Plants with large, multicoloured leaves were all around him. He walked in silence until he reached a stretch of open space.

He had finally reached Sorrow City.

Tall buildings with curved red tile roofs rose in a ring around a vast open square. As Rapach walked silently through the confined square, he saw intricate headless statues of people in various settings around him. They all wore long robes and held tragic poses—one was bent over, a hand on his chest. Plates and offerings were piled up below the statues, maybe by the people who had once lived there.

The city seemed empty. Rapach could not hear a single sound save for the flapping of flags attached to the buildings with thin ropes. The remnants of what once was a livid city.

In front of Rapach rose a pyramid of stone with a shrine at its top. Unlit torches lined the steps.

"Benu, we should go up to that shrine. It's the tallest structure around, and we'll have a better view of the city from there."

Rapach's ears perked up at a sound coming from a building next to them. He turned but saw nothing. Were they really alone?

"I'm probably just nervous," Rapach said to himself. He decided to ignore the sound and went up the dusty stone steps. When he reached the shrine, he saw a headless statue that had its arms stretched out to each side. There were many offerings around it—dried flowers and fruit—whoever this person was, the people must have adored him.

Rapach removed his goggles and stared at the city below him. It held a beauty he had never experienced. People seemed to have lived close to each other in the rectangular buildings, sharing the common space in the center where the statues were. They probably had a familial sort of bond with one another, just like the members of the Jerboa Clan. The noise of the flags flapping and the rush of the waterfalls behind him created a symphony that fascinated Rapach. Further away, there were other sounds. Was that the sound of the ocean?

"See anything, Benu?" Rapach asked. Benu jumped to the top of his head, burrowing into his hair. "Where are you, old man?" Rapach murmured.

Benu suddenly jumped. There was someone watching them from a balcony on a building to the right. It was a girl, no older than five years old. Rapach couldn't see her well from his position.

"Wait, you!" he called out. The girl ran back into the building and Rapach took off to follow her. He ran down the steps and towards the building he saw her in.

But before he could enter the building, Rapach froze, hearing a commotion at the entrance. He hid behind a headless statue.

A giant creature stepped from the building. Rapach had never seen such a menacing beast. It looked feline, with a black hairless body striped with orange and two bushy red tails. Its eyes were an intense red, as were its powerful fangs. It moved with a bizarre elegance. It had a shining silver circle on its forehead.

Even more terrifying were the five Purple Breathers riding the beast, exhaling miasma into the atmosphere.

Rapach's heart was racing as he felt the monstrous creature's every step creating tremors in the ground.

As he tried to better conceal himself behind the statue, Rapach noticed an open window in front of him. He took the chance, sliding slowly and carefully into the building, making sure to stay hidden.

Rapach found himself in a room that was filled with cushions and low tables. Everything was covered under a blanket of dust. He hid behind a child's bed surrounded by wooden animal toys, thinking that the room must have been inhabited by a big family.

He heard a deep growl as the creature got closer outside the window. Rapach crawled into the next room, trying to stay close to the floor, keeping the glass shield on his back out of sight of the windows.

He crawled into what seemed to be a dining room, where a big table lined with stone plates was surrounded with wrecked chairs, left upturned as if people had fled suddenly. Rapach hid under the long table, watching the dark, trailing robes of a few Silent People approaching from the room's entrance. One of them waited by the door as another floated through the room, exhaling a cloud of miasma from behind its mask.

Rapach hastily chewed on a blue flower as the thick miasma enveloped him. He could barely see in front of him. He breathed in the sweet smell and noticed Benu trying to quietly get his attention. Did the jerboa know a way out?

Rapach crouched and followed Benu, trying not to knock into anything. They quietly slipped past behind the Purple Breather who remained in the room, surveying it for anyone who could have been hypnotised.

They reached a set of stairs in the next room, and Rapach followed Benu up them.

On the second floor, they exited the miasma cloud. They were in a hallway with several doors that led to bedrooms on both sides. The walls were covered in clothes and flags, and there were pillars adorned with small stone statues. The girl Rapach had seen earlier was probably nearby.

He opened the door to the room closest to him, trying not to make any noise. The far end of the room led to the balcony where he had seen the girl. Outside, he could hear the monstrous beast breaking the stone steps as it climbed the pyramid.

Rapach felt a hand on his leg and jumped. The girl was behind him. She couldn't be older than five. She had round cheeks, a serious face, and two dusty pigtails. She was accompanied by another girl who appeared to be a little older than Rapach. She had short hair and beautiful eyes. Her expression was sceptical as she studied Rapach. Both of them wore bright dust-spotted dresses, and their faces and arms were painted with coloured lines. Rapach had never seen markings like that.

"Joie, behind me," instructed the older girl in an unfamiliar accent.

"But he has no scary mask, Nini."

Rapach bowed politely. "Greetings. My name is Rapach of the Jerboa Clan."

"There's no time for introductions," the older girl said. "It seems they've followed you here. Come with us."

The older girl slung the younger one onto her back to carry her. She pushed aside a flag on the wall and entered a concealed passageway behind it. Rapach didn't know what else to do but trail them.

They were now inside the walls of the building. The passageway appeared to have been constructed for hiding in. They could hear the beast outside breathing heavily, probably close-by. But the older girl kept on walking steadfastly until they arrived at a gap to the outside, behind the building. They climbed down some vines to reach the ground. Then the older girl pulled a big lever in the wall that opened a trapdoor on the floor leading outside.

The group climbed down a cliff and Rapach followed, careful not to slip on the muddy ground. After a few minutes they reached the bottom and found themselves on solid ground.

They were on the ledge of a high cliff, next to one of the waterfalls that cascaded over them into the ocean, where its white water mixed with the crystal-blue water below.

Rapach could not stop looking at the horizon. There was a small curtain of dust veiling the sun, but it was an amazing, rare view. The red light of the sun was beautifully reflected on the calm, infinite ocean. There were clouds in the blue sky, and he was sure he even spotted birds flying far away. It was almost as if he'd been transported to another world, where there was no dust or miasma.

"Is something wrong, boy?" the older girl asked.

"No, sorry. It's just that I have never seen the ocean before. It's so clean and big," Rapach said.

The girl smiled.

"It is. Hopefully these doomed lands don't spread their curse to where the horizon fuses with the sky. I'm sorry I didn't introduce myself earlier. My name is Nintai, and this little bug is my sister, Joie."

"Hello, kid." Joie said, shyly shaking Rapach's hand, not leaving Nintai's back. Benu leapt off Rapach's head and ran up to Joie. "Look Nini, a mouse!" she said.

"This is a dust jerboa, and her name is Benu," Rapach said.

"Well, you both should follow us," Nintai said. We have clean water and food at our house."

"Thank you," Rapach said gratefully.

They walked along the steep, rocky path beside the cliff. Rapach couldn't tear his eyes away from the impressive view. They walked underneath the white waterfall that passed in a curve overhead, the droplets of moisture cool on their faces.

"So, why did you come to Sorrow City, Rapach?" Nintai asked.

"I can't say. It's confidential, but I was told that's where I can find what I'm searching for."

"Well, there's not much I can do to help if you don't tell me," she said.

Rapach deliberated for a second.

"I'll tell you when I have some food. I just realised I haven't eaten in a long time." Nintai nodded. "That beast…what was that thing?" Rapach asked.

"That was a djinni," Joie said.

"We've seen some before, but never as vicious as that one."

"Djinni? I'm sure I've heard that term before." Rapach tried to search his memory.

"A beast made of dust. It's existed for many years," Nintai said.

That beast and its power, on the side of the Silent People. A chill ran down Rapach's spine.

After walking for a while, he followed the sisters into a cave in the shadows of a gigantic rock. They walked in darkness until a flickering light started glowing around the corner.

"Welcome to our current home, Rapach," Nintai said.

The cave looked like the inside of a house. Beds, chairs, and a little table were arranged in an orderly fashion. A tapestry covered the cold stone floor, and the space was illuminated by many candles. There were jars of clean water and baskets of fruits on the table.

On a cushioned chair sat someone wrapped in old clothes, waiting. He had long, dry hair and a wrinkled face with tiny dust spots all over. His ancient eyes stared into nothingness, devoid of any trace of emotion.

"That man…I think he's whom I've been looking for," Rapach said to Nintai.

CHAPTER XIII

FORBIDEN DUST

Erydis

THAT MASK, THE FUR, THE EYES. If the stranger in the lion mask was indeed the same person Rapach had spoken of in her dreams, it could mean only one thing: Rapach was real.

But as they entered the elevation chamber once more, Erydis noticed that no one seemed to acknowledge him, let alone as any sort of leader.

"You've arrived just in time," Ferus said to the new group. "Now, will any of you be so kind as to give me the key to the dust chamber?"

The man in the lion mask handed Ferus an intricate silver key without hesitation and walked back to stand next to Erydis, ignoring her presence. Ferus turned the key in the elevation chamber's second keyhole from the top.

The chamber vibrated and they all stood silently as it ascended. Erydis could hear the stranger steadily breathing behind his mask next to her. She wanted to steal another glance at him but didn't dare to—she knew what he was capable of.

Up until then, she had believed Rapach to be a figment of her imagination. An inexplicable dream. But this turned everything on its head. Silent

People, the Jerboa Clan, miasma, Rapach…they were all real.

And the stranger next to her could be the one who had tormented him. The man who turned Rapach's sister into one of the Silent People. Did Ferus know about all that, too? Did anyone in the city know? There was so much chaos in the far reaches beyond the fortress, but what could she do?

Erydis squared her shoulders. She had to try and find out what the stranger was planning in Dust City. And she would watch his every move like a hawk—it was the least she could do for Rapach.

"Ferus," Herra said, his gaze fixed on the key. "That silver key belongs to Liudmila. How did you obtain it? She's probably one of the most important people in Dust City, after the Emperor, of course. I cannot imagine there was no resistance."

"I appreciate your concern, Master Herra. But there are things I simply can't reveal, even to my own Vakandi."

The chamber came to a gentle stop and the doors opened to reveal what Erydis had only imagined over the years; a place where she could find the item that would make her shine as a dust mixer.

The dust chamber was a gigantic, noisy room containing an impressive spectacle of machinery. Several white pipes in the ceiling were connected to assorted machines in the room, emitting clouds of dust as they worked unwaveringly.

"I have to admit that you dusters have quite extraordinary inventions," Ferus said, clearly impressed.

"So, this is where the white dust is transformed into its many colours," Erydis marvelled.

"It took years for Valerios Kythera to engineer this chamber. This is a marvel of Fabrica," Herra said.

"How does it work?" Ferus asked, hesitant, as he probably realised the question was simpler than the answer. Herra smiled at his curiosity.

"Well, in brief, the white dust created at the top of the Tower travels down into different machines, where it is refined. We infuse it, boil it, and mix it with plants, minerals, and oils to create different types of dust. Of course, every type of dust is created using a different process. Some are more difficult to make than others and need more resources. But some are easily made.

"Then the different types of dust are moved to the chamber below, where you saw all the murals. We check their quality before distributing them to the population. But there are types of dust that only a mixer with a permit can use."

"The dust from the Tower," Erydis whispered excitedly to Eko, who seemed clueless about the dust.

"Some of the types of dust from Valerios's Tower are mined in the caves close to the mist, and others are created in this chamber or brought from far away. Follow me," Herra said, leading them to another section of the room, where the pieces of a golden machine were moving rapidly. Four expensive-looking jars, each slightly bigger than Erydis, sat atop a woven tapestry on the floor, each jar a different colour—silver, black, golden, and purple.

"Here it is," Herra said. "Years and years of research and discovery contained within these jars." The whole group leaned in for a closer look.

Erydis couldn't help but smile as she observed the deep colour of the dust. It seemed to glitter from the reflections bouncing off the dust lamps hanging from the ceiling. She had waited a long time to see this dust.

But her excitement was short-lived. She felt the ominous presence of the stranger standing silently behind everyone, ignored by all except Erydis. She couldn't focus, knowing what he'd done to Rapach. Why was he there?

"So what is this dust for?" Ferus asked. "Oh, let me guess, to create more weapons?"

His fellow Vakandi laughed; all except the stranger in the lion mask.

"These types of dust are believed to be too powerful and strange for people with no knowledge of how to use them," Herra explained. "Some are made with mysterious substances from faraway lands. But we'll get to that.

"The silver dust here is what we call the platinum dust. It is especially rare. It was brought to us some time ago from somewhere far northeast, where they use some sort of substance to create it. We are nowhere close to discovering its true power, but we believe it has something to do with the manipulation of metals. As I said in the Arma chamber, the morph blade is partially made of this dust, as well as a mix of purple and red. It's because of this dust that the morph blade can change its shape.

"The next type is black dust. It is also called naturally made dust. The Emperor has tried to make it inaccessible to the general public, but since it's found in nature, we've seen it being sold illegally in the Hidden Barrio. It hides inside rocks that have been exposed to the mist for a long time."

"A long time?" Ferus asked. "Months?"

"Centuries," Herra said. "We thought of it as useless when it was discovered. The people who tried experimenting with it found it too unstable to control. But then our genius Alchemia Master, Kemia, created the Obscura sub-discipline. She researched how to make this volatile dust into something more. It quickly became a frequently used dust at the Tower because of its tremendous power compared to all the others. It is similar to white dust, enhancing any elements mixed with it. But black dust triples that effect." Herra went silent for a few seconds before continuing. "Kemia insisted to the Emperor that more research had to be done on the dust to understand its dangerous instability. But Engyl ignored her, and now it's common for many dust mixers to use it.

"The next type of dust here is golden dust. This one is outstanding, made by *that* gold machine. It requires a huge amount of white dust to create, but in exchange, a spoon of it is ten times more potent than white dust! Of course, the disadvantage is the time and resources it takes to make. That's why we're very selective about when we use it. Only the fuel for my flying machine requires it as of now.

"And last, there's this creation," Herra turned to the jar filled with purple dust, his expression serious. "Purple dust is the most terrible, most dangerous dust that exists. It is still being researched by the Arma mixers."

Erydis stared at the purple dust. Her skin chilled as she felt the presence of the stranger in the lion mask weigh heavily on her.

"What does it do?" Erydis asked nervously.

"It manipulates cognitive behaviour. It can make people do anything or feel any desired emotion. It even has the potential of turning a good person into a dangerous, reckless psychopath. I still don't know much about it, as I am not allowed to use it. But if it were up to me, I would destroy this monstrous creation."

Erydis could only think of one thing—the curse that Rapach feared so much: the miasma.

"Is it difficult to make?" she asked, afraid to hear the answer.

"As long as there's a large quantity of black dust and a forbidden substance from the northern lands called purple grime, it is not. It was brought to us from the north, from lands the Emperor has decided to ignore. It is there where they process the ingredients to create this dangerous dust. Only the Arma Master, Liudmila, has the formula for it."

A disturbance at the other side of the room made everyone turn. It was Eko tripping over something.

"Ah! The musical instruments. Please, let me show you," Herra said, finding his smile again.

Ferus and Herra walked towards Eko, followed by the Vakandi. Erydis saw her chance to grab the dust she needed for her experiment. She started walking towards it but something made her stop.

The stranger in the lion mask stared at the purple dust as scooped some out and let it run slowly between his fingers. Erydis managed to hide behind the jar of golden dust a split second before the stranger looked over his shoulder cautiously. Then, as she peered surreptitiously from between the jars, the stranger grabbed several handfuls of purple dust and put it in a small sack. He hid the sack under his baggy robes and walked away to join Eko and the rest.

Erydis couldn't believe it. The stranger was the one using the dust, the one responsible for the miasma. Rapach was in danger, and she had to do something about it. She might be the only person who could do something. Erydis wondered if Rapach had managed to find Sorrow City. Maybe he'd have more answers when they returned to their shared dream.

But for now, that had to wait. It was her turn to steal some of the dust that she'd gone all that distance for. She grabbed fistfuls of gold and then black, enough for a full sack of each. She couldn't help but be impressed by the amount of resources that were needed to create all these different dusts. But it did come with a price—every time any dust was used, there was always the by-product of useless, grey dust. Just like the dust Rapach encountered every day. Erydis felt a little uneasy, conflicted for the first time about using it. But she couldn't let that hold her back, not when she'd gone that far.

She casually walked away from the jars, pretending that she'd been just looking at them up-close.

"So why exactly are there musical instruments here?" she heard Ferus ask as she approached the group. Eko had straightened the instruments back up against the wall while Erydis had been occupied with the dust.

"Lady Liudmila likes the privacy of this room," Herra explained. "Says she likes to play to the rhythm of the machines here. She created that instrument at the Inauguration Festival; the dust accordion."

"My friend Isaac was the one playing it," Erydis said to Eko.

Eko seemed too distracted to listen to her as he studied every instrument in awe.

"My little brother loves music," Ferus said with a smile. "Of course, we don't have fancy trumpets or accordions such as these, but we have our own kind of music. But now that you've found these to play with, I believe we adults have other matters to talk about. Shall we?"

Ferus walked over to the other end of the room, beckoning at the Vakandi and Herra to follow. The stranger in the mask followed them silently as well, leaving Erydis and Eko behind. What was that about? Erydis frowned, nervous about what it could mean. But she had to pretend as if she was unaware of anything—at least for Eko's sake.

"So you want to learn to play one of these?" Erydis asked. Eko nodded, eyeing a little string instrument. "I wish I could play one of these as well as I can mix dust."

Eko grabbed a small trumpet, perfect for his size, and attempted to blow into it unsuccessfully. Erydis laughed as Eko kept trying. She then thought of Rapach and his singing. She'd never had a talent for music, yet Rapach's repetitive five-note tune had firmly etched itself in her head. Rapach was real. He had to be.

She tried to whistle Rapach's notes again, but she could only sputter a terrible noise. Eko stared at her curiously and tried to imitate her terrible whistle on the trumpet.

A clean note followed by a small cloud of dust came out of the bell of the trumpet.

"There! That's the note I wanted to whistle," Erydis said. "Now try this…"

She whistled roughly again. Impressively, Eko managed to play the note perfectly. Right then, Ferus approached.

"Clever girl," he said. "I'm afraid it's your time to head out. You have been an incredible help to us Vakandi, but for the next part of our plan we must stay here. That is, until the time is right."

"Oh, did I do something wrong?" Erydis asked.

"Besides entering this Tower illegally and stealing prohibited dust? Not close. But I do promise to explain more later on, once things calm down."

Erydis blushed, embarrassed to have been caught stealing. "If you insist," she said and walked back towards the elevation chamber. Eko waved his goodbye and continued playing the trumpet.

"Farewell, and may our paths cross again one day." Herra bowed. Erydis smiled and gave a nod.

She turned her attention to the stranger in the lion mask, who was walking around silently, analysing the vast Tower's ceilings.

"Ferus," Erydis started as they entered the elevation chamber together. "Who's that man in the lion mask?"

Ferus stared at her, his smile fading slightly.

"The masked people who have arrived are Vakandi..."

"I know, but who is the one in the lion mask?"

"Why are you asking?"

"I'm curious."

Ferus stared at her for what seemed like an eternity.

"He's a Vakandi, that's all you need to know." Ferus inserted the key into the keyhole and they descended back towards the tunnel leading to the Hidden Barrio.

As Erydis emerged from the hideout, she was greeted by a spectacle of coloured clouds. In the Dust Ring, people were throwing dust marbles everywhere, creating small, vibrant explosions. Some played music on the street, celebrating while dancing and revelling with all sorts of food and drinks. The spirit of the Festival of Many Dusts was truly alive.

It's a shame Eko had to remain in the Tower, Erydis thought. He would have loved to see Dust City like this. But maybe it was for the best; amidst the partying, several guards were ordering citizens to remove their masks, some more aggressively than others. Little did they know that all the Vakandi were already inside the Tower. Since the Emperor had closed off the Tower's access to anyone entering and leaving, it seemed the people of Dust City were in for a big surprise.

But this also meant the man in the lion mask was inside, and there was no easy way for her to reach him. She felt truly lost. How was she going to find a solution to the riddle of the last few days?

Erydis sighed, then squared her shoulders. Worrying wouldn't change anything. It would be better if she focused on the celebration in front of her, she concluded as she walked the path towards the Emerald Barrio. The colourful dust on the streets looked beautiful, but Erydis now knew that it was all grey, useless dust disguised cleverly. Rapach had grown up in a place full of dust with no celebratory hue.

Erydis couldn't wait to dream of him again and tell him everything that had happened that day. But she still had some time before nightfall to seek Kemia's advice and work on her experiment.

The Dust Academy was still open. All the students were working hard before the Closure Festival. They feasted on big plates of food as per tradition, while correcting and tweaking their experiments in the hope of winning. Erydis realised she was still missing the last piece needed for her experiment—the Emperor's sceptre.

She went up the stairs towards Kemia's laboratory but stopped right next to the door. Someone was already inside.

"He was on his way here to pick up some dust, Kemia. You must have seen him," a familiar voice said, filled with worry.

"I need you to calm down, Kitri."

"But you must have seen where he went! I'm sure he was on his way here!" Kitri's voice was shaky.

Erydis pushed the door open. Kemia looked up at her as she entered. Kitri was sitting on the floor, crying.

"What's wrong? Is Trinos missing?" Erydis asked, alarmed.

"He is, dear," Kitri said, still sobbing. Her bright smile had faded. "Have you seen him?"

"I'm sure he'll be back home tonight," Erydis said.

"But he promised to help me close the store, and he's never late. You know that."

"Kitri, I know you're worried, but the city is in chaos right now," Kemia said firmly. "He might be late because the funicular is closed and the marble stairs are full with soldiers questioning people in masks."

"What if he got arrested?" Kitri asked.

"And why would he get arrested?" Kemia asked with a raised eyebrow.

"I've been helping them."

"The Vakandi," Erydis guessed. Kitri nodded.

"I just helped them to gain supporters. They approached me after they saw us selling purple paint at the market. They gave me some red coins to hand to those wearing purple dots on their masks."

"To join them at the hideout?" Erydis asked. Both Kitri and Kemia looked at her, startled. "I might be working with them as well," she admitted sheepishly.

"I was told that only those with red coins would be allowed into the hideout in the Hidden Barrio. Oh, please, Kemia, don't tell anyone."

"I'm working with neither side," Kemia said. "I have not cared for the Emperor's decisions since a long time ago, and the Vakandi can do as they please. They've suffered enough. So your secret is safe here. Now, go home and wait, Kitri. Try to get some sleep and let me work. If Trinos is still not there in the morning, I promise to help you look for him."

"I knew I shouldn't have helped," Kitri said. "Trinos warned me, and the soldiers probably heard something. Kemia, dear, thank you for your time." Kitri left the room, her cheeks stained with tears.

Kemia returned to a mix bubbling in a stone jar. "So you're helping them?" she asked, popping a smoke candy that was lying on the table into her mouth.

"I am," Erydis said, trying to appear casual as she inspected Kemia's mixture. "It was a good truce—help them out and finally gather Tower dust for my experiment."

"So you've finally seen what lies inside the Tower."

"It was unbelievable, Kemia! So much technology that I've never seen in any barrio. A sword that changes shape. A flying machine!"

"So Herra finally did it," Kemia mused.

"He did! At least, it's a small start for the sub-discipline Aera. He's so wise and admirable. He explained everything about the dust to me and even some of his mixing secrets."

"He's a great mixer," Kemia said with a smile, deep in thought.

"He supports the Vakandi, so when the Vakandi invaded the Tower, he gave their leader, Ferus, a tour."

"So, the mixers and soldiers are being held inside the Tower. And since Engyl has decided to lock the entrance to the Tower, there's no way he'll know of the invasion. Smart," Kemia said, analysing the situation. "He won't be pleased when he learns that, so you'd better be careful."

"The Emperor is not the one I fear." Erydis cast her eyes down to the floor.

Kemia stared at her. "Is there someone else bothering you?"

"Well, inside the Tower with the Vakandi, there's a stranger I don't trust. A stranger with a lion mask."

Kemia glanced at her and went back to her mixing.

"Why wouldn't you trust a Vakandi if they helped you get inside the Tower?"

"There's this boy I know. He told me that someone wearing a lion mask had kidnapped his sister."

Kemia stared at her.

"And who exactly is this boy?" she asked, an eyebrow raised.

"He's not from Dust City. He lives outside the fortress."

"I don't recall you leaving the city any time in the past." Kemia sounded sceptical.

"Well..." Erydis raised her head and breathed deeply. "I know you'll want proof of this. Especially you. But I had a dream about this boy, Rapach, who told me he was in danger. He told me about these woods filled with what he calls the miasma, and how these masked individuals called the Silent People are looking for him and his clan. He told me their leader was a stranger with a lion mask."

"But how...that's impossible." Kemia paused her mixing. She had a strange expression on her face that Erydis had never seen before. Did Kemia believe her?

"He's been in my dreams since the festival started," Erydis said. "I thought it was a projection of my imagination. That was until today, when I saw that stranger with the lion mask. Based on everything Rapach has told me, it has to be the same mask. And he was stealing some purple dust from the Tower." Erydis looked at her mentor nervously. "Do you believe me, Kemia?"

"Like you said, I need proof," Kemia said. "But I also believe I might have it."

Kemia pointed at Erydis's blue amber necklace. "The day of the Inauguration Festival, you delivered some black dust to me. You also told me that whoever sold you the dust in the Hidden Barrio was the same person who gave you that necklace."

"That's true! I started dreaming about that place when I started wearing it. Is it really connected?"

"I can't be sure yet." Kemia extended a hand. "I'll need a small piece of your necklace to study, if you don't mind."

Erydis nodded and unclasped her necklace. Kemia chipped off a tiny piece of the blue amber with a hammer and chisel and placed the fragment in a small glass flask. She handed the necklace back to Erydis.

"Don't stop wearing it. Come back tomorrow, and don't tell anyone else about this. I'll have to run a test."

Suddenly, the door behind them opened, making them jump. It was Thylac, looking alert and a little panicked.

"You! Knock before you enter," Kemia said.

"I apologise, Kemia. Erydis, you're safe." He sounded relieved.

"Well? What's the matter?" Kemia urged.

"We can't find them; the Vakandi. We've been searching in the six barrios and we've only managed to find a few supporters."

"Well, there are none here. Off you go."

"I was also wondering if you have the smoke candies I left here the other day?" Thylac asked.

"In the name of dust, right now?" Kemia grabbed a sack from under the table and handed some candies to Thylac.

"Sorry, I wouldn't have asked if I hadn't been working all night and day since the beginning of the festival."

Kemia shook her head as Thylac walked towards the door.

"Thylac," Erydis called, smiling. He turned to her. "I finally have the dust I needed for my experiment."

Of course, she didn't tell him about her entire adventure retrieving the dust from inside the Tower with the Vakandi's help. She felt a little guilty hiding this from him, but her experiment felt more important than the truth.

"Oh, fantastic! I just hope the contest won't get cancelled, with everything happening in the city," he said. "But anyway, what's left for you to finish?"

"Just hours of dust mixing and...the Emperor's sceptre," she said with a wide grin.

"The what?!" He yelled. Erydis thought she saw a glint of anger in his eyes.

"I know, I know..." she said. "You're supposed to protect the Emperor and all. But I really need it to finish my experiment. It's a useless relic that separates him from the rest of his people. It just makes shiny clouds of grey dust!"

"Why do you need it then?" he asked.

"What it does now is useless, but how it works is amazing."

"It's true," Kemia said as she continued her mixing. "It grabs any useful dust to create that useless grey trash. Quite expensive, for no reason."

"I need your help, Thylac," Erydis insisted. "And in exchange I guarantee you'll be speechless when you see my experiment working. Besides, it won't hurt the Emperor to lose his useless toy."

"But how am I supposed to…" Thylac stopped. It had just clicked in his mind. "You want me to help you sneak inside the palace during tomorrow's Festival of the Palace so you can steal it, don't you?"

"I do." Erydis grinned.

"Am I supposed to agree? And in front of Kemia?" Thylac asked, his eyes pleading for help from the Alchemia Master.

"I'm just focused on my mixing," Kemia said, pretending not to listen.

"Please, Thylac," Erydis said. "The people of Dust City don't need that stupid relic. And I won't need it for long."

"I'm afraid you're right," Thylac said. We do have bigger problems right now." He sighed, stroking his beard. "Very well. Tomorrow afternoon, we'll meet at the marble stairs. Wear your best outfit. Only for you, Erydis." He walked out the door.

Erydis jumped with excitement. She would be a thief in a pretty dress at the annual palace party.

As for the rest of the evening, she had hours of dust mixing and experimentation ahead of her.

Chapter XIX

Escape

Rapach

"A red envelope?" Nintai looked confused.

Rapach was in the midst of trying to explain why he was looking for the old man. But thirst and hunger were getting the better of him.

"Yeah," he mumbled, chewing loudly on a mouthful of a sweet-and-sour green fruit.

"A 'friend in red' had this package for him? But how did he know the old man was here?" Nintai asked.

Rapach grabbed a bowl of water and took a gulp to wash down his food.

"That's what he calls himself; a friend in red," he said, coughing from wolfing down his meal too quickly. "I don't know how. I have no idea who this person is or how he figured it all out. But the old man, how long has he been here?"

They stared at the old man, who was still sitting on the cushioned chair, staring emptily at the ground. He didn't seem to be listening or reacting to anything they said.

"He arrived here with us," Nintai said with a fond smile. "We've been here probably for a month or so. My sister and I were separated from our clan and we got lost in the forest at night. We then saw the miasma for the first time. We didn't know what to do, so we called for help in desperation. That's when he emerged from the dark. I remember we were scared of him." She laughed at the memory.

"He looked like a dirty beast," Joie added, playing with Benu's tail. The creature didn't seem to mind as she munched on seeds at a speed that matched Rapach's.

"He was a bit livelier when we first met," Nintai continued. "He even walked for hours, guiding us through these cursed lands, taking the safest routes away from the miasma, until we found this city. But since we don't trust these lands, we've decided to hide here. We've been living in this cave since."

"The old man just sits there. He just sleeps, eats, and almost never moves," Joie said.

"And… we are grateful to him for helping us, aren't we?" Nintai reminded her sister gently.

"Yes, Nini."

"She's not wrong, though," Nintai said. "He's been like that since we got here. I suppose he's saving his strength in case we have to escape the miasma again."

"I see…" Rapach said, touching the red package in his pouch. "Which clan do you and your sister hail from?"

"We're from the Amaru Clan from the far south. The curse reached most of our lands, and many of us had to search for a safer place to live. Our clan stands for the teachings of the wise djinni, which is the foundation our main village was founded on."

"A wise djinni? Like the one outside?" Rapach asked.

"Our teacher was kind and smart," Nintai said with a frown. "That djinni outside is evil."

Rapach took another bite of his food, pensive. He would have to be even more careful from now on. That old man knew something important enough for the man in the lion mask and the Silent People to be determined to find him.

The old man sat impassive, only blinking slowly now and then.

Suddenly, a shadow cast a pall over everyone in the cave.

"Nini!" Joie screamed, pointing at the entrance. A cloud of miasma was oozing into the cave, rapidly blocking out the sunlight.

"They found us! They're coming. We have to go." Nintai was frantic.

"But where to?" Rapach asked as Benu hopped close to his ankle.

"There is another exit. Come with us," Nintai said, turning towards the old man. "Excuse me, sir?"

But the old man was already standing up and was staring at the miasma with a glint of anger in his eyes. He swung a big cloth bag over his shoulder and walked towards a small gap in the rocks that Rapach had not noticed before. The man stopped just before entering the gap, seeming to wait for the rest of them.

Joie slipped through the gap first, followed by Rapach and Benu, Nintai, and finally the old man. Darkness surrounded them, except for the light coming from a crack of an opening on the other side of the cavern they now found themselves in.

The cavern was humid, with ponds between jagged rocks on the ground.

The group crouched silently behind some rocks, careful not to make their presence known, watching through the gap in the rocks as the miasma slowly seeped into the cave they'd just exited. Then some Purple Breathers entered through the gap, searching the area soundlessly, almost seeming to hover above the ground.

Rapach and the rest turned around and headed for the other side of the cavern, hiding behind the rock formations as they went. Benu leapt lightly towards the exit, undetected.

SPLASH!

The silence was broken as the splash echoed in the little cavern. Joie had tripped into a pond. She looked like she was about to cry. Before anyone could do anything, there was a horrific swoosh as a cloud of miasma enveloped them. The old man started running towards the exit.

"Rapach, hurry!" Nintai picked her sister up and sprinted out.

Rapach started running just as the masked breathers were getting closer. He saw that the old man was holding a rope at the exit. It was knotted to a rig connected to some rocks at the opening of the cavern. There was no time to waste; the Purple Breathers were fast approaching. Luckily, Rapach had anticipated that before they entered the cavern. He had grabbed a blue flower from his pouch , and quickly chewed on it, waiting. As the fresh scent filled his lungs, a Purple Breather grabbed him by the arm and shoved him to the ground. A cloud of miasma filled Rapach's surroundings.

But it had no effect on him, thanks to the flower. Rapach stood up, wielding his shield, and leapt a few steps back before running towards the masked Purple Breather. He pushed him as hard as he could, knocking him back into another Breather and onto the floor of the cavern.

Rapach took his chance to sprint out of the cavern. The second he was out, the old man pulled the rope and the rocks tumbled from the rig to the ground, partially covering the entrance.

Rapach heaved a huge sigh of relief. He was back with the group, all waiting with bated breath on a ledge that stuck out from the cliff face, and became a path as it went up. A second polluted waterfall cascaded next to them, the water pouring into the ocean.

"Why aren't you one of them?" Nintai asked, alarmed. "I saw you breathing in the miasma."

Rapach started to explain, but he noticed the old man looking alert. There was indeed something strange happening—he could hear the sound of rocks being crushed nearby, as if something heavy was approaching. They were not alone on the path.

"Nini!" Joie screamed, pointing skywards.

They all looked up and the blood drained from their faces. The feline djinni was crawling down the cliff face, digging its sharp, red claws into the rocks as if they were soft clay. Its red eyes, burning with menace, stared directly at them. It let out a powerful roar, causing the earth to tremble. Rapach had never heard such a sound from a creature.

They ran for the ledge, the djinni hot in pursuit. It almost flew off the ledge but recovered elegantly, effortlessly clawing for grip. Underneath its every step, the rock crumbled to dust.

"Run up the cliff! I'll try to distract it!" Rapach shouted, unfolding his slingshot and grabbing a sharp rock. He took aim at the beast's right eye, and the rock whistled in the wind on release.

It caught the djinni in the eye, stopping it in its tracks. It rubbed its eye and let out another fearsome roar as Rapach kept running, not knowing what else to do. He felt cold sweat streaming down his chest. We have no chance, he thought as he felt the tremors of the djinni speeding up in fury.

A dog's bark made Rapach turn. It was Pek, running up from the cliff path, followed by Danaa and other familiar faces!

It was the Jerboa Clan members, wielding their bows with sharp blue glass-point arrows. They shot rapidly and relentlessly at the djinni as they carefully advanced on the narrow path.

Another group wielded short swords of blue glass, while a third group carried large, rectangular blue glass shields and a pole with the clan's flag—the silhouette of a jumping jerboa emblazoned on a caerulean background.

The arrows hit the djinni but bounced off its strong body. The beast slowed down and angrily slashed its claws at the projectiles.

"Shields ready!" Danaa barked.

At the order, the clan members raised their shields and charged at the beast. Rapach felt a wave of pride for his clan as he ran alongside the others.

The first wave of men and women forced the djinni towards the edge of the cliff with their shields, causing it to stumble. The second wave, with Rapach in the middle, pushed the beast even closer to the edge. Finally, the last wave pushed the beast down the cliff, its roar growing distant as it fell.

But even thirty clan members proved insufficient in defeating the beast. The creature sank its claws into the rock face and tried to climb back up again.

"Come with me!" Danaa shouted to Rapach and the others while some of the Jerboa Clan shot arrows and threw rocks at the djinni clinging to the cliff below them.

"Retreat!" Danaa shouted.

They ran up the path to the woods nearby. Large boars were waiting for them in a clearing, snorting impatiently.

"How did you find us?" Rapach asked.

"Well, I knew somehow where you ran off to," Danaa said. "We can't overlook something that will give us some answers about their leader."

Danaa climbed onto a brown boar with yellow patches on its fur.

"You and the old man will ride with me, boy. The ladies will ride with Lu," Danaa said, pointing at a muscular woman.

Rapach and the old man climbed onto Danaa's boar.

"Are we riding that, Nini?" Joie asked, staring at another boar with green fur patches.

"Yes, Joie, and we have to hurry." Nintai lifted her sister onto the back of the animal as the rest of the clan mounted their own boars.

"We'll split up here. But everyone, meet me back at the camp," Danaa instructed. He made a strong blowing noise with his mouth and their boar took off towards the north.

They rode for about an hour, finally arriving at an open field with tall crimson grass, where a caerulean cube rested. A few tents had been pitched inside man-made holes in the ground. The tents were made of thick curved cloth that could withstand strong winds.

"Here we are, folks. This must be the mailbox marking south-east from the Central Camp," Danaa said. Benu gathered with Danaa's and Lu's jerboas, and Nintai and Joie went to rest in a tent.

Danaa dismounted the boar and helped the old man down. "Is something wrong with him?" he asked.

"I don't know," Rapach said. "He's been like that since I met him. He could have spent all his energy to escape Sorrow City. I wonder if I should give him the package while he's in such a state."

"I think ye'd best wait fer tomorrow, boy," Danaa said confidently. "We'll ride to the Central Camp. That way ye can tell us more about what happened. Today, ye all rest. Lu and I will remain vigilant in case that unfriendly beast finds us."

Danaa placed his hand on Rapach's shoulder.

"Ye've been very brave, Rapach. The clan is proud, as I'm sure dear Mat would be as well."

Rapach looked away, trying to hide his sadness. The thought of Mat moving like the Silent People and Purple Breathers was just too much. Was she walking like a Silent One, hypnotised by the man in the lion mask's curse?

He shook his head, trying to clear it. He had to accept it. Mat had become one of them and there was nothing he could do.

The Fourth Dream

1

Rapach had been waiting alone by the roots of the black tree for a while. He started to wonder if his last encounter with Erydis had scared her off. He had tried to stab her after all, but that was when he wasn't entirely sure if she was with him or against him.

After finding Sorrow City thanks to her precise instructions, he was confident that she was trustworthy. Erydis had saved his life more than once. She'd been on his side all along.

The dream world looked a little different this time around. Tall buildings extended into the distance, like those he'd seen in Sorrow City. But it was not only that. Shiny machinery hummed and clanked all around him, and the buildings in the distance looked like an infinite stretch of jars in different hues.

"You!"

The familiar voice behind him made him jump. He watched Erydis march towards him, her hands by her side in tight fists.

"Erydis, wait!" he said as she grabbed him by the tunic.

"You tried to stab me! If this weren't a dream, I wouldn't be standing here," she said angrily.

"Well, nothing happened, did it?" Rapach said apologetically.

"What if it had?" she retorted, pushing him to the ground.

"I'm sorry, alright? I don't know whom I can trust these days."

Erydis turned her back on him as he stood up.

"I know I can trust you now, though. I really appreciate your help, Erydis," he said.

"And now I know you're real after all," she said, facing him again. Her face softened and she grinned. "I saw him."

"Who?"

"The man who took your sister. The man in the lion mask. The mask had brown fur and small, scary eyes, just like you described."

A wave of mixed feelings enveloped Rapach.

"But… how? Why is he there? Where did he take my sister?"

"I'm not sure what he's doing at Dust City. But him being at the Tower, where the dust we use is created, can't be good."

"Did you follow him?" Rapach asked with a glimmer of hope.

"I tried to keep a close eye on him, but we got separated," she said. "But don't worry, tomorrow I'll be shadowing him to figure out his intentions." She gently placed a hand on Rapach's shoulder. He nodded, thoughtful. It would have to do for now.

"Anyway, did you find it? Sorrow City?" Erydis asked.

"I did, thanks to your directions! When I woke up, I was really close to the river and the rocks—just as you described them.

"I also found the old man I was looking for. He was being taken care of by two young girls, Nintai and Joie. They've been with him for a while. But the old man's mind is numb, far from reality. He was just staring into space.

"We were chased by Silent People! They even had djinni, which was almost like a large cat."

"Wait, a what?" Erydis asked, her eyes wide.

"Djinni. I know some of my clan members who helped us escape have encountered them before, but I don't think it was ever as big as this one," Rapach said.

"But the djinnis were all wiped out by our old emperor, Orn Ryk, hundreds of years ago!" Erydis said.

"Not in the Miasma Realm. They're rare, don't get me wrong, but they are alive," Rapach said.

"That's impossible," Erydis said, rubbing her temples in disbelief and a bit of awe. "I hope I'll get to see them one day."

She glanced at Rapach, who was grasping his pouch tightly. "How's your mission coming along? Did you finally deliver the package to the old man?"

"Not yet. I was instructed to wait until we find safer grounds."

"Can I see it?" Erydis asked, suddenly standing right next to him.

Rapach carefully took out the red package. But in a lightning-quick motion, Erydis grabbed it from him and started unwrapping it.

"No, wait!" Rapach gasped, but it was too late.

"Do you always do what you're told?" Erydis laughed, pushing him away with one hand. She then opened it. "Oh…"

Rapach froze. "What? What's in there?"

"Nothing…There's nothing inside that I can see, but I can feel a heavy weight under it, as if there's something."

She stretched out her palms. Rapach realised she was right—the red package was unwrapped, but there was an emptiness where its contents should have been.

"I don't understand," he said, puzzled.

"I have a theory," Erydis said with a knowing smile. "Since this is a dream, all the objects around us are details from when we are awake, like these jars and this package. A projection of our experiences in the real world. But you see only what it looks like on the outside, not the inside. This dream projects it as if there's nothing."

"That makes sense…I suppose," Rapach said. He couldn't think of any other explanation, and a part of him was relieved that he hadn't betrayed the trust of his clan by opening the package after all.

"Well, it was a good try." Erydis sighed, sitting down with her back resting against the black tree.

"I guess many of our questions will have to wait," Rapach said as he sat down next to her. "Erydis, you speak of so many things I don't fully comprehend. About the dust and the academy and your daily life. Can you tell me more about it all? Your city and the way you grew up, and how you came to know so much?"

2

"Well, there are so many parts to it," Erydis said. "Most of them are difficult to explain if you don't know much about dust or dust mixing."

"Do you like living there?" Rapach asked with honest curiosity.

"I do! I guess every city has its good qualities and a chaotic side, but there's so much I love. Looking up at the gigantic Tower every day, where the dust is made. The bazaar and the festivities. The food! All the flavours of stews, drinks, and candies.

"I do wish there weren't such a divide between us and the fancier people though. Even learning about the dust requires money if you want a proper education at the Geberus Dust Academy."

"You have schools for that?" Rapach asked. "That's incredible." He thought about the blue flower and its potential. That must barely scratch the surface of what Erydis knew.

"Yes," she answered, "but most people there come from rich families. The rest are hardly able to learn about what a complex, beautiful thing the dust is. If you learn how to use it well, there's no limit to your creations."

"That sounds magnificent!" Rapach tried to imagine it all as he lay on the white sand, staring up at the starless sky. "How did you start to learn about the dust? Did you go to this Dust Academy?"

"When I was little, my family barely had any money to send me there. So I started learning at my parents' restaurant at the food market. Aeri's Comfort Stews was its name. Mum loved mixing yellow dust to create new spices and infusions for her food. I remember when he gave her some jars with dust and mixing tools so we could learn together." Erydis went silent.

"He? You mean your father?" Rapach asked.

"Yes." Erydis swallowed. "We mixed spices, and sometimes we discovered new flavours. Some were delicious and others awful. But that's the only dust we had to mix, yellow dust, which is mostly used for cooking.

"But my Dad, Elias, was convinced by some people he met at the market to start experimenting with more types of dust. For the longest time, he would spend his time holed up in a room, mixing dust. He was terrible at it but was strongly against studying the art of mixing properly. He wanted to prove he could do it, but his mixtures were all unsuccessful. They all turned into useless, grey dust.

"But one day, he finally seemed to have got something right. I remember it was when I started to notice my mum distancing herself from him, the distance growing each day. She lost her radiant smile, and she couldn't hide her tears from time to time. I could not understand what was happening.

"One day, Mum decided to close her small restaurant and leave Dad. She begged me to go with her and to forget about Dad. I went with her, but of course I didn't stop loving him. It's almost impossible to forget so many memories and feelings when there's just too much to remember."

"He must have done something bad," Rapach said. Erydis took a deep breath.

"A year or so passed, and Mum fell in love with a young banker named Egi. He lived on the second level of the city. He wasn't a man of many words, but he was good to me—and more importantly, to my mother. It was her fresh start. She reopened her restaurant with Egi's help, and her smile returned once in a while. He even gave me my own bedroom when we moved in with him."

"And what about your dad?" Rapach asked.

"He remained in the Hidden Barrio, surrounded by crime and derelict houses. He had no money and no talent. I missed him. I missed him dearly. So each time I was out buying spices from the bazaar for Mum, I'd slip away and visit Dad in his worn-down shack.

"Most of the time, he'd be drinking dust-infused alcohol, too out of his mind to carry a conversation. Other times he was just furious, slandering Mum. And a few times, he was just crying. But he was always working, creating whatever mixture he could with the dirtiest tools, leaving his desk piled with grey dust that I sometimes cleaned for him.

"I remember that terrible day. He was crying desperately as I arrived from the bazaar. He refused to talk to me, so I left my bag full of spices with him, and went to the well to draw water for him to wash his face. But when I returned, he was no longer crying. He was calm, eerily so. As he handed me my bag of spices, he smiled and told me to hug Mum for him.

"When I got home, I gave Mum the spices she needed and a hug, which she accepted with her beautiful, radiant smile. But in my mind, I could only see Dad's anger and sobs. I was so sad that I skipped dinner with Mum and Egi that night."

A tear fell involuntarily down Erydis's cheek. Before Rapach could say anything, she continued.

"I woke up the next day, eager to help Mum. Strangely, she was still in her room. She was usually up hours before me. Her door was closed, so I opened it and saw them sleeping peacefully. I went closer and tried to wake her, but her eyes wouldn't open. I shook her, but she wouldn't wake up."

Erydis covered her face with her hands, openly sobbing, embarrassed that Rapach was seeing her this way. But he ripped a piece of material from his tunic and let her dry her tears with it.

"I'm sorry to hear that, Erydis," Rapach said softly. "Do you know what happened?"

"The Herba mixers said their hearts stopped suddenly in their sleep," she continued. "Then the soldiers took over their home, and I was sent to the Hidden Barrio to live with Dad. He was as sad as I was, but angrier than I'd ever seen.

"To pay for mixing tools, I had to work for him. He would give me money if I helped him deliver his special dust around the Hidden Barrio. He made the dust himself, and it was surprisingly popular. But he always warned me to never get caught by a soldier.

Rapach frowned as she said that.

"One day though, I was running from some particularly aggressive customers when I bumped into a soldier. I had yet to learn that that would be my luckiest encounter yet. His name was Thylac Siopi. He was so young and clumsy." Erydis laughed fondly.

"But he was nice to me. He kindly asked me what was in my pouch. I lied, saying that it was just spices for food; worst excuse in Dust City. He ordered me to hand them over but explained that I wasn't in trouble. He asked where I got them from, and I told him the truth.

"He told me that he would take the dust to a great mixer friend of his,

Kemia. Thylac told me to meet him at the same place in a week.

"He seemed trustworthy, so I agreed. I did not tell Dad about the incident, fearing he would express his anger at me, as he often did. And a week later, I returned to the same spot.

"When I saw Thylac again, he was very honest with me. He told me that Kemia had found an almost untraceable substance in the mixture my dad had been working on. It was a dust hidden in the spices that, when exposed to flames, released a toxic chemical. A poison that would stop anyone's heart in a matter of hours.

"Later that day, a group of soldiers asked me where my dad was. I didn't know what to say. It took me a while to connect things, since I couldn't accept it. Dad had created this poison, and I'd been helping him sell it to people with the worst intentions.

"And then it came back to me in a flash. That horrifying day. He had exchanged my spices for his poison, the only thing he had ever been able to create. It was the reason Mum and Elgi had died. They cooked those spices into their dinner. That man, the wicked stranger I called my dad, had murdered them."

Erydis closed her eyes and inhaled sharply, trying not to cry again.

"I'm so sorry, Erydis," Rapach said, his face full of concern. He thought of his parents, and how distraught he was when Mat was captured. He couldn't believe Erydis had been through so much.

"That afternoon, they arrested Dad," Erydis went on. "I saw them walking him out of his shack. He was fuming at me, shouting and swearing, almost as if he'd never loved me. As if he hated me. And at that moment, I realised the reason I wasn't dead. Had I not skipped dinner, I would have consumed the toxic dust too. That good-for-nothing will stay in jail forever, but I'll never forgive myself either. He made me deliver that curse to my mum.

"The guards threw me in the streets of the Hidden Barrio. I lived there for about a week, until Thylac came to my aid once more. That's when everything got better.

"He let me stay at his place for a few days until I could find a job. He would bring me food; he was very kind to me. I learned he was an orphan and he'd once lived on the streets as well. He saw himself in me, he said. And against all odds, he worked hard to become a renowned soldier. I remember hearing his story and feeling some hope for the first time in months."

"I'm glad you found each other," Rapach said with a gentle smile.

"Thylac introduced me to Kitri and Trinos, the owners of Dusty Corner, the best dust store in the bazaar. Trinos didn't want to hire me, but Kitri made him change his mind.

"Thanks to me, their business boomed. I'm good with people and numbers, and in about three months, I had earned enough money for a small attic in an old building. After a year, I managed to save enough money to study at the Geberus Dust Academy! It was that dream that got me through some long, dark times.

"It takes seven years to graduate from the academy, with each year getting more and more difficult. But since I was already teaching myself before I joined, the first year was a breeze. I was already working on my own mixtures while my classmates struggled to remember the colours and textures of the different types of dust.

"One day, I was working secretly inside a classroom when someone entered. It was the famous Kemia, who was once Master of Alchemia and who now teaches at the academy. She asked me what I was doing there. I told her I was working on a mixture that could be embedded inside a marble, and that it would become even more powerful than the common dust marble."

"A what?" Rapach asked.

"Oh, sorry. A dust marble is a marble that breaks to create a small cloud of dust when you smash it against the floor. We do it for fun."

"What kind of fun is that?" Rapach frowned, thinking of all the dust in the Miasma Realm.

"Anyway, Kemia told me to test it out, right then and there. I was shocked! I knew I could get in trouble but she insisted, saying she would protect me if it came to that. I threw the marble to the ground, and it broke into a gigantic red cloud. It worked! I was so proud! But numerous people were running out of the academy, thinking a fire had caused an explosion.

I begged a red-dusted Kemia not to tell anyone and she just told me not to worry.

"I thought they were going to expel me, but instead they moved me up to the fourth grade! Kemia had recommended me to the headmaster. I jumped three grades just because of that mixture! That's one of the happiest times I remember. I was so thirsty for knowledge. I stayed extra time in class, powering through piles of books every day. I was learning like never before, and I felt unstoppable."

Erydis smiled fondly at her memories.

"This makes me think that even in your complex world, you're one of the smartest people in it. And your friends seem to believe it, too," Rapach said. "How many years have you been at the academy now?"

"Well…I was expelled," Erydis said, still smiling, but glancing shyly at the floor.

"What? Because of the marble you made?"

"Some professors have wanted me expelled ever since that day, yes. One day, I was creating a mixture infused with red iron. It was meant to incinerate rapidly to act as a combustion engine in another experiment of distilled blue flowers and..."

"Erydis, I don't understand what you're saying," Rapach said, cutting her off.

"Well, the main problem was, to create a hotter incineration, I decided to rely on black dust. Black dust is an illegal type of dust that is extremely potent and unstable. My mixture was working perfectly right up until a stupid girl named Tulia caused me to trip and add more black dust than I intended to. The combustion got out of control, and the west wing of the academy was soon engulfed in flames, burning some students and a teacher. Luckily no one was seriously hurt, but when the headmaster heard I had used black dust, he expelled me. I had to swear not to leak any information outside the academy about black dust."

"Why did you use illegal dust then?" Rapach asked.

"Kemia had taught me of its potential. She told me not to fear it and that if I learned it well, I would know how to avoid its dangers. But I wasn't careful enough. I do regret it, you know. But at least I learned from my mistake and managed to fix it in time."

"So, you're still mixing dust?" Rapach asked quietly. He wasn't sure how to feel about Erydis's recklessness.

"I am! I'm very close to completing my best experiment yet! In Dust City, we have a Tower where the best mixers create new inventions, and if I show them my experiment, I might have a chance to work among them! That is, of course, after all the chaos in the city dies down."

"Everything sounds so complicated where you live."

"At least I don't have to run away from the miasma," Erydis said. "I wouldn't survive a day where you live."

"I know I'll never get used to the miasma," Rapach conceded. "It fills me with dread every time I see it. But it's not all bad where I live. At least we have each other in the Jerboa Clan."

"So, what's the story of this clan of yours?" Erydis asked. "Why are you all so restrained in sending messages?" Go ahead, dream boy. I've told you my whole story. Now it's your turn!"

3

"Well, you already know most of my story," Rapach began. "My clan, the Jerboa Clan, are tasked with delivering messages to connect clans and lost villages in our lands. We used to live far away from where we are now, in a land called the Jerboa Plains. Our main village, Jarburg, was a peaceful place, rich in trade and very welcoming of outsiders. My parents sometimes sing about those lands without dust or wars."

"But why would they leave such a place at all?" Erydis asked, amazed as she often was by these histories.

"Because one day, an unexpected visitor came to our lands. Something was rattling inside one of our many mailboxes around the village. A Jerboa Clan member opened it and saw a small boy hiding inside, weak and scared. He had a note with him, which was taken to the clan. It read as follows: '*A doom of dust has fallen upon the lands beyond the mountain chain that divides the east and west. A purple wind. A purple curse. We implore whomever receives this note to save us from forever speaking no more.'*

"We still have no idea how the boy survived crossing the mountains, and who wrote that letter for him to bring to us.

"A wise master read the message and a decision was made. 'We should not ignore this warning,' she told us. 'We shall travel to the west in search of an answer.'"

"And you all just left your village?" Erydis asked.

"Yes. Half of the village. All of those who were able and willing to travel far."

"Why leave everything behind? What if there was no truth to the note?" Erydis asked, sceptical.

"Because we received a call for help and our clan helps anyone who asks for it. It is what makes us who we are," Rapach answered.

Erydis felt something in her chest. She couldn't understand it, but she had a new respect for Rapach. His clan was full of brave, selfless heroes.

"We embarked on what we call The Voyage to the Miasma Lands," Rapach continued. "We asked our neighbouring clans to look after our village and those who stayed behind. We've been living in moving camps as we travel since then, and we have never heard anything from Jarburg again ever since we arrived in the Miasma Realm."

"Do you miss the village? Erydis asked.

"Well, I was born after we left, while my family travelled through the chain of mountains. But my sister used to tell me stories about our old village, where there was no dust and the grass was shiny and clean. The water had a fresh scent from the bright soil. She had no idea how much she would have to rely on those memories.

"The chain of mountains was merciless. I remember the piercing cold that didn't lessen even wearing leather we borrowed from the wild. You see, we tried not to take lives from the living. All the clan had back then was the hope to be of some aid to those in need.

"Most of us made it across. May the lost ones forever be remembered. When we descended from the last mountain, we saw the dust. It was everywhere, and we were not prepared for it.

"We created tools specifically to survive and to avoid breathing in the purple clouds. We fashioned blue glass into protective shields and goggles. After some time, we established our first Central Camp in the Miasma Realm. With that in place, we searched for people all over the realm. We were able to find and help some, but we also found those we fear. The Silent People and the miasma, which have claimed so many of us.

"But the Witness's luck was with us. We also realised that the Miasma Realm was rich with the blessed animal of the east, the jerboa. A new kind of jerboa that had adapted to the dust and thrived in those lands. They helped us through the shadows, and every member of the clan is accompanied by a jerboa after their first delivery.

"We roamed the lands for answers, but we found only more desperate notes asking for help. Who are the Silent People? What is the miasma? No one knows. One day, it just appeared and uprooted the people of the Miasma Realm.

"My sister has rescued many lost children, hidden in every corner of the land. Many were born after the miasma arrived."

"What's your sister's name?" Erydis asked.

"Her name was Mat, from my family, the Angarum. She was smart and strong. She became a major messenger in no time. She could get a sense of the land with just a quick scan, and she taught me how to survive in the cursed west."

"She sounds like someone with a lot of determination," Erydis said. She admired that in people.

"And she was," Rapach said, trying to forget the image of the stranger in the lion mask capturing Mat.

"What was she like when she wasn't out in the wilderness?" Erydis asked.

"She cared for my parents, and always helped them move the tent we lived in. She was always very active. And she danced like no one else at the Central Camps could. Half the clan wanted to dance with her, but she danced with no one–until she met Zelle, another kind soul who sheltered the lost children Mat and the rest of the clan rescued. Zelle and Mat cared for them as if they were their own. And together, they would dance like a flame in the wind. All of us, my parents included, would watch them for hours. It was mesmerising. And after they danced, we would all gather to tell stories and laugh for a while as if the miasma didn't exist, as we drank my favourite drink, red cocoa." Rapach smiled as he looked out to the horizon.

"Your family sounds lovely," Erydis said.

"They are. My parents taught us to be determined but always smile. I can't wait to see them after we wake up. I hope they're taking the news of my sister well."

"I'm sorry you're dealing with all of this, Rapach."

"I should be the one who's sorry. You've had such a dark past, not even the stranger in the lion mask deserves something like that."

"But I think he does," Erydis said, standing up. "He can't get away with what he put your clan through."

"Erydis, please, you have to find him and figure out his plan," Rapach pleaded.

"I'll try, I promise," she said, staring at the buildings surrounding them and the silhouettes of shadows walking in the distance. Rapach stood up next to her.

"This dream," Rapach said, "I don't understand it. But I'm grateful for it."

"What do you think of naming it?" Erydis asked, smiling.

"Yes, this mysterious place deserves a name," Rapach agreed. "A place where all we see and feel are reflected as if it were an echo of our memories."

"A place where we can be eternally safe from all the chaos of our lives, like a vault for our thoughts," Erydis added.

"An impossible dream." Rapach stared into her eyes.

"What about...the Vault of Echoes?" Erydis asked.

"Vault of Echoes. Yes!"

They smiled and talked for what seemed like hours more, until the clock on the tree ticked to the number four.

Day Four

Chapter XX

Jerboa Camp

Rapach

Rapach woke up in his tent feeling rested. He thought of Erydis and her stories. He was grateful to have finally learned more about her and the incredible place where she lived. Then he thought of the day to come and how he would meet his family soon at the Central Camp. He was excited to see them again, but he felt a sense of dread at having to retell how Mat became one of the Silent Ones.

Nintai and Joie were already awake and seemed ready for the trip ahead.

"Rapach!" Joie called out as Rapach stretched.

"It seems you're both looking forward to the trip today," he said as he slipped on his pouch and shield.

"We've never been this far away from our lands before. I'm so curious about this clan of yours, your traditions, your people," Nintai wondered aloud.

"Morning, folks!" Danaa approached them riding his majestic boar. His jerboa was resting on his shoulder. "The rest of the clan has advanced to the south-eastern provisions camp. We should not fall behind, as I fear a dust storm close by might fall upon us at night. But do not worry! For now, the three of you will ride together on one of the boars."

"Where's the old man?" Nintai asked.

"We believe the Silent People are searching for him, so we had to interrupt the poor elder's dreams and accompany him to the Central Camp with some extra security. I will go ahead to make sure everything is safe on your way there. Rapach, boy, please guide your kind companions through our camp."

Rapach nodded as Danaa swiftly steered his boar into the distance. He helped the sisters mount another boar's back and climbed onto the front to take control.

As they rode steadily, Rapach handed the sisters some seeds from his pouch. "I know it's not much, but I promise we'll have a proper feast when we get to the Central Camp," he said, feeding some seeds to Benu as she nested on top of his head.

"This boar; I've never seen one quite like it or as obedient," Nintai said.

"His name is Varah," Rapach said. "He is of a species we first rescued when we arrived at the Miasma Realm. We believe the dust had a great impact on the way some animals behave."

"Hi, Varah," Joie said, petting the side of the big animal as it snorted with contentment.

Crimson trees and grass surrounded them as they rode down an uncharted trail. The whistle of the wind through the leaves created a concerto of sounds as the wind blew fresher and cleaner than usual. Rapach hoped it was a lucky sign, but he could also tell that a dust storm was coming.

"How do you know where we're going?" Nintai asked. Joie stood on Varah's hindquarters, gazing at the new landscape as she leaned against her sister's back.

"Look at the tree branches," Rapach said, pointing upwards.

Hidden among them were small caerulean flags displaying the silhouette of a jerboa.

"That's the flag of my people. When we arrived at the Miasma Realm, we couldn't rely on the stars or the sun to guide us, so that's the only way we know. The jerboas are resistant to the miasma and hide in plain sight—and the Silent Ones can't sense or see them. Remember those flags, as they will help if you ever get lost. Just look for one of our caerulean cube mailboxes, and look up at the trees," Rapach said, his chest swelling with pride. "If we follow those all the way, we will arrive at one of the six provisions camps surrounding the Central Camp."

"What's a provisions camp?" asked Joie, her head looking around for flags.

"You'll see! We'll arrive close to evening."

As they journeyed on, the trees around them thinned out and the grass grew taller, rising above their heads. Joie fell asleep, hanging from her sister's shoulders, her little frame hidden in the shadows.

Suddenly, they heard a whistle. Nintai held Joie tighter, startled. "Was that an animal?" she asked Rapach, who shook his head with a smile.

He calmly placed his hands together in front of his lips and hooted thrice like an owl, each hoot louder than the one before.

A man stood up from among the tall grass. He wore the blue uniform of the Jerboa Clan and was folding a short blue glass sword into his pack.

"Welcome back, Rapach," the man said in a deep voice. "Danaa told me you would be passing through. He has already arrived."

"Thank you, Garah. I would stay and talk, but I need to hand over a package."

"So I've heard, Rapach. Everyone in the clan is talking about your mission. I won't intrude more. Welcome to the south-east provisions camp, companions," Garah said and took a bow. The sisters nodded, at ease. "Oh, Rapach. I'm sorry about Mat," Garah added. "May she be in the sight of the Witness."

Rapach nodded, but he anticipated more reminders of the loss of his sister as they got closer to the Central Camp.

Two watchtowers of thick, red wood overlooked the provisions camp. Rapach couldn't help feeling nostalgic as he remembered the provisions camps that he'd grown up in.

"So what exactly is this place?" Nintai asked, glancing a little nervously at the guards up on the towers with their sharp glass weapons.

"Well, it's a type of lookout. Eight of them surround the Central Camp. Near every provisions camp there are caerulean mailboxes that mark the borders of our territories. But we never stay in one place for more than a few years."

"Such a well-planned organisation," Nintai said, impressed.

"At these camps, we sort letters and packages for delivery," Rapach continued.

As Varah trotted into the camp, other boars were seen around them carrying around all sorts of parcels. "Some clan members deliver food, clean water, and weapons to other provisions camps for trade."

"Dogs!" Joie gasped.

To their left were dozens of dogs of all shapes, sizes, and colours, wearing jerboa goggles and pouches strapped to their backs. Some were resting, while clan members prepared others for upcoming travels.

"I guess you found our providers, Joie," Rapach said, laughing. "They deliver food and water to our messengers at the mailboxes before they start their missions. But if there's an urgent message, they run tirelessly for long distances. We're proud of them. Speaking of which..." A dog running towards them started to bark in excitement as Varah stopped and bent down.

"Greetings again, Pek," Rapach said. "Meet Nintai and Joie."

"Adorable!" Joie jumped off the boar to pet the dog with its tail wagging rapidly.

"He really is." Nintai smiled.

"You're not working right now, I see," Rapach said. "Join us!"

Pek barked again and scampered after them as Nintai helped her sister back onto the boar and they started walking again.

"What are those people doing?" Nintai asked, pointing towards an open tent with a group studying papers on a table inside.

"They're sorting letters and marking their destinations. They also send coordinates and short, coded instructions for the messengers."

"Do you know this code?"

"I don't. Only the experienced messengers do. Mat was going to teach me but..."

Rapach fell silent, almost as if he'd suddenly lost his speech. Nintai asked nothing more.

They passed small fields of crops and all sorts of free-roaming animals: boars, jerboas, dogs, wild lizards, and frogs. The sights and sounds that met them were like a familiar harmony to Rapach.

But as the wind lifted some dust, he could not avoid thinking about recent events. It was a tragedy, what happened to his sister, but at least he had rescued Nintai and Joie as well as that old man. As he glanced over his shoulder and saw the girls laughing cheerily at Pek's playfulness, he wondered what Erydis would think of them.

"What can you tell me about your people, the Amaru Clan?" he asked, as curious as he thought Erydis would be.

"We live in a more peaceful land, although we do have some problems at times. We also do our best to remain attached to nature. The lands of the south are as cold as they are ancient," Nintai said.

"And the food is better!" Joie said brightly.

"Does the Amaru Clan believe in the Witness?" Rapach asked.

"The Witness? Never heard about that. No, but we do think there's a link between our world and the world of spirits. Like I said when we met, we believe in the teachings of the wise djinni of the south. We've seen him, and he holds knowledge we've never encountered before. But he left us one day. Now he's a legend, but we've made it part of our lives."

"I don't mean any disrespect, but the Witness we believe in is said to be a spirit that...well...witnesses our world through the eyes of the living. I get a little lost in the story behind it, but I'm sure our ancients can tell you more once we arrive. Maybe our myths and legends are searching for the same greater truth."

"A more complex legend that's just a children's tale—that's really something," Nintai said, holding Joie who had fallen asleep again.

The dust-sprinkled sunlight slowly disappeared behind the trees as more people and animals started to surround them; traders, running dogs, and even more boars resting on beds of accumulated dust. A man was lighting torches on poles as dusk enveloped the camp, though the winds seemed to disagree with the flames.

"Joie, wake up, bug," Nintai said, tapping Joie's nose gently. "We're almost there, aren't we, Rapach?" Rapach nodded as Varah stopped at a pathway.

"We'll walk from here. Looks like Varah wants to rest on that bed of dust—boars from this region seem to be the only animals that enjoy it."

They dismounted and continued down the path. Soon, they arrived at poles bearing the Jerboa Clan's flag and guards guarding the perimeter. "Welcome to our home," Rapach said, feeling a warm sense of security as he looked at the flags. He entered the Central Camp.

Caerulean tents covered the flat fields beyond the flags. Some were small enough for a couple of people, while others seemed to be able to fit over a dozen. People walked free of fear, free to live. Families walked around, wearing clan uniforms and other assorted garments. Kids ran around throwing dust and giggling as hundreds of jerboas jumped around the people and tents. Outside each tent were small blue glass plates laid out full of kibbles for the jerboas. Nintai and Joie watched the scene with radiant smiles.

Benu, still on top of Rapach's head, looked curious but shy. Maybe she wasn't used to big groups of jerboas, Rapach thought, remembering how he'd found her all alone by the blue flowers.

"It's so lively here," Nintai said. "Are all these people from your clan?"

"Most of them, yes," Rapach answered. "Others are people who were once lost in these lands. They all ran from the miasma when it appeared and lived by themselves in the middle of nowhere until we found them. That's the whole purpose of delivering letters—to connect those who have lost their way."

"So you live in tents so you can keep moving?" Nintai asked.

"Yes. We want to search all over these lands, and we can't stay in one place for that. We move every few years. We analyse which of the provisions camps is safest and we turn that into our Central Camp. For now, it seems like the north-west provisions camp is the most dangerous. We've spotted many Silent People there, and the miasma also seems denser. The camps to the south and east were thought to be safe until we saw the monstrous djinni in the south-east. We might have to move back to the north-east if the ancients decide it's best."

"That's quite an organisation you have here," Nintai said.

"Still, it can help only so much. Being at the mercy of the dust storms, we have to keep changing our plans. However, we're very well prepared in case one arrives."

As they walked, Nintai noticed some clay furnaces. "What are they doing?" she asked, watching some people shovel dust and fine soil into the furious flames.

"This is where they forge blue glass," Rapach explained. "We use it for everything from weapons and tools to jars and plates. We don't have much in these cursed lands, but we do have more than enough grey dust. We discovered very early on that melting it with some fine soil creates a resistant, light glass with a unique blue tint."

"Does everyone have a shield like yours?" Nintai asked.

"No, only us outer messengers." This triggered Rapach's memory, taking him back to the many days of practice with Mat. He remembered how she said they should always protect each other and stay close on a mission, unless something major happened.

They approached a tent made of thick cloth, its corners fastened securely to the ground.

"This is where most of my family lives," Rapach said. "It seems they're getting prepared for the dust storm."

Rapach felt a heaviness on his chest and blood rushing to his brain. His family would have heard about Mat and were probably anticipating Rapach's version of the story. He would have to clear his mind to tell it.

They entered the tent through a double layer of thick tapestries, stepping down into a slight impression in the ground. The ground was covered in carpets, with blankets and beds in every corner. Candles of all sizes lit up the farthest walls of the tent, illuminating the center, where some people sat on cushions on the ground.

"Mom. Dad. Zelle. I'm back." They looked at him with gentle smiles, but there was sorrow in the air. "Family, these are my guests, Nintai and Joie,"

Rapach said, avoiding their grief-filled gazes.

Everyone remained silent, forcing Rapach to lift his head. His mama stood up. She had the same hair and golden dark skin he had, but with lighter, honey-coloured eyes. The many dust spots on the lower half of her face camouflaged her tears. She pulled Rapach into the warm hug he had so sorely missed.

"Welcome back, son," she said. "It seems your friends are tired. Please, take a seat."

Nintai and Joie bowed and sat down in a corner. They looked uncomfortable with the palpable tension and sadness in the air. Meanwhile, Benu slept on Rapach's head.

His papa was there as well. He had pale skin and thick blond hair, a bushy moustache, and tired black eyes. He was comforting a woman who was sobbing uncontrollably. It was Zelle. She was wearing a long dress, her light brown hair cascading down her back. Her peachy skin was covered in dust spots, almost like she had multicoloured freckles of multiple colours. She was still as beautiful as the first time Mat had introduced her to the family, but her green eyes were puffy and red.

"Rapach," she said in a fragile, soft voice. "Where's Mat?"

This was what he had been fearing since he arrived—to relate his story to his distraught family.

Chapter XXI

Dust Pearl

Erydis

Even though she felt like she talked to Rapach for hours in their dream, Erydis barely slept. She stayed up most of the night, continuing the work on her experiment. She was close to finishing it.

She raised her head. Balanced precariously on a pile of books was the thick glass sphere she'd borrowed from Kemia's laboratory. Since then, many hours had gone into adding intricate details to her experiment. With everything Herra had shared at the Tower, she'd gleaned a clearer idea of the Machina aspect that was left to create. And with the black and gold dust she sneaked out of the Tower, she had discovered that all her Obscura theories worked.

But the experiment was missing an important piece; the make-or-break aspect—the Emperor's sceptre. Of course she would add her own creative touch. If she could just get her hands on it today, then her experiment would be complete before the Closure Festival and the competition. But based on all she'd seen so far…what if the festival was cancelled?

She shook her head, trying to motivate herself. Yes, the competition might not take place, but she wanted to prove she was capable of doing something significant anyway. It had taken her many years to get to where she was. She trusted her theory, and if proved to be successful, the result would surely be remembered.

Erydis readied herself for a busy day. She wanted to meet Kemia and find out what her mentor had discovered about the blue amber. And then there was the palace party in the evening to go to. But Erydis's mind drifted to concern for Kitri. She'd been so upset, frantically searching for Trinos. Maybe he had returned to work at the Dusty Corner? He wasn't the sort to miss a day of work. He never let her have a day off. She smiled fondly at the thought and decided to check in with them first.

Erydis travelled to the Dust Bazaar taking her usual route, though it was a bit more patrolled than usual. When she arrived, she was surprised to see that the store was shut. She gingerly parted the curtains and saw a desolate Kitri, again missing her radiant smile, sitting next to Isaac, who was sketching something on a table. Still no sign of Trinos.

"He hasn't come back yet, has he?" Erydis asked, already aware of the answer.

Kitri shook her head, her emotionless face streaked with tears.

"I asked every person I could find in every barrio, but no one knows where he is. Thankfully, dear Isaac here is helping me make some signs to help with the search."

As always, Isaac's drawings portrayed perfect details. Trinos's gruff face looked exactly as Erydis knew him. Across the top, the sign read: "*Trinos Kontos was last seen at the Festival of Many Dusts. If you have any information about his whereabouts, please inform someone at the Dusty Corner store located in the bazaar.*"

"You don't think the Vakandi took him, do you?" Erydis asked.

"I asked the Vakandi," Isaac said. "No one knows who Trinos is."

"Did you ask the guards? Maybe they think he's on the Vakandi's side," Erydis said.

Isaac shook his head. "They haven't seen him either. Though they don't seem very concerned about helping us locate him."

"Their search for the Vakandi takes precedence," Kitri said, frowning. "Trinos didn't support the Vakandi. He trusts Emperor Ryk. We were even invited to the Palace Festival, but of course, we won't be able to go now."

"Thylac invited me, too," Erydis said. "Maybe I can sneak away and find out if someone knows something about Trinos's whereabouts."

"Please do, girl. Also, you're on your way to see Kemia, aren't you? Could you please tell her I'll be needing the help she offered yesterday? We could use all the support we can get in our search." Erydis nodded.

"Oh, and please take a few signs, dear," Kitri added. "Could you put them up in the academy?"

"Of course I will. I'll help you however I can, Kitri," Erydis said sincerely. She'd always had her differences with Trinos, but she knew how much those two loved each other.

During the Palace Festival, the Geberus Academy was closed to everyone . It was the last day students had left to prepare their experiments before the contest, so they and selected teachers had special access. This of course meant that Erydis had to enter the academy through her secret path on the second floor of the city.

But the funiculars were all closed, and the only way to the Palace District was up the heavily guarded marble stairs.

Weaving through the crowd took time, but she managed to get through a guard's interrogation while he checked her belongings. She grinned as she answered each question with a lie and walked away confidently.

As Erydis reached the second floor, she noticed a wall of guards protecting the entrance of the palace. Soldiers of all ranks stood guard vigilantly, wielding crimson longswords, crossbows, and Arma mixtures in bags attached to their belts. They searched everyone before allowing the crowd to enter the palace. It seemed like everyone was preparing for the party attended by the wealthy families. Tonight, they'll have an extra guest, Erydis thought.

She reached the balcony beside the academy's tower. The window to Kemia's laboratory was wide open. Erydis found the ladder and climbed it to enter Kemia's office.

As she stepped inside, Kemia was leaning on her desk. But strangely enough, she wasn't working on any mixtures today. Kemia turned as she heard Erydis come in and focused her deep eyes on her.

"Trinos is still missing, Kemia," Erydis said. "Kitri wanted me to tell you she'd be happy to accept your help now."

"I know, and as promised, I will help Kitri," Kemia said. "But I want to talk to you about something."

Kemia went silent as Erydis froze. It was unlike Kemia to address her this way.

"I suppose the proper way to begin telling you this is that, as you know, I've been working on an experiment lately," Kemia began. "It's taken several years of research, interrupted often by my teaching and various other experiments. But about a week ago, my efforts finally yielded some promising results."

Kemia opened a clenched fist, revealing a small black sphere in her palm.

"What is that?" Erydis asked, keen yet a little nervous at her mentor's attitude.

"This is what I call a dust pearl. I realised that black dust can be unstable in its capricious, pure form, making it very risky to carry around. So I delved into the old books of ancient Alchemia mixers to find a solution. I found out that concentrating the black dust in a solid mixture would make it much more manageable.

"This dust pearl is extremely powerful, Erydis. A single one of these is as potent as five average jars of black dust."

Erydis was speechless. She knew very well that the power of a tablespoon of black dust was enough to raze an entire classroom.

"That's incredible, Kemia!" she exclaimed.

"The process takes months, but if successful, you need only one jar of black dust to create it. I'm still studying it, and it is impressive what it's capable of. But this morning, I realised that I'm far away from uncovering the dust's true potential.

"The blue amber in your necklace uncovered something remarkable. The small fragment I took had such an intense effect that it would make the dust pearl pale in comparison."

"How much more powerful can it be?" Erydis asked. "Twice as strong?

Five times?"

Kemia took a small, glowing flask from a stand.

"This is a mixture infused with a dust pearl. Its intense power can be seen in its glow." She picked up another flask that was covered in drapes. As she uncovered it, an almost blinding light appeared radiating from the flask. "And this is a mixture infused with that tiny fragment of blue amber. Just that small piece is one hundred and twenty times more powerful than one Dust Pearl, to be precise." Kemia covered the flask again.

Erydis's eyes widened as blood rushed to her head. Just trying to comprehend that potential seemed impossible.

"I have a theory," Kemia continued. "As you must know, amber is formed from the sap of trees that existed hundreds of years ago. This sap, though, came from a tree with similar properties as the blue flower, which as you know has favourable effects on the respiratory system, but hundreds of times stronger. And somehow it has reached you…the amber from that blue sap."

Erydis couldn't wrap her head around what Kemia was saying. "The day before I started dreaming about the Vault of Echoes, a man gave me the necklace with the blue amber hanging from it.

"The Vault…of Echoes?" Kemia asked.

"Oh, sorry. That's the name Rapach and I have given to the place in our dream where we meet."

"I see. Who was this man, Erydis?"

"I…I don't know. I don't even know what he looks like. It was on the west side of the Hidden Barrio, and he was wearing a fox mask. He told me he had black dust to sell, so I bought some to bring to you. The man wanted to give me a present from faraway lands as a token of gratitude. He gave me the necklace, and I never saw him again."

"But why would he just hand you such a powerful object? That's what I don't understand. It seems a little too haphazard."

Kemia picked up a smoke candy from her desk and looked thoughtful as she breathed out red smoke through her mouth and nose.

"These dreams with Rapach must have something to do with it," she finally said. "But I don't know how a healing object is connected to this vault you speak of."

"So you believe me?" Erydis asked with hope.

Kemia nodded slowly with a faraway expression. "Erydis, I'll need more of this amber to continue my research. May I have another sample? I won't take much more than the last time."

Kemia looked into Erydis's eyes, much more politely than usual.

Erydis handed over the necklace and watched Kemia break off a slightly larger piece than the previous time. Kemia lifted the piece of amber, examining it in the light of a dust lamp.

"It's a little murky, but I can almost make out something in it," she said. "Usually amber has trapped leaves or even insects inside it." She turned around. "But as much as we might be distracted by this extraordinary event, I have to help Kitri find Trinos, and you have to prepare for a party," she said. "You should go ahead while I store this piece of amber somewhere safe."

Kemia returned the necklace to Erydis.

"Weren't you invited to the party at the palace?" Erydis asked, putting the necklace back on.

"I was, but I rejected the invitation as usual. I'm not particularly fond of socialising with those people, and I have many other things to do. I'll see you at the Dusty Corner."

As she walked down the busy marble stairs, Erydis tried to remember anything she could about the man who'd given her the blue amber. She'd noticed him before in the Hidden Barrio, wearing that signature fox mask and selling illegal dust, but she had no clue who he was. Curiosity washed over her as she thought of the amber and recalled every dream she shared with Rapach in the vault. There had to be some sort of logical explanation for it all. Perhaps a stroll through the run-down neighborhood would help her find the man with the fox mask, and it would be a good place to start searching for Trinos, she reasoned.

She passed a wall of guards just in time. They were preventing citizens from approaching the second floor unless they lived there or could present an invitation to the party at the palace. This level of security detail wasn't the usual protocol, but it seemed that security had been strengthened in case of a Vakandi invasion.

As she reached the Dust Ring, Erydis felt overwhelmed by the amount of surveillance she saw everywhere. Her experiment was not ready yet, and there was a strong chance the contest would be cancelled. An invasion would quickly escalate into something scarier if the Emperor caught wind of the Vakandi inside the Tower. The image of the clock in the vault came vividly to mind. At the rate everything had been escalating lately, she feared what the number five could possibly indicate.

She entered the Hidden Barrio. People knew her there and some greeted her as she passed. But she had no time to stop and speak to them. Before the party started, she had to meet with Kitri and Kemia to find—

A slight wind ruffled Erydis's messy hair and a fleeting shadow caught her eye. She froze. Was her mind playing games? Was that…?

Walking in the opposite direction a few steps in front of her was the ominous stranger with the flowing black cloak and the scary lion mask. Guards had been asking people to take off their mask at the Dust Ring, but no one really cared in the Hidden Barrio. Except Erydis. And she owed it to Rapach to find answers.

She followed the man as silently as she could, her heart hammering in her chest. Maybe he was the missing link, so she had to make sure not to lose him. The stranger swiftly turned into a dark street. A street she often had nightmares about.

She stepped into the alley to follow him, but the stranger was gone. In his place, undesirable memories hit her like a blinding light. In front of her was a dilapidated house she had tried valiantly to erase from her mind. The home of her dad, who had had her love but also lost it in an instant.

Erydis stood in front of Elias Nott's brick house with its cracked corners, twisted broken door, and thick curtains covering the windows. A wooden sign on the door declared: *Property of Dust City. Those who trespass will be persecuted.*

Her old home; her father's old lair.

Erydis tamed her nerves and stepped closer. It was eerily silent, and there was no light as far as she could see. Her time was spread thin that day, but she had to overcome her fear. Maybe she'd even find out who this stranger in the lion mask was.

She slowly opened the door and looked at the living room. Broken furniture lay everywhere, the walls were cracked, and it was cold from the lack of sunlight. It was just as dirty as it had been back then. A thick layer of grey dust blanketed the floor, and dust particles floated in the sliver of light that shone through a gap in the curtains.

She remembered walking across that little space to her father's mixing room. Turning towards it now, she noticed a flickering light coming from the crack under the door.

She cautiously placed her ear against the door but heard nothing. Maybe the stranger had taken shelter inside.

She lay her head on the floor to try and see through the gap below the door. She couldn't see much, save for a perfectly still shadow. Someone was standing in the middle of the room.

Erydis took a deep breath and shivered at the cold. She thought of Rapach and how his home must be even dirtier, with nothing but the endless grey dust everywhere. She reached for the doorknob and, as silently as she could, pushed the splintered door open slowly.

She quickly glanced around the room, which had changed since the last time she'd seen it. A table was crowded with mixing equipment—jars, flasks, and a furnace—all of it illuminated by a dust lamp in the corner. The strange thing was that the mixing tools were much cleaner than she remembered ever seeing them.

But even stranger was the person standing in front of her. He had his back to Erydis, unmoving. She instantly knew whose silhouette it was.

"Trinos?" She was almost breathless. "What are you doing here?"

But the figure did not reply or react to her voice.

"Everyone is looking for you." She walked around to face him. "Trinos?" Still no answer.

Erydis froze upon seeing his face. The chill was no longer just physical.

It was as if Trinos was dead. His eyes were blank and his jaw hung open, his arms hanging at his sides. He didn't blink or twitch. The only sign of life was an almost imperceptible breathing. His irises had a purple tinge to them—something Erydis had heard about too many times.

"The Silent People," she whispered, thinking about the Vault of Echoes; about Rapach's life and his terrorised face every time he described his sister becoming one of them.

Erydis grabbed Trinos's hand and pulled it, but he was rooted to the floor. Erydis fled in a panic, thinking of Kitri, who needed to know the truth about her husband.

She ran through the Hidden Barrio and the Dust Ring as fast as she could, bumping into disgruntled strangers, but she did not care. Many people were in danger, and she was the only one who knew what the Silent People and their leader, the stranger in the lion mask, were capable of.

The bazaar was crammed with customers. She slipped through the crowd and spotted Kitri and Kemia leaving the Dusty Corner to start their search.

"Kemia! Kitri!" she shouted. "I found him. You have to come with me. Hurry!"

"Is he safe?" Kitri started to sob. "Why didn't he come with you?"

"He's not himself, but he's alive. Follow me!"

They ran back to the Hidden Barrio as fast as they could, Erydis trying to explain what she had seen as they ran.

But as they reached the alley, a pillar of black smoke billowed into the sky ahead of them. Erydis's old home was ablaze.

"NOOO! TRINOS!" Kitri cried out.

Chapter XXII

Witness Sight

Rapach

Rapach's family fell silent after he tried to describe Mat's fate in the least painful way he could. After spending some time comforting them, he left the tent to show Nintai and Joie more of the camp.

"She was clever," Rapach said, smiling at the fond memory. "She was kind and brave. One of the best messengers and navigators of the clan."

"I'm really sorry, Rapach," Nintai said earnestly. "I don't know what I would do if that curse took someone dear to me."

She fell silent, watching Joie chase Benu and other playful jerboas. Her naive happiness was almost comforting.

Zelle emerged from the family's tent and approached them. "I'm sorry you've arrived at such an unfortunate time," she said to Nintai, with traces of tears on her dust freckles. "I didn't introduce myself properly. My name is Zelle."

"Greetings, Zelle," Nintai said. "Rapach has told us a little bit about you. I apologise for intruding while you're all suffering such a loss."

Zelle shook her head. "I should figure out a distraction from my own thoughts. Please, let me show you around the camp."

"Zelle, I can do it," Rapach said.

"I'll be fine, Rapach. She would have wanted me to."

They walked past many tents, until they reached one with childish, smudged paintings on its walls. Several children ran in and out of the tent as they approached, some pausing to look at Nintai and Joie with curiosity.

Peals of laughter greeted them as they entered the tent. Rough splashes of paint resembling animals and other doodles covered the walls, while children of varying ages played together with blue glass toys. Rapach spotted some figurines of warriors and animals amongst the toys.

A shy boy in a corner was carefully but excitedly feeding kibble to a pack of jerboas. Carpets and cushions were strewn all over the ground, some with toddlers napping peacefully on them despite the din.

"This is the tent for rescued children," Zelle said, managing a smile. "It was Mat's and my job to care for them. It was difficult at the beginning because we didn't have any experience, but over time, I believe we got it right. The kids seemed to enjoy this place so much that our clan's children came here to play, too. It's their sanctuary, free from outside dangers."

"I bet you would love to meet some new friends, wouldn't you, Joie?" Nintai said, but Joie seemed intimidated at seeing so many others of her age. "It must have been a difficult task to bring them all here from the cursed lands."

"It was." Zelle nodded. "Some of these children were rescued during Mat's missions and none of their families made it back, may the Witness watch over them. Some traders even left their children with us so we could teach them how to roam the Miasma Realm safely. But curiously enough, a majority of them were brought to us by a man we don't know much about. It seems it was his life's mission to walk the land in search of lost children," she explained.

"Zelle was one of those children, isn't that right?" Rapach said. Zelle nodded.

"I was about as old as little Joie here. My family were nomads who were traveling somewhere to the east, and on their journey they were taken by a dust storm that turned into a miasma storm. I managed to survive inside a broken log. A man in a silly animal mask came and offered me his hand.

He gave me water and food and took me to the Jerboa Clan. Then he disappeared."

The story made Rapach smile every time. Whoever had rescued Zelle had given all these children a new life, a new opportunity.

"Rapach!" Danaa was holding the curtain open at the tent's entrance. "The ancients are waiting to hear your tale, boy. And they've asked me to bring your guests as well."

"Is the old man coming with us?" Nintai asked.

"We've taken him to a tent. He's safe, but it seems he exhausted his energy during the trip. Last time I checked, the poor fellow was asleep."

"Thank you, Danaa, I'll be there shortly," Rapach said.

Danaa nodded and left.

"Who are the ancients?" Nintai asked.

"They're our elders," Zelle answered. "They make the important decisions, with some advice from selected youth. Do not worry, their wise words will warm your heart."

The wind had picked up speed and was blowing fiercely compared to that morning. People hurried back to their tents as soldiers watched over them. Zelle stayed behind in the tent with the children. She had given Nintai and Joie scarves and goggles to protect them for their walk to the ancients' tent.

Rapach knew he had to tread carefully with his words. *I should avoid telling them about Erydis for now and focus on the events of this mission,* he thought. But more importantly, he had to tell them about the blue flowers.

The ancients' tent was bigger than all the other tents and was flanked by several guards. Some were seated on boars, their jerboas hiding under their scarves. Benu, though, seemed to prefer hiding in Rapach's mop of hair.

Two guards parted the first layer of curtains to let them into the tent. In the waiting area, a lady with white robes cleaned the newcomers' clothes with a thick brush. After they were fairly free of dust, she bowed and parted the second layer of curtains.

Inside, numerous elderly people rested on cushioned beds. Some were playing bongos as they laughed, wrinkles furrowing their faces. Others donned intricate blue glass jewelry. Young servers offered them food and clean water respectfully. Joie seemed intrigued as she watched from behind her sister.

"In our clan, the ancients are highly revered," Rapach said. "They carry knowledge of many legends, and their advice is always thoughtful. I must ask you to show respect. I know not all clans are like ours."

"Our clans would work well as one, Rapach," Nintai answered.

In the centre of the tent sat four ancients in a circle, waiting with a young advisor. A bright blue carpet was laid out in front of them.

"We must sit there, if you don't mind." Rapach pointed at the carpet, hoping the situation wasn't too intimidating for the sisters.

As they settled onto the carpet, the ancients scrutinised Nintai and Joie with their experienced eyes.

"Welcome back, Rapach," an old woman with thick silver brows said. "And greetings to you, dear visitors. We hope you've found your visit to our grounds pleasant. My name is Akma."

"We couldn't be more grateful to the Jerboa Clan," Nintai answered. "My name is Nintai and this is my sister Joie." She bowed her head and Joie imitated her hastily.

"Nintai, Joie, this place is your home for as long as you desire," an elderly man covered in dust spots said. "I'm Ahau. And this is Cham and Ahez."

The woman named Cham, who had coiled braids, bowed. So did the bald man next to her.

"We've heard of the events that happened these past few days, but we believe you can enlighten us of the details," Ahez said in a soft, calm tone.

Rapach dreaded repeating the story, but he knew it was important for the ancients to know every detail. He took a deep breath and let the words flow.

The young assistant filled their glasses with clean water as they talked. After Rapach recapped everything, save for his dream with Erydis, everyone fell silent.

"It seems that the package must have something of utmost importance to the Silent People," Cham observed.

"But we will not open it. Our code of confidentiality must be respected," Ahau said.

"Let's leave the old man to rest," Akma said. "Meanwhile, we must prepare for the miasma storm that is to fall upon us early tomorrow."

"But I believe the old man must be presented with the package as soon as possible. We have escaped from the dust-created djinni—for now. This cannot wait," Ahez said.

Cham agreed. "Rapach will deliver it to the man once he awakens. All agree?"

All the ancients bowed in unison.

"I will fulfill my task," Rapach promised.

"Now," Akma said, her serious expression turning into a smile, "we wish to know more about these adorable girls. Please, tell us more about the Amaru Clan."

"We come from the southern lands," Nintai said confidently. "Our village is often at peace thanks to the wise djinni's teachings."

"Tell us girl, who is this wise djinni?" Ahez asked.

"He's a wise creature we were lucky to have encountered years ago. He taught us about the world of spirits and how to find and protect its essence in the world of mortals."

"Have you found this spiritual essence, my dear?" Akma asked.

Nintai and Joie exchanged glances.

"There are things our clan is forbidden to share," Nintai said. Rapach looked at her, puzzled as she continued. "At least, until our clan leaders unite."

"We shall respect the views of the Amaru Clan," Cham said. "But we believe in bridging clans, so we are open to any questions your young souls desire to ask the Jerboa Clan."

Nintai was thoughtful for a moment. "Rapach spoke about a spirit your clan believes in, the Witness. Can you tell me more about it?"

"Well, to better understand the Witness, you have to know our roots," Akma said.

"The story of our founder, the man who conversed with the Witness, has been passed down many generations. It is said that he was a man running from bloodshed. A man who believed in peace. A man who lost everything. And as he tried to find a land for his unfortunate people, he became lost in his wandering.

"It is said that the skies above him and the soil he walked on became infinite clouds, and from the emptiness, the Witness appeared. She is often described in the tales as a girl weaved from infinity. A girl who witnessed the mortal world. The man bravely asked her who she was, and she revealed that she was a being who would protect humanity. But even though her presence felt powerful, she asked the man for aid.

"She explained to the man that she could witness our world only through the eyes of a living being. She instructed the man to find a jerboa lost in faraway lands. When he found the small creature, the sight of the Witness would be revealed to him and with it the possibility to see beyond mortal limits.

"Even though the man did not know the power the Witness's sight held, he swore to find the jerboa and protect it with his life. The Witness, grateful for his words, extended her hand for his. As they connected, it is said his hand became caerulean blue and shone like a star.

"The Witness told him that his shining hand was a gift from her world and to use it carefully. Then the Witness, as impossibly as she had arrived, dissolved into the infinite clouds.

"The man journeyed back to his people and showed them the Witness's gift. Impressed by the man's tale, the people gathered to create the Jerboa Clan in a quest to discover the creature with the Witness's sight."

Nintai and Joie seemed enthralled by the legend. Rapach was familiar with it, but it had always puzzled him.

But then his gaze wandered to Benu and he wondered aloud: "When we find this jerboa with the Witness's sight, how will we know?"

"It is said the Witness will introduce herself to you," Cham answered.

"Maybe the world the Witness lives in is the spirit world to the Amaru Clan," Akma concluded, smiling at Joie.

Silence washed over them, the only sound being the howling of the strong wind outside.

"Any more questions or anything we should know about, Rapach?" Ahez asked.

Rapach pondered for a second. "Yes. There's something everyone should know."

All eyes were on him as he brought out one of the blue flowers from his pouch.

"This blue flower grows in the wild. When chewed, leaves, stem, and all, breathing in its essence will give a temporary immunity against the miasma."

"But how do you know this, boy?" Cham asked.

"I've tried it, multiple times, it works."

"It's true," Nintai confirmed. "He chewed a flower as we ran from the Purple Breathers back at Sorrow City. No one I know has come back after being exposed to that much miasma."

The ancients exchanged meaningful looks and nodded once.

"We must spread the word. We see only honesty in your eyes, Rapach," Cham said.

"Please order the messengers and merchants to seek these flowers immediately," Ahez said to the young assistant, who ran outside.

"How did you discover this, boy?" Akma asked.

Rapach hesitated before saying, "Someone told me in a dream."

"A dream?"

"Yes…a girl."

A fierce gust of wind hit the tent. Dust found its way in through a torn opening, which was immediately sealed by some soldiers.

"We shall hear more about your dream at our next meeting. Today, we must prepare for another miasma storm," Ahau said.

The ancients nodded in agreement. Rapach, Nintai, and little Joie bowed and took their leave.

As they walked back to Rapach's family tent, others were seen preparing for the impending storm. Some nailed their tents tightly to the ground, digging into the soil to keep out as much of the draft as possible. Walls of logs were also fashioned to protect the tents from the storm.

Rapach walked carefully, protecting the sisters with his round, glass shield, feeling the dust slide off it.

"The wind is gaining speed," he warned them, his voice slightly muffled under the scarf that covered his mouth and nose. "We should be fine inside our tent. Do not worry, we encounter a storm like this at least twice a year."

His family's tent had a wall of logs and mounds of soil protecting it. The inside had been dug deeper than before, but all the tapestries and candles were placed back on the ground.

Rapach's mother was cooking something savoury as Rapach's father played a tall drum with two thick sticks in a slow, steady rhythm.

"Welcome back. I hope the words of the wise were helpful," his father said as they entered. "I apologise for not formally introducing myself to you earlier, girls. My name is Dazish Angarum, and this is my wife, Pirrah. Welcome to the tent of Angarum."

"Papa, before I forget," Rapach said, handing him some blue flowers. "This blue flower will protect anyone who breathes its essence against the miasma. Chew it all, leaves and stem, and inhale its scent. You'll be immune for a while."

"How did you learn this, Rapach? Is this one of your games you used to play?" his mother asked, incredulous.

"No, Mama. It's a long story."

"Well, we aren't going anywhere soon with a miasma storm upon us, are we, Rapach?" his father said, still playing the drums. "But tell us about it as we have dinner. Zelle will be here shortly. We're waiting for her."

"Where is she?" Nintai asked.

"She took some food to the old man. He's resting in the tent next to ours," Rapach's mother said. "Rapach, little mouse, we also have a surprise for you to celebrate your first mission."

Rapach blushed as Nintai chuckled at the nickname. But then he saw his mother pouring a thick, red liquid into a glass jug. He knew that drink very well.

"Red cocoa," he said, beaming. "But I have yet to complete my mission."

"You still deserve it. As do your new friends. I'm sure they've been through a lot as well."

"What's red cocoa?" Nintai asked as Pirrah poured the warm, foamy liquid into glasses for everyone.

"It's a cocoa bean species that can only be found in the Miasma Realm. We grind it with dry spices and boil it with water or milk. A Jerboa Clan specialty."

"It's so good," Joie said with a trace of red foam on her lips.

"It tastes so rich and smooth," Nintai added. "Thank you, Pirrah. It's delicious."

The entrance curtain opened behind them.

"Dinner is ready, Zelle. Please get comfortable. Rapach has a story to tell us," Dazish said.

But Zelle was quiet as she brushed the dust from her clothes.

"What's wrong?" Rapach asked. She was acting differently than usual.

"I know who he is," she replied. Her face was difficult to read. "The old man. I remember him."

"Who is he?"

"He's the man who rescued me years ago. The man who brought me to the Jerboa Clan."

Everyone fell silent as she joined the circle with a faint smile.

"He has the same long grey hair, but it's whiter now. He still carries that leather sack with him," Zelle said.

"But how do you know it's him?" Nintai asked. "Didn't you say he was wearing a mask back then?"

"I saw the mask. I opened his sack and I saw that same comical mask. It has to be him." Her smile became wider. "I could not talk to him, though. I wanted to thank him for saving my life. But he's still deep in slumber. He must be too fragile now."

"If it's really him, then we owe him so much," Dazish said.

"I know this day has been eventful for us all, but we must eat something now," Pirrah said, serving them a thick plant stew with a flat cornbread on the side. "May the Witness preside over this peaceful meal."

After filling themselves with comforting stew, they drank more red cocoa and listened to Dazish play the drums, accompanied by Pirrah's melodic pan flute. Meanwhile, Zelle danced with fluid moves, a beauty Rapach had seen only in her dances with Mat. The song had no words and showcased her perfectly timed moves. Rapach sang a familiar tune, since his parents loved his voice. Nintai laughed as Joie tried to imitate Zelle but tripped over in her attempt.

After a while, Rapach told them about his experiences with Erydis and about the Vault of Echoes. But even after such an impossible story, he saw no disbelieving eyes in the tent.

"This has to be the Witness's will, somehow," his father said thoughtfully as he sipped more red cocoa. "I hope your friend will have more answers about this stranger in the lion mask in your next dream."

"But how can they mix the dust?" Rapach's mother asked. "It seems so useless and dangerous. It has brought drought and disease, and we've managed to contain it after much trial. But to use it? Seems impossible."

"Will you see her today? Inside this Vault of Echoes?" Zelle asked, intrigued.

"I hope so," Rapach said eagerly. Zelle laughed at his answer, making him blush. "That's not what I meant."

"Well, thank you for this great feast. I had such a good time that I forgot," Zelle took a gulp of cocoa, "about the children. I should sleep in their tent. I have to make sure they're safe. That reminds me; maybe you should sleep in the old man's tent tonight, Rapach. You need to deliver him the package when he wakes up and look after him."

"We can join you," Nintai said.

"No, please stay," Rapach said as Benu jumped onto his head. "My parents will take care of you, and you shouldn't be out in this wind."

Rapach walked to the old man's tent, shielding his jug of red cocoa from the wind. He noticed that most people were inside their tents while soldiers watched over the camp, protecting themselves against the gale with steady barriers. With such a fierce wind, the torches had been blown out and the flags were flapping violently.

The soldiers protecting the old man's tent nodded to Rapach as they let him in. They helped to block out the wind with their rectangular glass shields.

Inside, a few candles shed light on the old man, who seemed to be sleeping silently and deeply. Rapach placed the jug on a small table and arranged some tapestries and cushions for his bedding.

He looked at the old man and remembered how he'd helped Zelle and so many others from getting lost forever in the Miasma Realm. Now he looked so fragile and emotionless. Rapach had so many questions to ask him.

He grabbed his pouch and stared at the red package inside, making a mental note to deliver it first thing in the morning. He placed it aside, but something caught his eye.

The old man's leather bag was lying close to him, open on the floor. Rapach saw something peek out from the top.

He stepped closer. It was a mask. A monkey mask.

Chapter XXIII

Palace Party

Erydis

Erydis scrutinised her reflection in the frameless mirror. After a rigorous interrogation, the barrio soldiers had informed them that Trinos hadn't been seen anywhere close to the charred house. Kitri had seemed relieved despite the worry and confusion still etched across her face. Kemia had gently escorted her to the food bazaar to distract her and to come up with a new plan to search for Trinos. Erydis knew that until they got wind of more information, all they could do was to stay alert, especially at the Closure Festival. She had realised that she needed to start getting ready for the party at the palace, and headed home.

She pulled out a folded dress from underneath the bed; a dress she thought she'd never wear again. It was a gift from her late mother's husband; her most expensive dress, and yet she hated it. It was blue and shiny with a yellow ribbon wrapped around the waist. After slipping into the dress, Erydis tamed her scruffy hair, taking more time than she usually did. As she finally put the last strand into place, she sighed. "Such a hassle."

Erydis made her way through the city to the marble stairs, but it was difficult to weave through the crowd in her outfit. Soldiers had created a barricade to the second floor, allowing in only those invited to the party.

"Erydis!" Thylac emerged from the throng of people, wearing a silver helmet and ornate black-and-white robes.

"New outfit?" she asked with a grin.

"No, I wear it on special occasions like this. But look at you! It took me a while to realise it was you. You should dress like this more often," Thylac said.

"I hate it, but at least it's long enough to cover my old boots."

Thylac smiled before his expression became stern.

"Erydis, I heard about what happened while you were trying to find Trinos. What was he doing at that monster's house?"

The image of her father scrambled Erydis's thoughts for a second.

"I'm not sure," she said. "But he didn't look like himself. I think he might be in danger, Thylac."

"I promise I'll help you find him after this commotion with the Vakandi," Thylac assured her.

"So Engyl hasn't found anything on them?" Erydis thought of the Vakandi inside the Tower.

"Not a thing. And the Emperor's supporters are getting impatient. We even had to arrest some of them because they were breaking into houses in the Hidden Barrio to see if there were any Vakandi hiding there. But their doing so only creates chaos in the city, and we don't want to make things worse. On the other hand, however, we have the Vakandi supporters getting into fights with those loyal to the Emperor. I don't understand why Engyl is going ahead with this party at such a terrible time."

"Look at you, disagreeing with the Emperor! That's unusual." Erydis laughed.

"I just want all this to end."

"Maybe someone needs to steal his sceptre to teach him a lesson."

"Erydis, you have to be more careful, please. I can help you only this far. You'll get in, grab the sceptre, and leave immediately. If they find you stealing from the Emperor, they might punish you as if you were a Vakandi."

"Thylac, stop worrying. I'll be fine, trust me," Erydis said.

Thylac looked at the floor thoughtfully, rubbing his forehead.

"Erydis, before you go, I wanted to ask." He moved closer to her, staring into her eyes piercingly. "Do you know something I should know?"

Erydis's heart jolted, but she tried not to show it.

"What about?"

"Anything. Something about the Vakandi? Or about what Kemia has been up to? I know you brought her some black dust."

Erydis tried not to break her eye contact with Thylac, as guilty as she felt.

"You won't get in trouble, Erydis. I wouldn't do that to you."

She had to say something, and fast.

"Well..." Erydis pulled out the last blue dust marble marked with an E from her pocket. "I sold some of my special marbles to someone at the bazaar," she said. "He gave me a few Imperials for them."

Thylac stared at her quietly. There was a shadow of doubt on his face.

"Very well," he sighed. "As promised, I won't tell anyone, but don't sell those troublesome marbles to strangers. Your dust marbles were used yesterday morning to aid some arrested Vakandi to escape. Keep this a secret. Now, follow me, you have a party to get to."

The outside walls of the palace were covered in Dust City flags. Erydis saw white and black everywhere she looked—from the flowers and carpets to the serfs in their elegant robes, black leather boots, and small, flat hats.

The guests were in their best outfits, wearing outlandish hats and robes as well as walking sticks with complex carvings that had no purpose other than to display the extent of their wealth.

Thylac and Erydis approached a tall soldier at the palace's entrance. He was also wearing celebratory robes along with a belt that held several sharp weapons.

"Greetings, Thylac. And who's this young lady with you?" he asked.

"This is Erydis, an old friend. She will be joining the party as my guest." Thylac patted Erydis's shoulder.

"Oh, I believe I've heard your name in some of Thylac's stories," the soldier said. "And does Miss Erydis have a coin?"

"I have it." Thylac showed the soldier a white coin with the Dust City crest and his name etched under it. "Erydis, keep this coin close to you; it's your invitation to the party."

"Very well, welcome to Festival of the Palace," the soldier said, bowing with a smile.

"I'll see you after the party, Erydis." Thylac gave her a quick hug. "Please be careful," he whispered into her ear before letting go.

Erydis waved goodbye and entered the huge doors of the palace. She had never been inside it before, although she had often dreamed of this moment. She looked around in awe at the tall columns that flanked the entrance. Carved into the stone were the detailed, chiseled faces of the many emperors who had once lived in the palace.

She walked alongside the many guests into the palace plaza, surrounded by buildings with complex architecture supporting the many columns and arches. "Fit for an Emperor," she thought. Engyl lived in one of those structures, but she was not sure which. At the far end of the plaza were the imposing doors to the colossal Tower.

In the center were the palace gardens, warmly lit by dust lanterns as sunset retreated from the sky. Brightly coloured plants and trees, probably infused with dust, surrounded the guests. A band was playing—an accordion accompanied by string instruments. The music was a complex allegro.

A dozen uniformed servers were pulling out delicious food from a stone oven and placing it onto shiny plates. They had to be some of the best yellow dust mixers in the city.

Soldiers walked around smiling but alert as guests conversed on cushioned seats next to a fountain that had a statue of the Finder, Orn Ryk, in its centre. The statue had detailed robes and a replica of the Emperor's mask. A cloud of shiny dust emerged from its right hand, and from its left, a steady stream flowed into the fountain. *This has to represent the two main elements of dust,* Erydis thought. *Mist and water.*

"I was near the Geberus Dust Academy when I heard it," a woman nearby said in a scandalised tone. "That man working at the Dusty Corner, the grumpy one with the pretty wife, he's missing."

"Is he? But it can't be," her companion said arrogantly. "I saw him nearly an hour ago."

Erydis's ears pricked up as she tried to covertly get closer so she wouldn't miss any details.

"You mean here? At the party?"

"Yes, I believe so. He entered the palace but he looked…well, it appeared that he was dragging his legs as he wandered around. And he had this ugly stare, as if he were ill."

"Poor woman, Kitri, is it? Having to deal with a drunk like that."

"Yes, drunk. I believe he must have been drunk when I saw the man. He was alone, too, without the wife."

"Escaping her to look for young beauties at the palace?"

"Well, it would seem so, yes."

Erydis stood still, trying to think. Was Trinos really here? If he were, alcohol had nothing to do with his strange behaviour. He was a Silent One. After she obtained the sceptre, she knew she had to try and find him. Hopefully, that would also lead her to the stranger in the lion mask.

"Well, look who managed to trespass into this party," a familiar voice said behind her.

"Tulia." Erydis turned to face her. "Still working on your pyrotechnic cat?"

Tulia was wearing a golden dress with a big shiny ribbon pulling her hair back. Erydis had to admit she was as good-looking as she was annoying. Next to her, Kori wore a long green tunic and a friendly smile on his face.

"Erydis, you look so– so different!" Kori said shyly.

"Yes, it's a shame not even clean clothes can help you," Tulia said. "And let it be known that my experiment is doing well. I just ran into a little problem, but it's nothing I can't fix."

"Too bad your father can't help you like he always does," Erydis said. "I heard the mixers are inside the Tower, which is in lockdown to avoid an invasion."

Along with a few Vakandi, Erydis thought.

"I heard they might cancel the contest, with everything that's going on," Kori said, trying to avoid conflict between the girls. Erydis felt disappointed at that thought.

"What about your experiment?" Tulia asked, ignoring him. "Is it so pathetic that you've decided to make it a secret?"

"When you see it working, even you'll admit it's the best experiment you've ever seen in a contest," Erydis said with pride.

"Now that is funny. Let's go, Kori. They shouldn't see us talking to people from the Hidden Barrio."

"See you around, Erydis," Kori said with a friendly smile as Tulia glared at him.

Finally alone, Erydis thought as they walked away. She could finally focus on finding the Emperor in peace. Where could he be? Probably not in the gardens, otherwise all the guests' attention would be on him. Not at the Tower either, since it was in lockdown. That left only one of the palace's twin buildings. But which one?

She decided to climb a curved tree to get a better view of her surroundings. A few guests stared at her in confusion as she climbed, but she knew she'd be back on the ground before they became suspicious. As she reached the top, she looked down at the entire party.

Protecting the big doors to the Tower were vigilant, well-armed soldiers with heavy armour. Near the eastern building, more soldiers patrolled from north to south. Some stood alert by the doors while others stared down at the party from balconies on the top floor. Then she looked at the western building.

There were only two guards at the entrance. Engyl would never let himself be that vulnerable—he cared too much about himself. He must have taken his army into the western building with him for protection.

"Hey you, girl! Get down from there!" a voice shouted below her.

This wasn't good. Erydis climbed down gingerly, pretending to be afraid.

"You can't be up there," the guard said. "We'll have to take you outside the palace for interrogation."

"But, sir, I have a coin."

"We have to be sure you don't have malicious intent," the guard insisted.

"Sure, sir. I just need to tell my friend, Thylac, who invited me here."

"Thylac Siopi? From the royal guard? Let me see your coin again."

Erydis nodded, showing the guard the coin with Thylac's name inscribed on it, smiling on the inside. This guard was definitely of a lower rank than

Thylac.

"There's no need to talk to him. Just don't go climbing any more trees here, understood?" he said.

Erydis nodded innocently as the soldier walked away. Once he was out of sight, she slipped towards the western building.

The only way to enter, it seemed, was through one of the many windows on the first floor. It seemed like the best option, since the guards couldn't possibly watch every single one of them. Of course the windows were all closed, but they looked simple enough to pick.

Erydis spied a window in the corner, next to a big bush in the gardens.

She pretended to be listening to the ambient music as she edged closer to the window while humming off-tune. She glanced into the window—no guards, at least not in this room. She grabbed an uncomfortable pin from her hair, and leaning with her back to the wall, deftly found a crack in the window behind her. *Click*. The guards could not see her from this angle.

In a single move, she opened the window, swung herself over the sill, and dropped to the floor as silently as she could. She closed the window behind her and raised her head.

She was in some sort of guest room, decorated with a big stand that had books piled on it. She was close to a set of imposing doors with a silver frame.

"Let me remind you that these doors must remain open," a voice said on the other side of the door as the handle started to turn.

Erydis slid under the bed as two female soldiers entered. She saw the bottom of their robes—one ranked higher than the other.

"We have to maintain our vantage point. We don't want any of those Vakandi to catch us by surprise," the higher ranking soldier said.

"Understood, but..."

"Yes, soldier?"

"What about the third floor?"

"Emperor Engyl has asked for privacy. He said we soldiers must be focused on the entrances. Now, open the rest of the doors on this floor."

The ranking soldier walked away.

"Privacy...arrogant man," the remaining young woman whispered to herself just before leaving the room too.

If the sceptre had to be somewhere, the third floor would be Erydis's best bet. But it wouldn't be easy getting there with all the soldiers around. She crawled out from under the bed and grabbed a small mirror from the nightstand. Carefully, she crept behind the doors and used the mirror to look around the corner. A soldier stood tall next to the stairs going up to the next floor. As the young female soldier passed by him, he turned and stared at her with unmistakable attraction.

Erydis took her chance to dart up the stairs, quiet as a mouse, while trying to hide in the shadows of the tall pillars and behind columns.

On the next floor was a long hallway with many open doors. Near the middle of the hallway were the stairs to the third floor, being watched over by four guards.

"He's taking a long time to get ready," a guard said in a low voice.

"Quiet! I don't want to hear you complaining about our Emperor again or I'll make sure you lose your rank," a stocky woman of a higher rank ordered.

"He's probably practicing his speech anyway. He always makes sure he has it memorised before he speaks to the public. Smart man," another man said, sounding eager.

"Compared to you, maybe," the first voice said.

"That's enough! You, come with me. You two, keep watch until I return."

Two of the soldiers disappeared up the stairs.

"I'm afraid that soldier might be one of them Vakandi supporters," the genuine-sounding soldier said.

"He must be. He never behaved like this before this all started."

Crash!

"What in the name of dust was that?" the man asked.

"I don't know! Let's go check."

The guards rushed into a room a few doors down the hallway. It seemed too convenient to be a coincidence, but Erydis was thankful for the distraction and made her way up the stairs.

The third floor was dark, with warm light illuminating only some of the rooms. It was, as that soldier had suggested, unpatrolled by any soldiers.

Thick curtains covered the windows and all the doors were closed, except one. This door was bigger and of a more intricate design. That had to be Engyl's room, where the sceptre would be, Erydis reasoned.

As she tip-toed closer to the door, she heard nothing from inside the room. She peered around the door using the mirror. No one was there, but the Emperor had to be close, as all the lanterns in the room were burning.

She entered cautiously and scanned the room. In the middle was the biggest bed she'd ever seen, with over a dozen decorative pillows. The carpet on the floor had complex patterns, matching the walls. Behind some thin curtains were the doors to a wide balcony.

And then she saw it. Beside the bed was the Emperor's golden mask atop a pedestal—and hanging on the wall right above it, the sceptre. A golden relic with a thin, cylindrical handle and several holes on both ends to let out the useless, shiny clouds of grey dust.

Erydis approached the sceptre triumphantly. She couldn't believe it. She had prepared for this moment for so long. The last piece of her experiment. She just had to open the sceptre, rearrange a few pieces, and…

"The Vakandi menace must retreat before they destroy what we've built together," a powerful voice said, growing louder and closer to the room.

Erydis needed to hide. She scanned the room quickly, but there weren't many options. Her first instinct was the balcony, but what if the Emperor wanted to walk outside? Under the bed—but for some reason this massive bed had no space underneath it. Then she considered the cushions. It was risky, but she had no other option.

She threw herself among them, hastily covering every bit of herself. It probably looked a little bit askew, but it was the best she could do. She took shallow breaths so the cushions wouldn't move above her.

Erydis could still see through a small gap between the cushions. Someone entered the room. It was the Emperor in his imperial robes and tall, rectangular hat. He was reading a parchment as he bit into a dust-infused pear.

"...and the dust, the mist, and our river will prosper as we build a brighter future!" He was practising his speech.

He walked over to the bed and stopped.

"I assure you, their lies about the river… no," Engyl said, scratching something out on the parchment. "I must ask you not to believe their false claims and work with us to search for those traitors."

The Emperor put the pear and parchment down on the bed. He grabbed the mask and sceptre and walked towards a big mirror next to the door. He looked at his reflection and put on his mask.

"We shall not panic in this precious season of festivities. We shall celebrate the dust as we search every house in the city, our swords in hand. And we shall punish those who oppose us."

Then the balcony door slowly opened behind Engyl and a figure stepped inside the room. Erydis stifled her gasp.

It was Trinos, still with that soulless expression. He started walking towards the Emperor with an awkward shuffle, dragging his feet silently, almost as if he was weightless. Had he been hiding on the balcony for long? And how did he reach such a place? He couldn't have done it alone in the condition he was in. He grabbed something from a pouch on his belt without looking and kept moving towards the Emperor.

Engyl seemed too distracted to notice—until Trinos's reflection appeared in his mirror.

"Who in the name—"

Trinos lifted a hand and blew some dark dust into the Emperor's face.

Engyl immediately fell to the ground with a dull thud, and the sceptre clattered on the floor.

Trinos stared soullessly for a moment. He bent to pick up the unconscious man and threw him over his shoulder. He then grabbed the sceptre and left.

Erydis's mind was racing. The Emperor was still breathing, but what did the Silent People want with him?

Trinos staggered into the hallway, carrying the unconscious man as if he were weightless. Erydis slid out from under the cushions and followed him. She peered around the door and saw Trinos stop next to a closet in the hallway. It opened from the inside. Trinos stepped in and closed the door behind him.

Erydis waited, confused. She had expected someone to exit from the closet.

Sure enough, the door opened once more and someone emerged.

Engyl? No, it couldn't be.

Someone dressed as the Emperor stepped out of the closet, straightening his robes. He was wearing the golden mask and had the sceptre in one hand.

He closed the closet door behind him.

"I am ready," he bellowed to the soldiers as he walked down the stairs.

Erydis considered following the imposter, but she couldn't stop thinking of Trinos. The imposter was taller than Trinos, so it couldn't be him.

She opened the closet door, her mind made up to follow Trinos instead. The inside of the closet was dark, but she could just make out the Emperor lying on the floor in his undergarments next to some soldiers' robes.

Suddenly, a hand stretched out towards Erydis, trying to grab her. It was Trinos.

"Trinos, it's me!" She hoped the man inside the Silent One could hear her somehow, but there were no traces of him left in that vacant stare.

Trinos flailed his hand at her again, but Erydis jumped back, pushing him forcefully back into the closet. She closed the door and jammed a chair under the handle. She heard him rattling it.

"Sorry, Trinos, but I'll do whatever I can to stop the Silent People," she said, thinking of Rapach.

The soldiers were all gone now, having followed whom they thought was the Emperor outside. Erydis easily made her way down the stairs and out the first floor window. She just had to avoid the two guards near the main entrance.

Outside again, she hid next to a bush, from where she could hear two voices.

"I need more guards at the palace entrance and more vigilance around the party. Tell the soldiers at the Tower doors to move to the main event," the imposter said, still sounding very much like Engyl.

"But, my Lord, you specified that we should watch over the Tower," a soldier answered.

"I want to make sure no one interferes with my speech tonight. What I have to announce is of utmost importance."

"Very well, sir." The soldier bowed and ran back towards the Tower.

The imposter walked towards the middle of the garden, surrounded by a dozen soldiers. People stopped talking to observe him with admiration. He walked up a stage that had been set up next to the Orn Ryk fountain, waving to his followers exactly as Engyl would.

The sceptre in his hand exuded a cloud of shiny dust. The crowd went silent.

"Welcome, citizens of the Palace District, and distinguished guests of the many barrios," the imposter said. "We come together in this celebration to remember the Finder. He who created this Tower for our future so we can today live in prosperity with the help of dust, our most precious resource that leads us into advancement in knowledge and technology. I ask of you to always respect it and help our city discover its every possibility."

The crowd applauded. Erydis almost believed it was the actual Emperor speaking.

"Nevertheless," he continued, "we should not ignore what has fallen upon us. The Vakandi have come once more to terrorise our people. They come to take away everything we stand for, and for the first time, they've managed to enter our city. But do not fear. We've been planning for this situation and I assure you—you will be safe soon.

"We'll find them. We'll search every house and imprison and punish the traitors."

The crowd cheered. But Erydis noticed some exchanging uncomfortable glances.

"If they want dust, we shall show them its power."

More cheering followed, some faces truly inspired by the horrific speech.

"But today, we must celebrate this magnificent evening to remember those present, all who work to make our city a better place—"

Erydis suddenly felt a slight tug on her sleeve. She turned and gasped as she saw Eko wearing expensive clothing, the dust spot on his neck concealed.

"Eko? What are you doing here?!"

"...in which everyone should reflect on our future," the imposter continued. "I ask you to applaud yourselves. To the bankers, who keep Imperials and dust flowing throughout the city, we applaud you!"

A smattering of people looked puzzled, but they applauded the bankers, who bowed proudly.

"To the families of our soldiers, who are here while our bravest people protect our city, we applaud you!

"To the families of the best mixers in the city, who are locked inside the Tower to protect the dust, we applaud your patience."

The cheering grew even louder. Erydis noticed Tulia by the fountain, Kori patting her back.

"And," the imposter's voice grew sombre, "to those whose families perished in useless wars. Those who are barely surviving with a polluted river. Those who believe in justice, and who will not accept more lies. Those who promised the Vakandi to return to the Mist Grounds. We raise our hands!"

The party guests looked alarmed, but hundreds of hands rose in the air. Some were clenched in fists, others held spears and swords. The Vakandi had found their way out of the Tower and were cheering while the guests looked confused. Soldiers exchanged glances with one another, their weapons at the ready. It was too dangerous to attack the invaders, with so many innocents in their midst.

"Now, before anyone decides to attack us..." The fake emperor said, taking off his mask—it was Ferus, with his usual wide smile. "Let it be known we have gathered weapons and explosive dust from inside the Tower. And if you still want to see Engyl 'the liar' Ryk alive, you'll cooperate."

Ferus pointed towards the third floor of the building Erydis had just come from. There, on the balcony, the hypnotised Trinos was holding a dagger to Engyl's throat.

"While you were enthralled by my speech, we locked you inside the palace. Yes, ladies and gentlemen, we were waiting for this party from inside your precious Tower. Every guard and mixer inside are safe, and I recommend that those soldiers who are listening drop their weapons, for your companions' sake."

Soldiers looked furious but hesitant, everyone looking at their superiors for orders.

"Drop your weapons!" An elite soldier shouted with an air of defeat. The order echoed across the plaza to all the soldiers.

"Why so much tension?" Ferus asked, still smiling. "After all, I would hate to interrupt your Festival of Many Dusts. That's why I come bearing magnificent news. Tomorrow, at twilight, I invite you to a festivity of our own, celebrated for the first time in Dust City. Tomorrow, we celebrate the Festival of Sorrow!"

The Vakandi cheered at the announcement. Eko seemed happy as well, until he saw Erydis's face.

She didn't know what to feel anymore. When she'd first talked to Ferus, she thought they deserved their rebellion. But since the Vakandi had the upper hand, the contest wouldn't be taking place the next day.

What made Erydis even more uneasy was that the Silent People and the man in the lion mask seemed to have helped the Vakandi. They had taken Trinos, and Ferus was aware. Maybe his intentions weren't as noble as she had first thought.

So what could she expect from the Festival of Sorrow?

The Vakandi proceeded to march every guest and soldier inside the Tower. Erydis saw Tulia and Kori walking in one of the lines. They looked so scared, she felt sorry for them.

Erydis followed Eko to the eastern building. Ferus was sitting on a cushioned chair in the living room, his feet on a table. His mask was pushed up to the top of his head, and he still wore the Emperor's robes.

"Erydis! I did not think I'd see you at this party," he said. "And you have no idea the panic attack I had when I saw you walk into the Emperor's room. I bet you never expected that, did you, me waiting in the closet until the Emperor was brought to me. Ha! Not that I'm not happy to see you, but what are you doing here?"

"I was looking for that." Erydis pointed at the sceptre, which was placed upright next to Ferus.

"For this experiment of yours? But that trivial contest is not taking place anymore, didn't you know?"

Eko stared at Erydis in silence.

"Of course I know. But I really want to finish my creation." She couldn't hide what she felt towards him at the moment.

"Very well, I have no use for it." He extended the sceptre to Erydis, who accepted it.

"Now, I want to know, what did you do to Trinos?" she asked.

"Trinos? Who's that?"

"The man who abducted the Emperor!" she was shouting now. "The man you used to take over the palace! The man who will not be the same ever again!"

Ferus's smile disappeared.

"He helped us restrain the Emperor while I pretended to be Engyl. You shouldn't worry about him anymore."

"He has a wife waiting for him!" Erydis couldn't contain herself.

"Be grateful he's not dead," Ferus said calmly with no regret on his face.

"But he's not alive either!"

"Erydis, this is war. I made a promise not to kill anyone unless we need to."

"So, you hypnotised him? You made him one of them?"

"Who's them?" Ferus sounded confused yet irritated.

"Don't lie to me! You know whom I'm talking about!"

"Erydis, enough."

"This is his fault, isn't it? The man in the lion mask!"

"I said enough!" Ferus stood up. It was the first time Erydis had seen him angry. "Now, you will go down to the Mist Caves and back to the hideout before we seal the tunnel to the Tower. Eko, take her with you and return. If you try to intervene, Erydis, I will not be so kind to you."

Erydis stared at him defiantly. But Eko pulled her dress lightly, and she had no other option but to follow him into the Tower.

Eko and Erydis were in the Hidden Barrio hideout, under the trapdoor where she'd first met Ferus. They were sitting on a rug, their faces illuminated by a dust lamp in the corner.

Erydis was angry and speechless as she stared at the flickering light, trying to get her thoughts in order. Eko wrote something on one of the chairs.

I'm sorry about my brother. He doesn't usually act like that.

"It's not your brother who scares me, Eko. There's something deeper going on, something difficult to explain."

Eko stared at her with concern.

"Do you know what happened to my friend Trinos, the owner of the store I work at?"

Eko shook his head.

"Someone used this cursed thing called the miasma to hypnotise him, and I'm afraid your brother knows this person. He was there when I was at the Tower. Eko, do you know who's behind the lion mask?"

Eko looked doubtful, but he started writing on the chair again.

I never met him. No one has, except my brother. Ferus says he's Vakandi's heir.

"Wait, never met him? So he's never been to Sorrow City?"

Eko shook his head. Erydis couldn't make any sense of it.

"Eko, I'm afraid this stranger in the lion mask has evil intentions. It's difficult to explain, but I know a friend whose sister was taken by him. Please be careful."

Eko nodded.

Erydis felt terrible. She hadn't managed to find out anything useful for Rapach, and on top of that, Dust City was in danger.

At least I have the sceptre—if I can ever finish my experiment in this mess, she thought.

Eko suddenly pointed at her necklace.

"You like it?" she asked, and he nodded. "It was a gift from a stranger, and turns out that it has incredible power. This blue amber right here helps me enter a place where a good friend needs my advice."

Eko seemed confused at her words, but he didn't seem to care. He lifted the necklace slowly.

"You want to see it?" She took it off and passed it to him. "I'll just need it back before I go to sleep."

Eko nodded once more and held the blue amber up to the light. He then started polishing it with his robes.

"What…what are you doing?" Eko pointed at the amber. Erydis looked closer, holding it up against the light. Kemia was right. Amber sometimes contained leaves or insects trapped in it. But this one held something very different.

Inside, curled into a ball, was a tiny jerboa with a torn ear.

The Fifth Dream

Erydis opened her eyes. She was back in the Vault of Echoes, lying next to the black tree.

But something was different inside the vault this time. It was as if there was a fierce storm around her blowing dust to the far horizon. Erydis was sure she'd never seen such a violent storm in Dust City. So this was probably happening on Rapach's side.

Near her were large lamps like the ones she had seen in the Emperor's bedroom. She noticed that there were also several houses in the distance, where a wild fire blew with the storm. Erydis felt uneasy, remembering her father's home crumbling into ashes, as well as her argument with Ferus.

"The weather is fierce in the Miasma Realm," Rapach said, walking towards her.

"Will you be safe?" she asked.

"Tonight, maybe. Tomorrow, we'll see. How are things in Dust City?"

"Rapach, we had our first victim of the Silent People."

Rapach stared at her. "Did you know the victim?"

"Yes, he's my boss. No… my friend. Was."

"I'm sorry to hear that, Erydis. What would the stranger in the lion mask want with your city?"

"I don't know," Erydis said. "But I learned something about him. He's Vakandi's heir, one of the three masked kings of ancient times. It seems there's only one person who knows about it—the Vakandi's leader, Ferus."

"Why would he be the only one to know about it?"

"I don't know. I don't know whom to trust anymore, Rapach. I don't think the Vakandi have the good intentions they promised me."

"Or maybe the stranger in the mask is the one with the cruel intentions,"

Rapach suggested.

"Maybe...maybe they are unaware of what the hypnotised did to you and the people in the Miasma Realm. I know the one person I can trust is Eko. I told you about him in our last dream. Maybe I can tell him to convince his brother about the man in the lion mask and the Silent People."

Erydis closed her eyes, trying to think of a solution, but nothing came to mind. Rapach looked at her. He had never seen her with such a defeated expression.

"Erydis, wouldn't this be the reason we're here?" Erydis stared at him. "Maybe we were brought to the Vault of Echoes to solve whatever is going on. There's still one more day."

Rapach pointed at the clock, which was pointing at the number four.

"It has to be," he continued. "Maybe we already have all the pieces to solve this puzzle. We just need to think."

Erydis looked at Rapach. His face had an inexplicable confidence, as if somehow he believed in the impossible.

"You are right. We can't give up now," she said. "We have to trace events back to the beginning. When did you first dream about the Vault of Echoes?"

"When we met. I had never seen this place before that," he answered.

"What happened the day before you had the dream?"

"It was the day I started the mission. Mat and I tried to go to Rabaska Lake, but we ran into some miasma. It was also the day I met Benu."

Erydis froze.

"Benu, your jerboa?"

Rapach nodded.

"The first time I dreamed about the vault was a day before that, the day I got this blue amber." Erydis took out the amber. "And before I went to sleep today, I discovered what was inside. Look."

Erydis held her amber against the light from one of the dust lamps. Rapach got closer. Inside, curled into a ball, was a jerboa. Rapach couldn't believe it.

"Your jerboa Benu and this jerboa must be connected," Erydis said, a faint smile on her face.

"This must be what the legend of the Witness was referring to!" Rapach said excitedly.

"The Witness?"

Rapach quickly told her about the legend of the man who saw the Witness, and how she gave him the task to find the jerboa with her sight. Erydis was sceptical at first, but there had to be a connection.

"So if you find the right jerboa, you will find the sight of the Witness?" she asked.

"Exactly. What if this is her vision, Erydis? What if the Vault of Echoes is what the legends describe?"

Erydis was still unbelieving. "But your legend says to find a jerboa," she said. "How come there are two of them?"

Rapach thought for a second. "I don't know. Maybe the legend is wrong and it's more than one?"

Erydis was silent, unconvinced by his theory. She stared into the amber, looking at the shape of the jerboa inside, trying to think.

"Rapach," she said suddenly, her eyes wide open. "Does Benu have a torn ear?"

Rapach nodded slowly.

Many thoughts shuffled inside Erydis's head, almost as if she understood better now how to join the dots.

"Rapach, Benu and the jerboa inside my amber are not two different ones. They are the same!" She got closer to him and lifted the blue amber to the light again. "This jerboa inside my amber is Benu!"

Rapach froze.

"But…how?"

"This is why you don't know about dust mixing! This is why you didn't know about the flower!"

Erydis gave a big laugh, making Rapach more confused.

"Rapach, we are from different times!"

Rapach blinked repeatedly, realisation dawning on his face.

"That's why you know so much!" he said. "That's how you knew the blue flower would help me! You live in the future!"

"That's what I think, too," she agreed. "Maybe we are here to fix something."

"But how?"

Rapach thought of something. "Maybe I need to fix something in the Miasma Realm. Maybe if I fix it in the past, I will save your city from falling into the man in the lion mask's hands in the future!"

"Something tells me that there's more to it," Erydis said doubtfully.

Rapach gasped. "But Erydis, what about the miasm—"

Suddenly he vanished into thin air. Something had happened on his side. In his time.

Erydis felt confused. Something could be wrong with their theory, and it was too late to figure it out. She turned to the clock and saw the hand moving to the last number. The last day to fix it all.

Day Five

Chapter XXIV

Miasma Storm

Rapach

Rapach woke up breathless. Something had shaken him. He thought it was the fierce wind outside, but it was Zelle trying to wake him up. She looked worried.

"Rapach, the southern provisions camps have been attacked," she said shakily.

"When?"

"While we slept. The camps were prepared enough to contain the attack, but it seems they were outnumbered by Silent People. A provisions dog came with a message. It says we should leave before they arrive."

Rapach stared at her. There were no lies in her eyes.

"Leave the Central Camp? But where would we go?" He tried to sound calm.

"I don't know. The ancients are holding a meeting outside while everyone is getting ready to escape. I'll go tell your parents."

Rapach jumped up and pulled on his gear. The old man was up already, holding his leather sack and wearing goggles and scarf. His eyes were a bit more alert than the day before but still emotionless.

They went outside, where the wind pushed against them mercilessly. People were gathered in a circle, with the ancients, carried on the backs of strong men, in the centre. Nintai was there too, protecting her sister Joie from the dust storm. Fortunately there was no trace of miasma, but it was just a matter of time before it would arrive.

"We don't have much time, my dear clan," Akma said from the back of a tall man. The wind was blowing her ancient hair in all directions. "A miasma storm is coming from the west as we speak, and I fear to tell you that Silent People are marching to our camp along with that monstrous djinni."

People looked at the ground. No one panicked as they awaited their instructions.

"We shall escape to the chain of mountains to the east, back to our ancient lands where no miasma exists. I am sad to say that we cannot fix these cursed lands. Most of us will march now alongside the dogs and boars, but some will have to stay and fight."

"We promise we won't let them reach you," Danaa said from astride a boar, wielding a glass spear and a square glass shield.

"But thanks to Rapach, we have found an aid against the curse of the miasma. He has discovered that the blue flower has the power to make us breathe through miasma. "Instructions on its use will be explained by the people carrying them to you all. Go now, run to the east."

Bags of blue flowers were passed around the group. Nintai and Joie grabbed many, and so did Rapach. Together they munched on one each in preparation for what was to come.

"We need to take care of the old man, Rapach," Nintai said.

Rapach nodded.

The old man was close to them, waiting for them while staring into nothingness, as he often did. Rapach then remembered the package, and he wondered if whatever was inside was of any use.

Suddenly, the sound of a roar mixed with the howling of the wind. They had heard it before—the roar of the monstrous djinni.

The sound came from the south, where a cloud of miasma was slowly appearing. People started running and riding away on their boars, while brave soldiers waited, munching blue flowers.

Then Silent People emerged from the miasma cloud. There was a whole army of them, Purple Breathers wearing purple armour, fast approaching in their odd gait.

They had with them powerful swords of steel, and clouds of miasma came out of their masks, carried forward by the storm.

"Attaaack!" yelled a Jerboa Clan soldier, charging at the army of Silent People.

The rest of the soldiers ran with him, but before they reached their objective, something big jumped out at them.

It was the djinni. He swiped at the soldiers with his sharp, red claws, throwing soldiers into the distance as the miasma washed over the skies. Just as a fierce battle started, the feline djinni stared at the old man behind Rapach.

"Run!" Rapach yelled. "Run!"

The djinni ran towards them with fury as they tried to escape. Surprisingly, the old man was sprinting with all his might.

A spear flew into the monster's face, but it shattered into pieces. It stopped the beast in its tracks for a while.

A dozen soldiers on boars encircled Rapach's group to keep them safe.

"Rapach," Danaa said, focusing on the feline that was glaring with fury. "We will hold this beast up, boy. Most of them Silent People marched to the east to pursue our clan. Go west and look for a stone house in between two hills. If…I survive, I'll meet ya there. Protect this old man, this is yer mission, boy."

The soldiers ran towards the feline, attacking it fiercely as Rapach stared in horror.

"Rapach, we have to go," Nintai said.

Rapach looked back at the battle for a second. He knew he had no other choice but to go west, where the miasma was thicker.

"Sorry, Danaa. Sorry, my dear family. Benu, take us west as fast as you can."

Benu jumped from his head, trying not to be blown away by the wind. She jumped swiftly ahead to take the lead, and Nintai, Joie, Rapach and the old man followed her closely.

The small group walked west, munching on blue flowers as the wind blew curtains of dust and miasma over them. They had managed to escape the Silent People, and there was no sign of the monster. Rapach was trying to cover everyone behind him with his shield, so the going was slow. Benu was giving small jumps to go forward, but the wind kept pushing her back. Rapach grabbed Benu and placed her in his pouch. She had done enough.

"Rapach!" Joie pointed to something nearby.

Rapach turned around. The silhouette of a house was just where Danaa had said it would be. Just in time too, since it would only be a matter of time before everything was blanketed by the storm. Good thing they had taken a high dose of the blue flowers to protect them against the miasma, but the effect wouldn't last a full day.

Rapach and Nintai opened the tightly shut door to the stone house. After letting everyone inside, they covered the entrance to keep the miasma and dust out.

They surveyed the inside of the house. There was nothing but a few candles and shredded rugs on the floor. The house had two small windows on opposite sides, each sealed with a wooden panel. Whoever lived here once knew the dangers of the miasma.

"It's quite dusty in here, but at least there's no miasma," Nintai said.

The old man slowly lay down on a rug, leaving his leather sack at his side. Joie sat down next to him, her eyes brimming with tears.

"Nini, I'm scared."

Nintai sat down next to her, silently rubbing her sister's head. Rapach stared at them, trying to think what to do, but nothing came to him. He thought of his family, Danaa, and the rest of his clan. He had left behind everyone he loved.

Erydis

Erydis had been working on her experiment since early morning. She had woken up when Rapach disappeared from the Vault of Echoes, and was still trying to think of a solution. Was Rapach really from the past? If so, what could he do to help her?

At least her experiment was finally complete, even though the competition was cancelled. Every piece was perfectly placed for it to work. She stared at her beautiful creation.

She had painted the sceptre in a dark purple hue, since gold reminded her too much of Engyl and too little of herself. On the base of the sceptre she had drilled some holes, and on top of it was her most elaborate creation: the thick glass sphere she had gotten from Kemia, pierced through its centre. Its material was extremely resistant, so making the hole through it was what had taken the most amount of time in the experiment. At the side of the sceptre was a knob that acted as a trigger for the experiment. A few spins and everything would be set in motion.

It was finally ready. Although it seemed useless now with the competition being cancelled, she still wanted to show Kemia its potential and seek her opinion.

As she walked to the Dust Ring, all the scared people gathered in the streets reminded her of the previous day's events. It had been a disaster. One group was shouting at a soldier.

"We only know that the Vakandi have taken over the Tower and the palace. They have taken our people hostage, including our Emperor," the soldier said.

"The Vakandi leader also said there would be some sort of parade at twilight, so we have to be careful with how we handle this."

"We should do something about it!"

"The reason this happened is because the Emperor decided to celebrate through an invasion!"

"We should go to the palace and kick that scum and their supporters out of this city!"

"Everyone, calm down," the soldier said. "We don't want the people inside the palace to get hurt!"

"Yeah, of course you don't want them to get hurt! They are from the second floor, the rich people! If they were people from the rest of the barrios, we wouldn't be having this argument!"

The argument grew louder as people started talking over each other.

"Everyone, listen! We must remain calm!"

"No, we must gather everyone at the marble plaza to prepare for a counterattack!

"You are all wrong," said a woman standing at the head of a big group. "Think of how much they've suffered! They just want justice for what the Emperor did to them! If we stay calm, we can fix this!"

"Shut up, you traitor!"

"Calm down or we will take action," the soldier warned. Other soldiers looked on, defiant.

"Let's gather at the marble stairs at twilight," a tall man said. "Whoever is against the idea of counterattacking the Vakandi will be seen as our enemies."

There was silence as angry stares were exchanged, and the groups slowly walked in opposite directions.

Erydis had never seen people arguing like that. And the worst part was that she didn't know which one to support. The Emperor who polluted the river and killed thousands of Vakandi, the Vakandi who seemed to have joined the Silent People, or the angry people of Dust City, who seemed determined to act even though they didn't know the full story.

She felt completely alone. It seemed like the only other person who wanted to stay away from the conflict was Kemia.

The academy was empty. Many of the students were at the Tower with the Vakandi. And since the contest for the best experiment was cancelled, the rest of the students had no reason to be there. But even though the academy looked sadder than before, Erydis knew there was one person who would not stop experimenting.

She ran up the stairs of the academy tower to Kemia's laboratory, carrying her experiment lovingly. It was no surprise that the door was shut. Erydis was about to knock, before she heard Kemia talking to someone inside.

Erydis pressed closer against the door and placed her ear against it.

"...to think that I was trying to help you..."

Kemia sounded angry, which was rare.

"You know I spent hours searching for him with Kitri? We searched everywhere and there he was, with you all this time. I see no more of him in those eyes."

Erydis froze.

"That's why you needed the dust pearls, isn't it? They are no toy. You should stop right now."

Whoever she was with remained quiet, waiting for her to calm down.

"Do the Vakandi even know about your plan? Does she, if you truly care so much for her?"

The other person took a deep breath. Erydis needed to see this other person. She looked through the keyhole, but she couldn't see them from that angle.

"Did you believe I was going to be on your side if you told me the truth? I knew about your sickening experiment, which is more of a curse. You're just like the people at the tower. I thought you wanted to use it only on the king and some soldiers if they were in your way. But Trinos?"

Kemia finally appeared in Erydis's line of sight. She was looking down at her table as if regretting her experiment. Someone walked towards her.

Erydis pressed even closer to the door, trying to get a better look at the stranger. But then, the door suddenly opened.

She stumbled into the room and looked up.

"Erydis, go!"

But before she could move, someone put an arm around her neck from behind her, immobilising her. She looked up at the stranger's face. It was Trinos with his soulless stare.

The man in the lion mask approached her, grabbing something from a bag on his belt.

"No, stop!" Kemia shouted.

But it was too late. He blew green dust into her face, causing her to choke. As darkness took over, she surrendered even as her fear grew.

?

ERYDIS OPENED HER EYES. SHE WAS INSIDE THE VAULT OF ECHOES AGAIN. She must have been knocked out by the stranger in the lion mask's dust. She was afraid of what was happening outside the dream, but maybe she could use this opportunity to tell Rapach what she had just seen.

But Rapach was not there. It seemed that the vault was empty this time. Around her were nothing but infinite white dunes under a dark sky. Not even the tree was there, which was a first.

Maybe she was having a normal dream.

Then a laugh echoed in the empty space. It somehow felt familiar, yet there was something strange about it. It was the sound of a girl giggling. The sound came from everywhere, but Erydis could not see anyone around her. She stared in all directions but saw only infinite white dunes, and nothing else.

Then another laugh resonated, this time right behind her. Erydis turned and finally saw the giggler. In front of her was the silhouette of a little girl, almost like a shadow staring at her. But Erydis couldn't quite make out her face.

"I'm looking for someone," the girl said in an echoing, naive voice.

"Sorry?" Erydis was trying to make sense of what she was seeing.

She stepped closer to the girl to try and see her more clearly. She could see the curves of her outline and the reflection of her skin, but she could also see through her, almost as if she was transparent. And inside of the little girl, Erydis could see stars, lights, colours, and shining clouds. She couldn't understand what she was seeing.

"I'm looking for someone," the girl said. She had a strange accent and spoke as if she were older beyond her years. Her large eyes shone with a cerulean light.

Erydis was speechless for a moment, but she had to figure out who or what this girl was.

"Who?" she asked.

"I was hoping you knew." The girl giggled again. "But you haven't seen this person. Or maybe you have but didn't notice."

Erydis was confused. She wanted more answers.

"What's your name? What are you?"

The girl went quiet and giggled once more.

"I go by many names, given to me by different people. The girl of infinity. The being from the fourth universe. But I like the name dear Rapach has for me."

Erydis hesitated. "You're…you're the…"

"I am, Erydis. The Witness. Many think of me as a savior, but their wishes are often spoken in vain. As to what I am, this will be a riddle for you to solve. In exchange, I can tell you where we are.

"This Vault of Echoes, as you call it, is a room in which I can gather two souls from different times. But I am restricted by the rules of the universe.

"They can be scary if you break them. I witness your universe through the eyes of a living being.

"With you and dear Rapach, I see your times through the eyes of one living being that is close to you—the jerboa, Benu."

Erydis gasped.

"You are a smart girl. And you were correct.

"Through Benu's eyes, I can see your universe, but I can't touch it for that will disrespect the rules of the universe. But through the Vault of Echoes, perhaps I can give you aid."

"Aid? What aid can you give me?" Erydis asked.

The Witness giggled.

"To answer would mean to go against the rules. Sometimes the universe must flow by itself. But it all relies on you."

The girl was fading away as if she was dissolving into space.

"Why tell me this then?!"

"Aid will come to whom aid provide. And also, you wouldn't believe in my existence otherwise."

Everything around Erydis went black.

"Erydis, Rapach," the Witness said, giggling.

Chapter XXV

The Festival Of Sorrow

Erydis

Erydis woke up in a blur. She was sitting in a comfortable chair. She tried to focus her gaze, but she could hardly make out what was in front of her. She felt weak as a room took form in front of her.

She was in an elegant dining room with heavy curtains and some dust lamps illuminating the room. She was sitting at the end of a long table. This had to be somewhere inside the palace.

"Erydis?"

She felt a chill when she heard that voice, a cold block sinking in her stomach, but she didn't know why. At the other end of the table was a silhouette.

"Erydis, you're finally up," the smooth voice said. A horrifically familiar voice.

She suddenly realised who it was.

Her limbs went numb and the blood drained from her face. Her eyes ran over his pale skin and messy hair, like hers. It was him. He who she thought she would not hear from again. It was her father, Elias Nott.

"You…" She was breathless.

"I was waiting for you to wake up. Dinner will be here shortly, my dear."

Her father was smiling at her with an expression that could easily be mistaken for nostalgia.

"What is happening?" Erydis asked groggily.

"This must be confusing for you." He laughed. "But don't be afraid. The Vakandi are taking good care of us. Erydis, I waited so long in that horrific cage for this moment, when I would see my girl again."

"You should have stayed there."

Elias's smile faded momentarily.

"Now now. I know you don't mean that."

Erydis smashed a fist on the table.

"You killed my mother! And had I eaten on that day, I, too, would have died from that poisonous mixture!"

"But Erydis, I didn't mean it. You weren't hungry, remember? I was sure you wouldn't die—"

"Nonsense! You didn't care about me. You were just jealous of Mum finding love with someone else!"

Elias stood up. "They deserved it! You don't know how much I suffered!" A tear rolled down his cheek.

"So, what now?" Erydis asked. "Will you hypnotise me with your dust? Force me to be your daughter again as a Silent One?"

"Hypnotise? You mean like that old bag Trinos? Not me. I'm not responsible for that. But you betrayed me. You told that soldier, Thylac, about my business. Because of you, I was in hell, Erydis. And you'll pay for it all."

He stood up and placed something on the table in front of her. The lion mask.

"I'm supposed to show you this."

"What for? To intimidate me?"

They stared at each other in silent fury.

Then the door to the room opened. It was Thylac, and behind him, Trinos with a plate of stew in one hand and a long knife in the other. Thylac was staring at Elias angrily.

"Erydis, are you alright?" he asked. "You didn't hurt her, did you Elias?"

"Ah…I see my dinner is finally here!" Elias said. "And you, the man who wouldn't mind his own business. I see the Vakandi have finally caught you. I hope they kill you, Thylac."

"What is happening, Thylac?"

"Erydis, everything will be fine," Thylac said.

Trinos gave Thylac the plate of food and went to stand next to the door with the knife. Thylac walked slowly towards Elias and placed the plate in front of him.

"I see the Vakandi have made an obedient slave of you," Elias said as he sat down and grabbed the cutlery.

"Remember that poisonous mixture you used to kill Aris?" Thylac asked, his face fraught with disgust. "The one you gave to Erydis, and which could have killed her as well?"

Elias was confused.

"What about it?" he asked.

"Your food is full of it, and you will eat it," Thylac answered.

"What?" Elias looked down at the food he was about to eat. "How dare you! This can't be true."

He stood up again, looking furious.

"Erydis, do you know who Vakandi was?" Thylac asked, catching her off guard. "He was one of the masked kings, the one who wanted to use the dust with care. That's what the Vakandi say. He was a man who sought peace. A man of courage who fought for the people. Not like Orn Ryk, the Finder, whose ambitions took over his mind.

"The Vakandi knew men would use dust for violence and murder, so he tried to fight back. But he failed and returned to Sorrow City."

"Why are you telling me this, Thylac?" Erydis asked.

"Many people from his clan know that, but not many know what happened when he got to Sorrow City. When he returned, it is said he went mad and experimented with dust to find a mixture to exact revenge on Orn. But he never managed to create it."

"What in the name of the dust are you talking about?" Elias asked, confused.

He walked towards Thylac, but the soldier blew something into his face from his hand. Elias stopped. Then, slowly, he went back to his seat. He looked sick.

Erydis was scared.

"Thylac, tell me what is happening."

"Many people don't know many details about Vakandi. In our murals in the Tower, they portray him as a horrible man, but in truth, he was rather attractive. And many in the Vakandi Clan know him by the mask he wore."

Thylac traced the lion mask on the table with his index finger.

"It can't be true," Erydis said, tears streaming down her face.

Thylac took a small bottle of green liquid from his robes and poured some drops on the mask.

"Erydis, I'm sorry I couldn't tell you before. As an apology, I have a present for you." He put on the mask and looked at Elias. "Eat it," he said.

"No!" Erydis shouted. But her father started eating the poisonous stew hastily, his jaw moving oddly.

"This is for all the incurable suffering you caused Erydis and her mother. Prison did not teach you any trace of regret, and for that, I serve you justice."

Elias stopped eating and his face fell lifelessly onto the plate, breaking it. He was dead.

"Why, Thylac, why did you do that?" Erydis cried.

Thylac hugged her.

"He's finally gone, Erydis. You don't have to be afraid of him anymore."

"What have you done?"

"I gave him what he deserved. Just like I did to that exploitative, ungrateful Trinos who never treated you right."

"You're Vakandi's heir. You're the man in the lion mask."

"I am," he said with a calm smile. Was he the same person Rapach had seen? "I have so many questions for you, Erydis. Why did you ask Ferus who was behind this mask? You were so curious about me, even though only three people—Ferus, Herra, and Kemia—knew about my plan and me being part of the Vakandi Clan."

"Kemia?" Erydis asked in disbelief.

Someone knocked on the door and the hypnotised Trinos opened it. There stood Ferus, wearing the mocking mask, with Eko behind him. He lifted his monkey mask to stare at Erydis with concern.

"I see you finally told her," Ferus said, his voice filled with happiness. "Eko, Erydis, I present to you our true leader, Thylac Siopi."

Eko's mouth hung agape.

"Eko, thank you for all your help." Thylac said, extending a hand to Eko. But Eko simply stood still, looking defiantly at Thylac. He then took a step back.

"Forgive my brother," Ferus said. "He will grow to understand things later on. Now come. It is almost time for the festival."

"Very well. Let us walk, Erydis." Thylac handed her a bag. "I believe you had this with you before I put you to sleep in Kemia's office. Today you finish this small experiment. But I promise you, I will make sure you become a great mixer."

Erydis's experiment felt so useless now, but she carried it with her anyway. She walked with Thylac in a daze, trying to make sense of everything that had happened.

She was only vaguely aware of her surroundings as they walked through the palace and up some stairs. She felt weak, simply moving in whichever direction she was nudged.

"I know you have doubts about all this, Erydis," Thylac said. "It was all set in motion before I met you.

"As I've told you before, all my life I wondered who my parents were and where I came from. But I never told you the only real clue I had was my lion mask. I always treasured it and kept it home in secret to avoid a thief taking it from me, like what happened with your lost djinni mask.

"One day, I woke up to a strange sound in my home, so I took my sword and ran to the entrance. It was Ferus. Before I could attack him, he smiled at me and calmly asked if my last name was Siopi.

"I was puzzled at the whole situation, but I nodded. He asked me if I knew who my ancestors were—that got my attention. Any trace of my roots was of great importance to me. I told him I didn't.

"He then asked if a mask had been given to me. A lion mask. I did not answer right away, of course. But Ferus kept on smiling and told me something that would change my life forever.

"He told me that I was a Vakandi, one of the people whom I had been to war with several times. I didn't want to believe him, but he persisted. He told me that he needed my help to stop the war. I asked him, 'Why me?' And he just said, 'Look under the fake fur on the right side of the mask.'

"I did as I was told, and there it was. The name Vakandi Siopi carved into the mask. Ferus then bowed and said, '*You are Vakandi's heir, and we need your help to reclaim the Mist Grounds.*'

"He needed my help to invade Dust City and stop the Emperor from continuing to pollute their waters and lands. I did not know what to say. But Ferus simply said, 'Go and search for a pipe in the Mist Caves. There you'll see grey dust leaking into the river. If you then believe in our cause, use the river's current to send us a message in a bottle. We will be sure to catch it.'

"So I did as he said. I went to see that hidden pipe. Such a horrible thing, and Engyl knew all about it. It was then that I knew I had to come up with a plan, and just as Ferus asked, I sent a message in a bottle. I simply wrote: *I saw it. I'll be ready for your arrival a day before the Five Festivals.*"

Erydis listened to Thylac's story in disbelief. She couldn't blame him for helping the Vakandi. She couldn't deny she would have done the same. But killing her dad like that...she would not have believed he was capable.

When they got outside the palace, Erydis saw Vakandi standing all along the fortress walls. They were gazing down at the people outside the palace. Thylac and Erydis stepped close to the edge, next to Ferus. They stared into the chaos of the streets below. Eko, however, was not there.

Armed soldiers formed a wall in front of the palace gates as people yelled on the marble stairs. Some were angry at the soldiers, while others argued amongst themselves. They were all enraged about different concerns, wanting to protect what they thought was best for them.

The soldiers pointed their sharp weapons at the angry mob, while the soldiers on the rooftops pointed their crossbows at the Vakandi, not daring to shoot. Erydis could not see how the situation could be resolved without a battle.

Thylac was still talking. "... but how did they manage to bring so many people into the city without raising the alarm? Yes, Ferus had climbed the wall without being seen, but that would be dangerous for most people.

Of course, the best solution was to bring the Vakandi in from underneath the city, through the underground river. But to do so, I needed help from someone inside the Tower."

"Master Herra," Erydis guessed. "He trusts you."

"Indeed. Knowing that Herra was a spokesman of peace and a long-time friend, I asked him for help to dig a tunnel from the caves under the tower into a small house I bought in the Hidden Barrio. He took some time to convince, but he simply asked me to do things peacefully. It took months and some of Herra's Machina inventions, but I finally created a path for the Vakandi to enter the city through the underground river.

"But I still had another task to finish. I needed to find a way to invade the city without killing the innocent. The idea was given to me by the Arma and Alchemia Master, Liudmila. One day, we talked about the dust during one of my shifts at the tower. Then she told me about this new form of dust capable of manipulating cognition. Mind control—the purple dust."

Erydis gasped silently. She knew the answer, but hearing him saying those words confirmed what she feared.

"Liudmila told me that she had found an ancient formula to create a mixture that was the solution to not killing innocent people. The formula was started by Vakandi Siopi himself and was finished by Liudmila with the purple dust. A mixture that would not kill anyone, but could subdue an army. It was perfect, and I didn't even ask for it."

A masked Vakandi approached Ferus, who then approached Thylac.

"We are about to start the parade, Thylac," Ferus said under his mocking mask.

"Let's begin," Thylac said.

A clean note from a trumpet pierced the air and the people of Dust City fell quiet. The doors of the palace opened and the soldiers stepped back, pointing their weapons to whatever was about to appear.

An orchestra took to the street, walking down the marble stairs towards the marble plaza below. Masked Vakandi walked with people from Dust City, playing accordions, trumpets, bells, and guitars. Erydis felt afraid as she listened to the fake cheerful music.

Behind that orchestra was a group of people wearing animal outfits.

Some of them were mixers, others soldiers and people who had been at the palace party. Erydis saw people she recognised, like Tulia, Kori, and Aerzzo. They all walked with that soulless stare, moving oddly. The people outside started screaming with horror as they recognised those who roamed in the group. Marching in front of them was Eko under his monkey mask, playing the trumpet.

"The Festival of Sorrow," Thylac said, smiling. "I have to thank another person who helped me, but I don't see her anywhere."

"Kemia…" Erydis said, disappointed in her mentor.

Thylac nodded.

"I knew I wouldn't be able to finish that formula without the unstable black dust. So I asked Kemia if she could help me to finish the mixture to stop the war. And she helped me well. She showed me an experiment of hers. The dust pearls, which had such a powerful effect, was all I needed to finish my mixture, along with all the purple dust, which I could get from the dust chamber in the tower.

"She gave me the dust pearls when you asked me to help you get into the palace."

Erydis recalled Kemia giving something to Thylac that day.

"I had to try the mixture on someone. I decided to give it to Trinos since I never liked the man. I kidnapped him and took him to Elias's house, your old home, where I crafted the mixture. It was a success, but then you spotted me walking on the streets of the Hidden Barrio. You went to your old home and ran to alert the others after seeing Trinos. I had to eliminate the evidence by burning the house down.

"But the mixture worked. That was all that mattered. I recently found a proper name for it."

Eko started playing a grim song on his trumpet while the rest of the orchestra went quiet. Erydis had heard it once before. Six notes repeated over and over, sung by someone she knew in the Vault of Echoes.

"Do you want to know the name I've given to that powerful mixture, Erydis?" Thylac asked.

But Erydis knew exactly what he was about to say.

"Miasma."

As people danced in the streets below, Erydis finally understood. She had made a terrible mistake. This was the real beginning of the curse that would spread through the land.

"Rapach, I'm sorry."

Rapach

The stone house was dark and the wind outside fiercer than before. Joie and the old man were sleeping. Nintai watched over her sister with concern, silently feeding Benu.

Rapach felt there was nothing else he could do to help them other than to wait patiently. But he was worried that the wind would get even stronger.

He wondered if Erydis was in danger from the Silent People and whether he really was from the past. He wondered if he could do something to help her in her time.

Rapach glanced at the old man. He had to give him the package, but he also knew the old man needed to rest to recharge in case they had to go out again.

He noticed that the old man had fallen asleep with something in his hands. He was holding on to it tightly. As he got closer, Rapach noticed the old man was holding the monkey mask Rapach had seen inside his leather sack the previous day.

He took the mask slowly from the man's hands to put it back in the leather bag, but he couldn't stop himself from admiring it.

It looked as old as the man did, with scratches everywhere and dust caught in the irregular gaps. As he tried to clean it, Rapach noticed a deep scratch on the back. He tried to rub it out, but then he realized it was not a scratch. Something was written there.

He squinted to make out the words.

Then he felt the wind knocked out of him as he saw the name written on the mask.

"Erydis Nott."

Chapter XXVI

The Grand Finale

Erydis

All that time, she had been trying to understand where Rapach came from. At first, she thought the vault was a dream, a projection of her subconsciousness. Then she thought Rapach was just someone real from far away. And finally they had realised that he was from a different time; the past. But they had been wrong.

Rapach, her friend from Vault of Echoes, was from the future.

Then she thought about the clock in the vault. Maybe the clock meant she had five days to fix the horrible future Rapach was living in. But how could she do that when there was no one who could help her in Dust City? Not even the two people she cared for the most, Kemia and Thylac.

Everyone stared as the Festival of Sorrow started. The hypnotised danced, unnaturally synchronised as Eko kept playing those six notes Rapach once sang, and musicians with accordions played at his side.

"It wasn't easy," Thylac said. "To create something like the miasma took me a long time. But now that I see its full potential, it is overwhelming how easy it is to use."

Thylac placed his hand on Erydis's shoulder. She was listening, but her mind was trying to unravel a knot of thoughts.

Eko suddenly stopped playing, turning to locate Erydis. But a dancer led him away from the stage.

"Look at all of those who inhaled it," Thylac continued casually. "They walk and stare in an odd manner because they are in this state of slumber where they are conscious enough to understand my orders. Now, remember the green liquid I poured over the mask?"

Erydis nodded, her eyes glistening.

"When I inhale it, I can manipulate anyone who inhales the miasma. That's the effect of mixing the–"

"Purple dust."

"Exactly. You have always been so clever. Now, look..."

He moved his hands as he spoke some words in a language that didn't make sense to Erydis. Suddenly, the lifeless-looking people started dancing together in couples as the music continued. The people watching the parade looked scared, not knowing if they should run or stay.

"The language I use is an ancient dialect I learned long ago," Thylac said. "But to make them follow my instructions, words don't really matter. What matters is my thoughts. Saying things aloud is just me playing around."

As he talked, a man wearing nothing but his underwear started dancing in the centre of the plaza, his movements comical yet haunting.

"Engyl has joined the Festival of Sorrow." Thylac laughed and gestured towards the dancing man. "It was always frustrating to obey him. It was difficult to stand by my beliefs while carrying out his commands. I do not wish to kill him, just to make him act like the fool he really is. Now, Engyl, dance on one foot."

The Emperor obeyed, hopping on one foot as the soldiers around him looked terrified.

"Now, crawl like a dog and lick the people's feet."

The Emperor obeyed once more, immediately dropping to the ground and licking the feet of the man beside him. The man stepped back, screaming. Thylac and several Vakandi laughed. But to Erydis's surprise, some of the other Vakandi looked like they didn't approve of what was taking place.

"Horrible...that's horrible," Erydis whispered.

"Now watch this." Thylac spoke a string of words in that ancient language again, and the soulless people grabbed members of the audience to make them dance with them. Some danced along, confused, while others fought back.

More hypnotised people kept moving to the centre of the plaza as the accordion player continued playing his haunting tune. Erydis knew something was wrong when she saw Eko walk away.

Erydis noticed that one of the accordion players was Isaac Droka. He had been hypnotised as well.

Suddenly the accordion players did something to their instruments, which started emitting purple clouds. Everything turned into chaos. People tried to run away, fight back, but the plaza was rapidly getting shrouded in the purple cloud. *This must be the miasma Rapach had talked so much about,* Erydis thought. As people breathed it in, they stopped fighting, their stares turning soulless.

Some of the Vakandi started applauding and cheering, while others watched in fear.

"This is the only way, Erydis," Thylac said. "This is just a necessary measure to avoid war and the death of the innocent."

Erydis felt a chill. She hated to admit it, but she agreed with him. It was this or death.

"I ask you, as your old friend, to help me in the reconstruction of this city. Erydis, will you join me?"

Erydis looked at the people desperately running away from the miasma as the Vakandi closed the doors to the palace. It was a horrifying sight. She had once thought the arrival of the Vakandi was exciting. Now she deeply regretted it.

She didn't have any option but to join Thylac. Or did she? She couldn't make up her mind. Was this really better than death?

"Thylac, can I think about it first?" she asked. "I need to calm down."

Thylac stared at her from behind the lion mask. "You're not a prisoner, Erydis. You're my friend. I'll wait for you at the palace. I'll make sure those who slumber help you in and out of the main doors. When you get back, I want to show you the festival's grand finale."

Erydis nodded. She took one last look at the Marble Barrio below them. Everywhere she looked, people were now dancing mindlessly to that haunting tune. Those who had not managed to run away had joined the parade. The Vakandi had won.

Not knowing what else to do, Erydis slowly walked home. People were scuttling around the streets, trying to find places to hide from the miasma. There was crying and yelling as some of the hypnotised took over the Dust Ring to dance and spread the miasma with their accordions. Erydis wondered why they didn't seem to be coming after her too. Perhaps Thylac had ordered the Silent People to avoid hypnotising her.

She debated with herself. Was Thylac right? After seeing the horrified faces of the innocent, Erydis didn't know anymore. She wanted to leave it all behind. To forget about Thylac saving her life before, to forget about admiring Kemia, and forget about that clock with the five numbers. Why hadn't the Witness told her what to do?

She climbed up the ladder to her home, took off her satchel, and took out her experiment, setting it on the desk. Then she sat down and simply stared into space, grateful for the silence. There she could finally think.

She looked at the useless notes on her desk. Her experiment had all been for nothing. Even if it worked, she could not see how it would help her now. She had no one.

Then Erydis heard a noise. Someone was climbing the ladder outside. Eko's face appeared from behind the entrance curtain.

"What are you doing here?" Erydis asked coldly.

Eko entered the room, but he was not alone. Kemia's face appeared behind him, a stern expression on her face.

"You…you knew…" Erydis started. Her blood was boiling with anger.

"Erydis, let me explain," Kemia said, Eko watching them silently.

"Why should I listen to you? Will you lie to me again, like everyone else?"

"Erydis, I don't ask for forgiveness. I just want you to hear my version of what happened, and then you can judge me as you should."

Erydis stared at Kemia defiantly. As angry as she was with her, she still couldn't help being curious about what she had to say. Erydis nodded.

"Before I completed the first dust pearls, months before the Festival of Many Dusts started, Thylac came to me," Kemia began. "He told me who his family was, and how much he wanted justice for the Vakandi Clan.

"He had one of the most complex formulas I'd ever seen. It required the use of purple dust, which not many have researched. I did not understand how Thylac had gotten it, but he told me if I helped him, the mixture would have the power to subdue every soldier who fought back.

"I'd seen what the Emperor and Liudmila were capable of, Erydis. They took all my black dust research and used it to create horrible things, inside and far from Dust City. You have no idea how many people suffered because of them.

"So I agreed to help Thylac. I explained to him what he had to do, and he did it. The only missing piece was a large amount of black dust. So I offered Thylac the dust pearls when they were ready.

"During the Inauguration Festival, Thylac introduced me to Ferus, who asked me if I knew people who could join their cause. I suggested you, Erydis. You are always smart with your decisions, and I was sure they could help you finish your experiment. So Ferus sent Eko to find you. And help you did, Erydis."

"So that's how you two know each other," Erydis said to Eko, who looked as miserable as she felt.

"He did it for his people, and he believed Thylac, like I did," Kemia said. "But then you told me something very curious the day Trinos went missing. You told me about Rapach hiding from Silent People and the miasma. And you also told me about their leader, the man in the lion mask.

"There was no way you could have found out about our plan, much less know about Thylac's mask, so how could you know so much? I thought that perhaps the blue amber around your neck somehow gave you visions. Visions of something that was about to come. Rapach told you about a miasma that did not exist yet, and told you the person responsible was a man with a lion mask. I'd never believed in premonitions, but this was remarkable."

Erydis felt the weight easing off her shoulders. She couldn't explain how she knew it, but she believed Kemia was telling the truth. Maybe, after all, Erydis had people she could trust.

Kemia continued. "If your prediction is true, and Rapach told you of a land covered in miasma, that means Thylac wants to use the miasma for more than just subduing the Emperor and his soldiers. I didn't believe it until this morning when he showed me the first hypnotised, Trinos. Then I was sure of his real intentions. If he hypnotised someone who has no correlation to the Emperor, then he would not hesitate to use the miasma against other people.

"Now that I know my theory is right, I believe the reason you met that boy in the Vault of Echoes is to stop Thylac."

Erydis felt the blood rush to her head.

"But I don't understand...how can I do that…"

"That's for you to discover, Erydis. But I believe I can assist you. Good thing you showed me the blue amber and its great power. I spent nights researching it further, and I found something. You see, I thought the miasma had no antidote. I couldn't find a way to reverse the effect of the hypnotism it caused.

"When you inhale the miasma, the body enters a sleeping state where consciousness is dependent on someone else's orders. The good thing about the miasma is that it seems to have an anti-ageing effect; although I don't believe someone would trade ageing for an eternal slumber. But I found a way to reverse the symptoms of the miasma. Your blue amber has amazing power indeed. It did not take me long to find a way to use it against the terrible purple mixture."

Kemia opened her pouch and took out four flasks with shining blue gas in them.

"This is the essence of blue amber, which is the only antidote to the miasma. I want you to have it. But beware. The antidote in each flask is only enough to save one person, so use it wisely."

Kemia handed the flasks to Erydis, who stared at the blue essence in awe. "But why me?" she asked, suddenly feeling overwhelmed.

"Erydis, look around your room. All those plans on the walls, the mixtures on your desk. You are my brightest student."

Erydis stared at Kemia. To hear her mentor say that took her breath away. Kemia glanced at Erydis's experiment on the desk.

"I now understand what your experiment is meant to do," Kemia said. "If it works, you will be surprised by its potential. You are brilliant, Erydis, and as you know, I don't say that lightly."

Erydis froze, but she felt a flame burning inside of her.

"Kemia, why does this sound like a farewell?" she asked.

"I must leave Dust City," Kemia said. "I need to hide from those people who would exploit my discoveries, and I want to learn to understand where your blue amber came from. I would ask you to follow me, but if there is something you can do to stop this madness, you should go back to the palace and find it there. Thylac trusts you more than anyone else, so I doubt you're in danger—for now.

"Just remember, Erydis, that if you think hard enough with that brilliant mind of yours, nothing will stop you. Not even time."

Kemia then opened the entrance curtain with her hand and looked at Eko standing next to it.

"Eko, take care of Erydis. You are now her most important protector. Do you understand?"

Eko puffed out his chest and nodded. And just like that, Kemia was gone.

Erydis knew there was nothing she could do about it. She thought of running after her, asking her why. Why was she going away at a time like this? Why was she leaving her behind with such a big task and no real answers? Then she looked at the flasks in her hands. Deep inside, she was sure the way out was in her head. She just had to think.

"Eko, we have to go back to the palace," Erydis said. "Maybe I can convince Thylac to stop this madness, but we still need a second plan in case everything goes against us."

Eko stared at her and then started writing on a loose leaf of paper lying on her desk.

If anything goes wrong, we must get out of Dust City. We can go down to the Mist Caves under the tower and get out of Dust City through the underground river. My clan and I reached the caves on rafts that were hid-

den there.

Erydis nodded. "Eko, sorry for not trusting you before. We have to do this. The life of a good friend and the future of these lands depends on it."

Erydis quickly packed the flasks and her experiment into her backpack and slung it over her shoulders. Then she and Eko ran towards the Hidden Barrio together. That was where most of the city's people had fled to; to hide in the shadows of the second floor while the hypnotised wandered through the other barrios. Erydis had never seen the city like this, so dark and dangerous. For a moment, she missed the boring days of working at the Dusty Corner. This made her think of Kitri. She hoped she was safe.

Eko and Erydis managed to reach the marble stairs, where some of the Silent People were still dancing. The miasma had dissipated. As they went up the stairs, Erydis looked at the Vakandi observing the city from the fortress. Some looked on with a sickening smile, some with a sort of regret on their faces. She even saw some of them dancing in the plaza. It seemed the miasma had claimed some Vakandi, too.

As they approached the doors to the palace, a Vakandi saw them coming and whistled to someone to open the doors. Inside, many Vakandi were cheering and dancing to haunting music being played by a group of hypnotised musicians in the gardens.

Around the fountain in the middle of the garden were some Vakandi throwing fruit at the statue of the Finder, Orn. Ferus was there too, toasting his fellow clan members with a golden cup. Then he saw Erydis and Eko.

"Little brother! You're finally here!" He lifted his mocking mask and drank from the cup. "For a moment there, I thought you had become one of those."

As he walked towards them, a Vakandi man approached Ferus and grabbed him by the tunic.

"What have you done?! You promised us you would use that thing against the soldiers, not against innocent people! My brother was there!"

A group of Vakandi grabbed the man and threw him to the floor.

"This is the best option we had," Ferus said, fixing his tunic. "And I promise you, I'll make sure to bring your brother back to his senses, but not today."

"And when will that be?!"

"That is something I have to talk about with a certain someone," Ferus said, turning to face the tower. As he did, his smile faded.

"We are looking for him, Ferus," Erydis said, as the Vakandi looked at her. "Where is Thylac?"

"He is waiting for you next to the doors of the tower." Ferus stared at Eko. "Brother, we should talk about what just happened."

Eko shook his head and gesticulated.

"What's gotten into you?! Erydis and Thylac need to talk alo—"

"Eko is coming with me," Erydis said firmly.

The Vakandi laughed at Erydis's reaction, but Ferus's smile faded.

"Very well then, but when you're done, I want to apologise to you both. I know this was a great surprise to everyone." Ferus's face was a mixture of sadness and regret.

Erydis walked away. Eko glanced at his brother with disappointment as he followed her.

Thylac was waiting for Erydis in the shadows next to the tower doors, his hands folded behind his back. He was wearing the imposing lion mask and staring at Erydis silently as she slowly approached him.

This was it. She had to handle this moment smartly and carefully if she wanted to convince Thylac to do things right.

"Erydis, thank you for coming back," he said. "Did you have enough time to think everything through?"

Erydis was thoughtful. She had to play her game well.

"I believe so," she said. "I do not agree with controlling people this way, but I understand the purpose."

She waited for a reaction, but Thylac just stared at her for what felt like an eternity.

"I know you don't agree, but I want you to look around us," he finally said. "Even amongst the Vakandi there are disagreements.

"Many didn't like the idea of the miasma, which I was afraid of. I even saw doubt about my methods in Ferus's eyes. But I am sure it is necessary to bring peace to this senseless rivalry. I promise."

Erydis looked at Thylac thoughtfully, thinking that he could be right.

"Now I invite you and Eko into the tower," he said. "There are more important matters I need to discuss with you."

Suddenly the doors to the tower were opened from the inside by a group of Silent People. Erydis gasped.

Not only Trinos was among them, but also Kitri, Isaac, and Herra. With them were people she didn't know personally but had regularly seen in Dust City. People she once didn't even care about, obeying the man she had once trusted the most, their eyes staring soullessly from purple irises.

But Erydis tried not to react. She had to be strong.

"Why are we going inside?" she asked. "When is your grand finale starting?"

Thylac stopped, turning slightly to face Erydis, and pointed to the sky.

"It has already begun," he said quietly.

Erydis felt her skin crawl as she looked up at the sky. Giant clouds of miasma were streaming out of the tower from the windows on the top floors. The clouds were slowly covering the night sky without anyone noticing.

Eko looked at Erydis and then stared skywards as well. He looked petrified.

"Come inside, Erydis," Thylac urged.

Erydis remained frozen, looking at Eko, who seemed ready to run to his clan and tell them what was upon them. But she knew that it would be too late. She grabbed Eko's arm and pulled him inside the tower with her. She felt horrible for doing that, but it was for Eko's sake.

He tried to push Erydis aside and whistle for his brother as the clouds of miasma invaded the city, but it was too late. The doors to the tower closed behind them.

Eko broke free from Erydis's grip and ran to the closed doors. He stomped on the floor with fury, throwing himself at the doors that would not open.

And then they heard it. Vakandi everywhere were screaming and shrieking. People were thumping on the tower doors.

"Thylac! Thylac!" It was Ferus. "This is not what you promised us! This is not what Vakandi would have done! YOU TRICKSTER!"

Eko was banging on the doors, tears streaming down his face. If he had a voice, he would be screaming for his clan, his family, his brother.

And then came the silence. A kind of silence Erydis had never heard in Dust City.

Eko fell to his knees, slumping against the doors. Thylac looked at him without saying anything. A hypnotised Herra was walking towards Eko, dragging his feet.

"Eko, hear me out," Erydis said. She pushed Herra to the side, stealing something from his pocket, then knelt down next to Eko. "You have to be strong. This is how it has to be."

"Now it's done," Thylac said. A scary air of freedom surrounded him as he removed his mask. "I finally fulfilled the desire of the Vakandi to take back the Mist Grounds. Now we wait for the miasma to extend through the lands, and we'll build a prosperous empire. No more poor or rich. All working towards a single purpose—progress and technology.

"And Erydis, when the time is right, we'll find a way to bring everyone back from their slumber."

"We will," she said, trying to smile.

"But Erydis, I can't trust anyone else except you for such a task."

"What? But Eko—"

"No, Erydis, look at him. He'll fight back. I can tell by his rage."

Eko was not even trying to hide his anger.

"When everyone is ready, I'll bring Ferus back first, I promise," Thylac said.

Erydis looked at the floor, thoughtful. Then she nodded. She turned to Eko and extended a hand to him.

"Eko, please come here."

But he was scared and shook his head.

"Please, Eko, hold my hand. This is how it needs to be."

Eko stared at Erydis, breathing rapidly. Although he looked doubtful, he took her hand. As she stared at him seriously, a faint smile appeared on her face. She winked at him.

"Close your eyes," she whispered. Eko obeyed.

With a quick movement, Erydis threw her last blue dust marble to the floor. One with the letter "E" on it. It exploded, filling the founder's chamber with an immense blue cloud. She pulled Eko to his feet and they ran to the elevation chamber in the centre of the room.

They stepped in and Erydis quickly inserted the key she had stolen from Herra into the keyhole with the words Mist Caves on it. The doors closed and the elevation chamber started its descent.

"Sorry if I scared you, Eko," Erydis said as both of them tried to clean the intense blue dust from their clothes and faces. "That was my last special marble. It seems we will have to escape now."

Eko stared at her and bowed with a hand to his heart. He then smiled at her with a grateful expression.

"This is not over, Eko," Erydis said. "We still have to leave and get as far as we can from the miasma." The elevation chamber stopped and its doors opened. There was no one in the cave.

"Seems like everyone is at the parade. This is our chance, Eko."

Eko nodded, and together they ran in the direction of the river. But then they heard the elevation chamber close behind them and ascend again.

"We have to hurry!" Erydis said.

They ran swiftly and soon reached the river. It was flowing at a dangerous speed as they ran along its edge against the current.

Eko took the lead. He pointed at a dark passage to the side of the river. There, very well hidden amongst the rocks, were the rafts the Vakandi had used to reach the city.

"The only way out is towards where the clear water becomes polluted," Erydis said, looking at the darkness far ahead. "I'm not sure where it goes, but we have to hurry and risk it."

Together they pushed one of the rafts towards the river, but it was heavier than they thought, and dragging it was difficult because of the irregular ground.

The going was slow, and just as they got close to the river's edge, they heard the doors of the elevation chamber open.

"Hurry!" They pushed the raft into the river with all their might, which was taken by the current.

They ran alongside the river and Eko jumped into the raft just as Thylac appeared behind them, some Silent People with him.

For a moment, Erydis saw herself jumping onto the raft with a smile and letting the current take them away from Dust City.

But she stumbled, and the raft drifted away from her, now on the polluted side of the river. She got back up and ran as fast as she could, but she couldn't reach the raft. The raft got caught on some rocks and rocked violently from side to side in the strong current, almost throwing Eko overboard.

Erydis thought about leaping into the raft, but the water was moving too fast and she didn't want to risk falling into the polluted water.

She stared at Eko, who looked at her with concerned eyes while trying to keep his balance.

"Erydis, please stop," Thylac said from behind her. "Admit it, it's too late to escape."

"Please, Thylac, you have to stop this madness," she said.

"Erydis, I promise you I will. We'll search for a cure to the miasma when the time is right."

"What if it's never time? What if they are never ready in your eyes?"

"They will be, when I discover a cure."

"What if a cure already existed?"

Thylac went silent.

"What's inside that bag on your back?" Thylac asked, concerned. "Did Kemia gave you something?"

"What if there were a cure right now, Thylac?" Erydis's voice was breaking.

"The people are not ready," he said. "I can't let a cure exist until it is time. I need you, Erydis. I need your mind, for the sake of this city. You're more useful to me awake."

"And Eko…does he need to be hypnotised?" Erydis asked.

"Not for long, I promise."

Erydis considered her options. The raft had drifted too far away for her to jump onto it now, and refusing Thylac would mean being hypnotised. Just the thought of losing her will and freedom sounded like a nightmare.

She saw how Eko was barely able to stay on the raft, still stuck on the rocks.

"Erydis, it's over," Thylac said. "Please, you're like a sister to me. The one person in Dust City I care for the most. I need you to help me. But for now, I need Eko on our side, and I need your bag."

Erydis stared at him.

"Why do you need it?"

"I know you have your experiment in that bag. And that might not be the only thing in there. You wouldn't be carrying it around all this time if you thought it was worthless.

"Why are you so obsessed with that experiment of yours? Don't you understand that you don't need it anymore, that if you join me, you will have the whole Tower and all the dust to yourself?"

Erydis thought about it. The possibilities were endless with that much dust.

"Decide now, Erydis! Will you join me?"

"I'm sorry, Eko," she whispered.

She took the bag from her back and threw it towards Eko. But it missed the raft and the current carried it away.

"Go now, Eko!" Erydis shouted. "Fix it all! Find the cure! Find my experiment! Don't let them catch you!"

Thylac and the Silent People approached Erydis. Eko stared at her for a moment. Then he closed his eyes and pushed hard against a rock, freeing the raft. The current swept him into the darkness of the cave ahead, away from Erydis.

"A cure?! What have you done?!" Thylac asked angrily.

"Thylac, I know the future," Erydis said. "The miasma will grow, and you'll destroy many clans and cities. I know you won't stop, but I promise you. He will find you hiding in the miasma, and he'll save the Jerboa Clan, our city, and the Vakandi. Surrender now or await your end."

Thylac took his mask off and stared at her with fury. Then he started laughing.

"So you choose to lie again. Very well."

Thylac took some purple dust from his pocket and blew it gently towards her. As she stared at him, her vision became purple.

"Ra…pach," Erydis said as she felt her body go numb and her vision blurred.

"We could have become great, Erydis."

Then everything became darkness. But her smile never faded.

Chapter XXVII

Blue Sparks

Rapach

Rapach stared at the Monkey mask.

He was trying to understand why the words Erydis Nott were written on it. He thought the old man was the one the legends spoke of. A lonely man whistling, looking for something dear to him. Then he heard he was the monkey-masked man, rescuing lost children like Zelle. But after seeing her name there, a terrifying thought came to his mind.

What if the old man in front of him knew Erydis? He couldn't believe it.

He had to ask him.

Carelessly, he shook the old man who was sleeping on the floor. Nintai looked at him, curious. The old man opened his eyes, looking hopeless.

"Sorry to wake you, but I need answers to this," Rapach said, holding the monkey mask and pointing at the name Erydis Nott.

The man stared at it and closed his eyes again. But Rapach persisted.

"This girl...Erydis. I dreamed about her, and she helped me more than once with her wise advice."

The old man opened his eyes and looked at Rapach. Something flickered in his eyes.

"Erydis was your friend, wasn't she? You're the mute boy she told me about; Eko."

The old man stared at Rapach, searching for signs of a lie. He sat up and with a slow movement started searching for something in his tunic. He took out some folded pieces of paper and a pencil. He wrote on it, focused, as fast as his age allowed him. Rapach waited as he wrote. Finally he finished writing and handed Rapach a page.

"I do not comprehend how you know this much about Erydis. But believe me, she was the greatest person I ever met. She was intelligent and kind in her own way. But I broke a promise to protect her the day the man in the lion mask, Thylac, surprised us all and used that cursed miasma against his enemies and the innocent alike."

Rapach looked up at the old man. "Thylac? The man who once rescued her from her father?"

Eko nodded.

Rapach felt an anger like he never had before. He groaned and continued to read.

"The only person Thylac planned to save from the miasma was Erydis. But she did not surrender to his offer of power, not even thinking she would be hypnotised. As a last sacrifice, she helped me escape through the underground river, and I cowardly accepted her aid. I promised to protect her. But I broke that promise close to seventy years ago."

Rapach was speechless, not only because his friend, Erydis, had been taken by the miasma, but at realising that her theory about time was almost spot on.

But she had been wrong about him being from the past. He was from the future.

"Rapach, what's wrong? Your hands are shaking," Nintai asked. Rapach kept reading as the old man continued writing furiously.

"The polluted river took me in its furious current, far from the miasma that was slowly but steadily spreading through the lands. I was trying to solve the task she gave me before I escaped, to find the antidote to the miasma and to recover her experiment from the river. Fortunately I'd seen this experiment of hers before, and I knew its shape well.

"I spent years hiding from the Silent People, who searched for me as I scoured the river trying to find the bag she threw into the river that day. On my journey, I found many people lost in the lands and I helped them, just like the hero in the monkey mask in Erydis's stories. I felt like I had a reason to live.

"Years went by, and I finally found the flasks containing the blue amber essence, and the scepter that was part of her experiment. Some I obtained by trading with people I met on my journey. Others I found by luck. I found the flasks containing the antidotes, all of them. But I believe her experiment was still incomplete when I found it."

The old man took a trumpet, four flasks, and a black sceptre from his leather bag. Inside the flasks was a blue gas.

"If I'm not mistaken, there's a missing piece that should go on top of the sceptre. A piece I never found. Decades have passed, but I still don't know why Erydis held on to her experiment with such care. It has to be important. Once again, I broke my promise."

A gust of wind howled outside of the stone house, and Joie woke up. She rubbed her eyes and walked over to look at what they were reading.

Rapach couldn't believe it. There, in front of him, was Eko, the child who once upon a time helped Erydis.

"Could it be..." Rapach wondered.

He grabbed his pouch and took out the red package he was supposed to deliver to the old man.

"Sorry I didn't get a chance to tell you this before," he said. "But the reason I've been trying to find you was to give you this." He handed the package to the old man.

"On behalf of Jerboa Clan, I declare your item delivered," Rapach said.

Eko stared at the package with renewed hope.

As Rapach, Nintai and Joie looked on, he opened it.

Inside was a blue sphere of thick glass. Everyone except Eko wondered what it was. He broke into a smile.

Eko placed the sphere on top of the black sceptre, where it clicked into place. It fit perfectly. He looked up at his companions, smiling happily and victorious. He had finally fulfilled his promise to Erydis.

"What does it do?" Rapach asked.

Suddenly a strong wind hammered against the covered window, causing it to crack. A thin trail of miasma started seeping into the stone house from behind the window covering.

"Get behind me!" Rapach instructed, grabbing his shield and pointing it towards the window. "Quick! Munch on a blue flower!"

Everyone obeyed, including Eko, who didn't seem to care about anything else but Erydis's experiment. He was turning a knob on the sceptre when suddenly the window exploded into shards and a thick cloud of miasma hit Rapach's shield.

The miasma enveloped them, making it hard to see. Rapach couldn't hear anything beyond the howling of the wind. *We are doomed*, he thought.

Then he heard something whirring. The sound grew more audible as blue sparks sputtered from the sceptre in Eko's hands. Suddenly a blue flame appeared on top of the sceptre, like a torch of blue fire that illuminated the purple miasma around them.

In an instant, the miasma—and the grey dust around them—spiralled towards the sceptre and was swallowed by the blue torch. White dust fell out from an opening in the bottom of the sceptre.

It was an amazing yet terrifying spectacle, watching the typhoon of purple miasma sucked in by the dancing blue flame at the top of the sceptre.

Everyone looked at Erydis's creation in awe. Then they started laughing in disbelief, relief on everyone's faces. Even Eko looked like the kid inside him had taken over his old self, as if he had been revived after all those years.

So this was what Erydis had planned so very carefully. If Rapach understood her world correctly, she had successfully recreated the technology of the tower which she spoke of —just many times smaller—and instead of disposing of grey dust, this device could transform any dust into usable dust. This meant they finally had a weapon against the miasma.

Staring at the sceptre in Eko's hands, Rapach thought, *This can give us another chance.*

They stared into the blue flame, hopeful, until all the miasma inside the stone house was absorbed and transformed into white dust. The blue flame slowly died.

"What is all this white dust?" Joie asked, grabbing a fistful from the ground and throwing it into the air.

"That, I believe, is the dust that people used at Dust City," Rapach said. "Unfortunately, I believe no one here knows how to use it. Do you, Eko?"

Eko shook his head.

"Now that we have this, we have to go back to help the Jerboa Clan, Rapach," Nintai said.

Eko patted Nintai on the arm and handed the sceptre over to Rapach. He reached for a piece of paper and wrote:

"Going back there will be too dangerous. Silent People will be following us all the way to the east. We do have a weapon against the miasma, but we do not have the strength to fight them. However, there's something important you must know. Thylac controls the Silent People by using a tonic on his mask, Erydis told me. Assuming he uses it often, we have to make sure to take it off him in order to stop him from giving orders to the hypnotised.

"Now that most of the Silent People are distracted in the east, we shall go west, to the place now known as Miasma City."

"Miasma City?" Rapach sounded concerned. "Does this mean that Dust City is now Miasma City?"

Eko nodded and continued to write.

"After I escaped, Silent People sealed the underground caves where the river was, making it impossible to enter like we, the Vakandi, once did. But I remember that Erydis's friend, Kemia, escaped Dust City using a different route. At first, it was just a theory, but after searching many years, I found the path she took, though I have never returned since the miasma took over the place."

Rapach nodded while Nintai looked confused.

"There're many things I have yet to understand, Rapach," Nintai said. "But Joie and I will help as much as we can."

Rapach nodded, and Benu jumped onto his head.

"I promise to tell you more as we walk. Please, Eko, guide us to this path," Rapach said. Eko nodded and gripped the sceptre tightly, a spark in his eyes. They packed their things hurriedly and left the stone house, walking west in single file as the storm continued to rage around them.

Rapach used his shield to protect them from the wind, while Eko used the sceptre to illuminate their path, spinning the knob to create the blue flame that continued to swallow the miasma around them, leaving a trail of white dust.

Nintai carried Joie, who looked scared but was as determined as her big sister.

Benu was in Rapach's hair, looking at the horizon as they followed Eko.

Rapach realised the miasma had become much less menacing. He smiled fondly, thinking of what Erydis had done for them.

After walking for a while, Eko pointed at a well in the distance. It looked dry, with grey dust caking its walls.

When the party reached it, Eko climbed down, clinging onto crimson vines in the inside of the well. The rest followed him, descending into the dark abyss below.

At the bottom of the well was a cave.

Eko reignited the blue flame, and together, they walked in silence, tracing the hidden route to Miasma City.

They walked for what could have been a full day, only stopping to rest and eat a few times. At least they were safe from the dust storm in such a humid place. The silence was overwhelming at times, so Rapach told Nintai, Joie, and Eko everything that had happened to him over the last five days.

"So you've seen it," Nintai said, convinced.

"I've seen what?"

"The spirit world. Talking with someone from the past can only happen there," she said.

"Well, I suppose that's what it was. But Erydis is no spirit. Eko knows."

Eko nodded with the silly smile of a child.

"So the plan is to go into Miasma City, find Erydis, stop this Thylac, and somehow use only four potions to save everyone affected by the miasma," Nintai said, sounding genuinely concerned. "Sounds a tad too ambitious, if you ask me."

"But if we're careful and as silent as the shadows, we might be able to make it," Rapach said confidently, barely believing it himself.

"But we don't know what is waiting for us on the other end. None of you know how much this Dust City has changed since you last saw it," Nintai said. "The dust you speak of, if its power is real, I doubt we have any chance against the Silent People."

Nintai glanced at her sister with concern. The way she was looking at Joie reminded Rapach of how Mat used to watch over him on their journeys. He realised that he had to do for Nintai what Mat would have done for him.

"I know you're worried," he said, thinking of what Mat would have said if she were there with them. "I know this is dangerous, but the Silent People are out there. If we don't stop them, they'll take my clan first and then spread to the south, to yours."

"Rapach, we might have a weapon against the miasma, but I bet they have technology we have never seen," Nintai said. "If they know we're there, I don't know what our fate will be."

"Nintai, think about it," Rapach said. "Right now, of all the people in the Miasma Realm, we are the only ones with knowledge of the miasma and how it started," Rapach said. "I know it's a lot to ask of you. We might not be many and we might not be the strongest of our clans. But we are the only ones who can do something to stop all this."

"And how exactly will we do that?" There was a slight tremor of panic in Nintai's voice now.

"His mask. The lion mask. We need to take it from him, don't we, Eko?"

Eko nodded, patting Rapach on the back. Nintai stared at them, holding Joie's shoulder. Joie squeezed her sister's hand. "Nini, I trust the jerboa boy," Joie said. "If we don't help him, no one else will."

Nintai's gaze lingered on Joie, seemingly unconvinced, but then she smiled faintly.

"You're braver than your sister, little bug."

She looked back at Rapach and Eko, took a deep breath, and nodded. "As silent as the shadows it is, then."

They walked deeper into the cave for what seemed like a really long time, not stopping to rest again. Finally, they saw a hint of the end. A light was shining through from between some stones and packed dirt above them, and they could hear faint sounds from an unknown source.

"Is this it, Eko?" Rapach asked. Eko nodded, looking full of life, as if he'd been conserving his energy all those years just for that day.

"Joie, from now on, we have to be quiet and alert, understand?" Nintai asked.

"Yes, Nini." She hugged Nintai around the waist.

"Benu, are you ready?" Benu jumped up and down twice on Rapach's head.

"Is everyone ready?"

They nodded nervously, staring up at the rays of light above them. Rapach turned and slowly started removing bits of dirt and pebbles from around the cracks where the light was shining through. Suddenly, the rocks gave way and tumbled down from above them, and the group jumped out of the way. There was now a narrow opening in the cave above them, wide enough to fit through.

Rapach hoisted himself up through the gap and peeked out cautiously.

To his surprise, there was no miasma. He seemed to be between two buildings that were very close to each other, which would explain why this entrance to the cave had not been discovered. Once he was sure the area was clear, he climbed up and out onto the ground above the cave, gesturing at the others to follow him. He pulled them up one by one.

"I'll check around the corner," Rapach said once everyone was out. "Eko, can you come with me? You're the only one who has been here before, so we need to know where we are."

Eko nodded, and together they walked to the end of the narrow alley. They peered into the street carefully, each covering a corner. They couldn't quite understand what they were seeing.

People were going about their business—merchants hawking, soldiers marching, couples walking hand in hand, children playing.

But something was amiss. Although their actions seemed normal at first glance, something didn't feel quite right. They all had a soulless stare and a forced expression on their faces, as if it was all an act. Even though their activities seemed to be normal, the way they interacted with one another and moved were unnatural.

Then it dawned on Rapach. Someone was forcing these people to act as if everything was alright in the city.

Suddenly, a group of Silent People walked right in front of him. He jumped, thinking that they were going to be attacked. But the Silent People simply passed by as if he were invisible. Could it be that the Silent People were unable to see them?

In a moment of boldness—or what Mat would have called stupidity—Rapach stepped out into the wide street. All around him, people continued going about their day. All of them ignored him. It was like he had stepped into a ghost city where its citizens lived every day in the same way, merely imitating the lives they once had.

He felt sad. These people once had dreams but were denied their lives because of the curse. It was all Thylac's fault.

His thoughts were interrupted by more Purple Breathers approaching. Unlike the rest of the people in the street, this group moved with purpose and seemed to be searching for something. Rapach darted back to the gap between the buildings where he had left the others.

"Are you mad?" Nintai asked, breathless. "You want to get us all caught?"

"Something was amiss," Rapach said. "I had to do it, and I learned something. From what I deduced, the Silent People with no masks are forced to live the same way they used to. They didn't even glance at me as I walked next to them.

"As for the Purple Breathers, they are the ones we should be careful of. It looks like they're looking for something or someone."

"Phew! I thought we would have to run and rescue you," Nintai said. "What about you, Eko? Does the city appear like it was before?"

Eko already had a piece of paper out and was writing quickly.

"The people seem to be acting just like they once did in Dust City, but they are not themselves anymore. Just like you said, Rapach. As for the city, there are a few differences.

"The second floor of the city, or the Palace Barrio, is gone, and what once was the Hidden Barrio now has walls around it to protect the Tower.

"Another big difference is the fortress surrounding the city. There appears to

be many towers that weren't there before. And all the towers are connected to the main tower, in the middle of the city, by bridges."

"All these changes to the city," Nintai said, half-impressed, "they were made in only seventy years?"

"With the way these people are acting, I wouldn't be surprised if they were forced to build everything," Rapach said. "With so many people working together, it doesn't seem too crazy to be true." He frowned at the thought of people having to work so hard against their will.

"I suppose so," Nintai said. "But if it's been so long since the people were hypnotised, why don't they look old?"

Rapach hadn't considered that before. Nintai was right. The people walking the streets were all hypnotised, but if they had been living in Dust City before they fell victim to the miasma seventy years ago, then why wasn't everyone as old as Eko?

Joie tugged at Rapach's hand. "Eko is still writing."

"Before Kemia left the city, she mentioned that the miasma has an anti-ageing effect. Silent People are still the same age as they were when they got hypnotised. They don't age."

Rapach thought for a moment. "If this is true, then maybe Erydis is still the same age she was in the Vault of Echoes. Unless Thylac found an antidote to wake her up from the miasma's effect."

"Then Thylac must have aged, though?" Nintai asked.

"Unless he found a way to stop aging without the miasma. But there's only one way to find out." Rapach looked up at the Tower in the middle of the city. "He must be in the Tower."

Suddenly, Benu hopped off Rapach's head. She jumped up and down on the ground.

"Benu, this is not the time to play," Joie said.

"No, I think she wants us to look at her," Rapach said.

Benu jumped out into the street.

"She wants us to follow her!" Rapach said excitedly. "Let's go! But be careful, and watch out for Silent People with masks on."

They walked slowly through the wide street, following the jerboa in single file. An unnerving silence reigned in the streets. None of the Silent People were actually holding a conversation, they were just pretending, strange droning sounds coming from their mouths without forming real words.

Suddenly Rapach saw another group of Purple Breathers searching the streets, exhaling miasma from behind their pearly masks.

Although Rapach and his entourage were no longer worried about the miasma, they couldn't risk being found out by Thylac.

They hid behind a tent where a hypnotised man was pretending to sell trinkets. The Purple Breathers stared at the store for a few tense seconds but then moved along.

Rapach and the others waited for the Breathers to disappear around a corner. Then they emerged from their hiding place and caught up with Benu. She continued weaving through legs and crates, leading them towards one of the new towers next to the wall of the city.

The group reached the doors, which opened and closed as the hypnotised entered and exited. Above the doors was a sign that read "*Dijenia Tower*".

"What is Benu doing?" Nintai asked. "Where is she taking us?"

Rapach studied their surroundings. "I believe she wants us to go into this tower and up to the bridge that connects to the main Tower in the centre of the city."

Benu jumped up and down a couple of times.

"How does Benu know where to go?" Nintai wondered.

"I believe Benu has been here—inside Erydis's blue amber. She must have been freed from the amber at some point in the past and somehow managed to leave the city, ending up in the Jerboa Grasswoods, where I found her."

"Poor Benu…you've travelled a long way."

"We should hurry inside," Rapach interrupted. "Benu, can you go inside and see if there are any Purple Breathers? Can you do that for us?"

Benu stared at him and hopped through the gap under the door.

As they waited, Rapach thought of Erydis. Was she still a prisoner in that place, like all the people of the city? He wondered if she was still hypnotised or if Thylac regretted what he had done and brought her back from slumber.

Benu wriggled back out from under the door, looked at them, and went back inside again.

"Let's go!"

Rapach pushed open the doors to reveal an elegant entrance hall. Statues of feline-looking djinni were facing them from opposite corners. On the wall, in big letters, were the words: "*In memory of the brave beasts of dust.*"

"That looks like the djinni that attacked us," Nintai said. "But what is this place? It looks like some sort of monument to the djinni, as if they were all dead, but they're not."

Eko wrote:

"Many years ago, the founder of this city, Orn Ryk, obliterated every djinni in these lands. Nevertheless, over the last decades, I've seen a few, all of them working for the Silent People. I fear that Thylac brought them back somehow."

"In the lands in the south, the djinni never died. They're rare, but they belong in the wild," Nintai said.

"Let's move on," Rapach said. "I see some stairs ahead. They might lead us to the bridge."

They went up the stairs, following Benu's lead. Their surroundings started getting darker as they walked to the upper floor, where an open door led to a low-lit chamber.

"I can't see anything," Joie said.

Rapach pointed at a lamp that was giving off green light in the centre of the room. "Maybe we can use that," he said.

They approached the lamp, which barely cast any shadows in the chamber.

"So this is how they use the dust," Rapach said, observing green smoke spiraling from the lamp. "How do I make it brighter?"

"Nini, I can hear something in the dark," Joie said.

Rapach finally found a knob on the side of the lamp, which he turned, growing the flames inside the lamp and illuminating the chamber with a powerful green light.

Then they saw what was making the noise.

All around them were red metallic cages. Inside were creatures with colourful patterns on their skin—some were small and had tiny wings while others looked like wolves with abnormally large tails. There were also some feline-looking animals, similar to the one that had attacked them, but smaller.

"Djinnis." Rapach looked around at all the beautiful yet abnormal creatures.

"But look," Nintai said, pointing. "That shiny, silver circle on their heads. Only djinnis that follow the Silent People have them. In the lands in the south, I never saw that mark."

"The djinni that attacked us had it, too. Maybe that's how they are controlled—via the mark," Rapach said.

"No, look at this." Nintai pointed at a table with open books. "Here it reads: *'Fifth group of man-made djinni did not respond to orders. I will order Aerzzo Chimara to create a new specimen and get rid of the rest by the end of the season.'* Man-made djinni? How is that possible? Using the power of the dust?"

"Nini, we can't let them die," Joie said, looking at a rabbit-like djinni.

"I know, Joie, but for now we have to stop Thylac," Nintai said. Rapach had to agree with her, but he, too, felt sorry for the beasts.

Eko approached them and started writing on a piece of paper on the table.

"I have a plan. Rapach and Nintai, I believe those big doors at the side of this room lead to the bridge. I'll have to ask you to cross it to reach the central tower while I keep Joie safe with me here. Please find Erydis and stop Thylac."

Rapach stared at him. This room was probably going to be the safest place for them, so it wasn't a terrible idea. "I guess there's no other way, is there?"

Rapach looked at Nintai, who nodded.

"Joie, please look after Eko," Nintai said. "He will need your help."

Joie threw herself at her sister and hugged her.

Eko patted Rapach on the arm and handed him the sceptre.

"Thank you, Eko. Please be safe."

Eko smiled at him before putting on his monkey mask.

Rapach and Nintai walked to the doors leading to the bridge, and looked at each other . Rapach grabbed Benu and placed her in his pouch. Then, slowly, he grabbed the cold handle of the door, which was vibrating from the fierce wind outside. He closed his eyes, knowing that real danger awaited them behind the door.

"Mat, Erydis, we're almost there," he whispered as he pushed the door open and felt the wind hit his face mercilessly.

Chapter XXVIII

Shattering Glass

Rapach

Their hair and clothes flapped in the wind as they stood on the bridge, staring at the central tower at the other end, an imposing silhouette against the sky full of moving clouds.

They could see the city below them. Traces of dust hit their faces as they walked towards the tower. Rapach could see the strong and imposing fortress around them, giant mills rotating at a dizzying speed, pushing away clouds of dust and miasma. That explained why there was less dust and miasma here compared to other parts of the Miasma Realm.

But before he could share that insight with Nintai, a wall of aggressive wind almost knocked them over. They grabbed the crimson railing of the bridge, looking at the ground below. Rapach felt dizzy.

"At least there are no Purple Breathers here," he said as he walked on, sticking close to the railing.

"I don't think we'll be this lucky once we enter the tower. Rapach, do you hear that?"

He strained to listen, but it was difficult to hear anything over the wind. Then he heard it; the sound of machinery grinding in the wind. At first he thought it must be coming from the mills on the fortress, but he was wrong. The sound was closer.

Rapach finally saw the source of the sound. Not too far from them, close to one of the small towers to their left, was a flying machine Rapach had never seen the likes of.

It was round and black and made mainly of metallic blades rotating at an incredible speed. On top of it sat a Silent Person that seemed to be controlling the flying machine with a round wheel and levers as the wind pushed it from side to side. Behind him sat two Purple Breathers who searched for intruders using orange lights.

"How is that possible?" Nintai asked.

"Down!" Rapach instructed. "Stay crouched under the railing. Hopefully we can make it to the other side before they see us."

They took cover behind the railing and did their best to scramble over to the other side as quickly and carefully as they could. But the wind was against them, slowing them down.

Rapach could see the black flying machine through the gaps of the railing.

They were halfway over the bridge when the flying machine suddenly got closer to them. Rapach signalled at Nintai to stop and they crouched down even lower. Orange spotlights swept the area close to them several times. Rapach closed his eyes, hoping they would go away.

Eventually he could not hear the machine anymore. Confused, he stood up. It was gone.

"We should hurry," Rapach said.

Suddenly, the machine flew straight up from under the bridge and hovered above them, shining a blinding light on Rapach and Nintai.

They froze as the flying machine got closer to them.

"What do we do now, Rapach?!" Nintai asked, grabbing the railing tightly.

Rapach was just about to run to the tower, when a noise suddenly came from below them on the streets.

Dozens of beasts were charging out of the doors of the tower they had just left. They ran wildly through the streets. The hypnotised population ignored them, but the Purple Breathers ran towards the chaos.

"The djinni!" Nintai said.

"Joie, Eko." Rapach smiled.

This was the perfect distraction. Rapach kicked off the floor, pulled Nintai's arm, and ran as fast as his legs could take him to the central Tower.

The Purple Breathers on the flying machine started throwing spheres covered in sharp spikes at them, which pierced the stone ground where they fell. Rapach didn't know what they were, but he knew he didn't want to be hit by one.

They reached the doors of the central Tower and tried to open them, but they were too heavy.

"Push!" Rapach shouted.

"I'm trying!" Nintai groaned.

Suddenly the spiked spheres exploded where they fell behind them, causing severe damage to the bridge and shooting rocks in every direction. Rapach had never seen a weapon that could do that.

"The bridge won't stand much longer," Rapach said as he pushed against the door as fast and hard as he could.

Something whistled and an arrow hit the door right next to Rapach's neck. He and Nintai stared at it, scared, as they kept pushing.

For the first time, the wind was on their side, pushing at the heavy doors and finally blowing them open with a loud bang. Rapach and Nintai quickly stepped inside as a couple more arrows passed near them. As they closed the heavy doors behind them, they saw a big section of the bridge collapsing onto a couple of buildings below.

It was finally quiet after they shut the door.

"I hope Joie and Eko are ok," Nintai said.

"Me too. But I'm sure we're the ones in bigger danger right now." Rapach stared at the room in front of them.

There was no one there, only several stands with jars containing dust of many colours. On the walls were ancient murals depicting Dust City and its history. It looked like it had been recently painted over. One of the murals showed the man with the lion mask and below it the words "*Vakandi's heir takes back the Mist Grounds.*"

"Seems like someone didn't like the old murals in this room," Nintai said.

"Now, where do we find Thylac?" Rapach wondered out loud. He took Benu from his pouch. "Benu, where is he?"

Benu jumped towards the middle of the room to a closed circular chamber. Rapach approached it and pulled at the door, but it wouldn't open.

"Seems like it needs a key," he said, staring at the keyhole.

Benu froze as if listening, then suddenly jumped away to hide behind a jar of dust.

"What's wrong, Benu?" Rapach asked. Then he heard something. The central chamber was vibrating as if something inside of it was making its way up towards them. "Nintai, hide!"

They ran and hid behind a stand full of jars, quietly staring at the chamber's door in anticipation.

The metal door slid open and two figures emerged. At first glance, they looked like Purple Breathers, but something was different about them.

They wore fake crimson fur around their pearl-like masks, and each wielded long, curved crimson swords in their hands and carried a short bow and quiver on their backs. They wore imposing thick red armour and walked out of the chamber in that smooth, odd gait Rapach knew so well. Each had a silver key on a chain around their necks.

"Rapach, they each have a key!" Nintai whispered. "But how do we get it?"

Rapach racked his brain.

"Taking the key from them will be impossible without getting caught," he whispered back. "I think we should remove their masks and...I suppose we'll take it from there. Perhaps we can use one of the potions on them. I must ask you to help me fight. You can take my dagger. I'll use my shield."

Nintai gave a nod, scared, as she grabbed his blue glass dagger.

"This is like a rodent fighting a lion, but I guess we don't have a choice," she said.

She was right. The Purple Breathers knew they were hiding in the chamber. There was no way they could get out of it safely now.

"Seems like they're searching in different parts of the chamber," Rapach said. "You stay here. I'll go to the other side. We'll get the masks off whomever is closest to us. Munch on a blue flower now."

Both of them took a blue flower and placed it in their mouths.

Rapach walked slowly between the stands, trying to be as quiet as he could.

Luckily the sound of the heavy armour the Purple Breathers wore was a giveaway of their whereabouts.

Rapach peeped out from between a couple of jars filled with dust. The tallest Purple Breather was getting closer. He stopped to listen, a mere two steps away from Rapach.

Rapach could feel beads of cold sweat dripping from his forehead and was worried that even his heartbeat was loud enough to be heard.

The tall Purple Breather turned his back, exposing a thick belt securing his mask.

This was Rapach's chance.

He jumped onto the Purple Breather's back and yanked at the belt, but it was fastened too tight. The Purple Breather started exhaling miasma from his mouth as Rapach kept pulling on the mask's belt till it broke.

Rapach fell to the floor with the mask in his hands. In front of him was a muscular man with a white beard and a scar on his cheek. His eyes were soulless as he raised his crimson blades. Rapach scrambled up and raised his shield just in time.

The impact of the swords threw him back against a stand, but he recovered quickly and shielded himself before the Purple Breather attacked him once more.

Rapach was flung to the ground. As he recovered, he noticed his shield was chipped. The sword was powerful enough to have done that.

He ran away from the Purple Breather, turned around, and charged with his shield in front of him. He was vaguely aware of Nintai facing off with the other Purple Breather somewhere behind him.

Rapach crashed against the Breather, hitting his head against the shield, making him dizzy for a second. The enemy was thrown back against a stand, sending the jars on it crashing all over him. A cloud of multi-coloured dust rose in the air.

Rapach waited for him to stand up, but the Purple Breather could barely move under the debris.

"Rapach!" Nintai was holding her injured arm as the unmasked hypnotised she was fighting approached her.

Rapach sprinted to stop the hypnotised Breather but missed and rolled on the ground. He got up, ignoring the pain in his arm, and stared into the enemy's eyes.

But the enemy was no stranger.

It was Mat. Her eyes were not the same as those he once knew, but her skills still were.

"Sister!" he called, but she showed no reaction. She raised her blades and attacked him, each slash landing on his shield until a crack appeared in it.

Nintai took an empty jar and bashed it down onto Mat's head. Mat then spun around and swung her blade wildly. Rapach took his chance to charge at her.

"Sorry, sister," he said as he sprinted.

His shield crashed against her, breaking into a hundred pieces. Mat fell to the ground, dropping her blades, and breaking the jar on her head. Before she could stand up, Nintai grabbed her legs and Rapach sat down on her chest.

"Your sister is a tough one!" Nintai said.

"The toughest," Rapach replied with mixed feelings. Benu jumped to his head. "You have the antidotes in your pouch, don't you, Nintai?"

Nintai grabbed one of the flasks and gave it to Rapach, who looked at it.

"This was made seventy years ago. How does it work?"

"Seems like there's gas in it. Maybe she needs to inhale it," Nintai said. Mat was still flailing around trying to free herself.

Rapach took a deep breath and placed the flask under Mat's nose. There were only four flasks. If this one failed, it would be a great loss.

He uncorked the flask, releasing the thick blue gas, which Mat inhaled slowly.

"Please, sister. Please, you have to wake up." He stared into her soulless eyes.

She slowly closed her eyes and stopped breathing, all her strength leaving her body.

"No, no, no, no, sister!" Rapach shook her as he cried, "Please, Mat, I need you. Please come back."

Nintai placed a hand on his shoulder gently. "I'm sorry, Rapach. It seems seventy years has rendered the antidote ineffective."

But at that moment, Mat's left eyebrow twitched. Then she frowned and started coughing as she tried to sit up.

"Sister?"

Mat opened her eyes. The purple shade in them had faded and her amber eyes had returned.

"Rapach? Where am I?" She tried to move and groaned. "Why does everything hurt?"

"Mat, you're back. You truly are."

Rapach wanted to hug his sister tightly but had to stop himself because of her pain.

"What is happening?" She looked around the room, confused. "We were at Rabaska Lake. Where is the man in the lion mask?"

Rapach nodded.

"He got a hold of you and hypnotised you with the miasma," he explained. "Many things have happened since that day, but all you need to know right now is that we found that man, and we're in his city."

"Wait, how many days has it been?" Mat asked. "It feels like it wasn't that long ago."

"It's been almost a week, Mat."

"It feels like I slept for a couple of hours." She struggled to stand up and picked up the crimson blades. "So we're in his city. Are we trying to get him?"

Rapach nodded.

"His mask...that's how he controls the Silent People. I believe he must be on the top floor of this tower, isn't he Benu?"

Benu jumped up and down twice.

"Then let's get going." Mat stared at Nintai. "Hello, I don't believe we've met."

"Nintai," Nintai said with a polite nod. "Rapach, we should hurry."

"Mat, we need the key hanging from your neck," Rapach said. Mat gave him the key and they walked to the round chamber in the middle of the room.

They stepped in and looked at the five keyholes on the wall. Next to the top one was the inscription *Dust Machine Chamber*.

"Rapach, behind you!" Nintai said, alarmed.

He turned to see the hypnotised man he had been fighting against. The man raised his blades. But before he could make a move, Mat lunged at him, taking him with her as she crashed to the floor and rolled out of the chamber.

"Go!" She turned her attention back to the hypnotised man and they started to duel.

Rapach froze, not knowing what to do. Nintai quickly took the key from him, inserted it in the top keyhole, and turned it.

"No, Mat!" Rapach couldn't stop the metal door from closing in front of him, and as the chamber rose, he turned to Nintai. "Why did you do that?"

"Rapach, do not underestimate your sister. This is our only chance. We can't risk unnecessary battles!"

"But we have three more potions! We can use one of them on the man!"

"Think about it, Rapach. If Erydis is really up there and we use one on her, that will leave us with two—one to research the cure and the other as a backup."

He knew she was right, but it was hard for him to admit it. He had gotten his sister back just to leave her behind again.

He could hear the faint sound of machinery above them, getting louder and louder.

"This is it." He took Erydis's sceptre from his belt. "We are so close. And you're right, Nintai. I shouldn't underestimate my sister."

The elevation chamber stopped and the doors opened.

Nintai and Rapach were silent as they entered the room in front of them. Covering every bit of the wall was what seemed like a mechanical rig, rapidly working as it released clouds of white dust. Much of the ceiling was covered in purple tubes that connected to another machine next to hundreds of jars containing purple dust. Rapach had never seen such machines in his life, and he was sure this one had to be one of the most complex pieces to have ever existed.

The room was illuminated by lamps hanging from the ceiling. There didn't seem to be any humans around.

"What is this place?" Nintai asked.

"This must be the machine that creates the dust from the mist. Erydis told me about this; the chamber at the top floor of the tower, a chamber she never got to see."

As they walked, they saw desks covered with piles of books and mixtures. Someone had spent many days there studying the dust.

They walked through the room, not spotting anyone—until they saw the doors to the balcony, on which two figures stood looking down at the city, their black and purple robes flapping in the wind. Both of them were wearing masks. One wore the lion mask and the other a mask with two long ears and a beak. The lost djinni mask. Erydis's mask.

Rapach started shaking as he stared at them. Erydis had grown up. She was almost as tall as the man in the lion mask. This puzzled Rapach, but this was no time to dwell on it.

Suddenly, the couple turned.

"So, you're the ones who caused the disturbance at Dijenia Tower," said a powerful, male voice, which must have belonged to Thylac. "I have to admit, I never thought anyone would reach this far in the Tower. Nobody gets here before falling victim to the miasma or the ones who slumber—unless I want them to.

"But you? A couple of children? I'm impressed."

The masked couple stared at each other. "Erydis…I wonder if this is what you meant."

"Thylac, you have to stop. Let Erydis go," Rapach said as he took a step forward.

"I don't know what you know about me," Thylac drawled, "but if you've heard of me, you'll know that getting any closer will be a terrible mistake. For each step you take, I can kill someone from the Jerboa Clan."

Rapach froze as he felt Benu squirm on top of his head. It was true. Thylac could kill anyone caught in a miasma storm.

"Did that mute boy, Eko, bring you here?" Thylac asked. Rapach said nothing. "He and that coward Kemia were the only ones who escaped the city. I searched everywhere for Eko, for ages, but he hid well. Well enough to bring you here, I suppose. But what intrigues me the most is how does this concern you? What's your name, boy?"

Rapach stared and spat, "Rapach, and Erydis told me to stop you."

"Rapach?" Thylac laughed. "So this is no coincidence. I thought you would be older. She spoke of you before, many years ago. I don't understand how this is possible, but you came too late. What did you think would happen? You'd kill me? Right now, as we talk, Silent People are marching here to get you. Did you think that distraction at the Dijenia Tower would help? Are you that stupid?"

Rapach took another step forward. In an instant, Thylac had a crimson knife pressed against Erydis's throat. Rapach froze, gritting his teeth.

"Do you want her to die?" Thylac asked softly. "Admit it. There's nothing you can do now."

"Leave her alone, or I'll put an arrow in your chest!" someone said from the side. It was Mat, holding a bow and pointing the arrow at Thylac. The cord was tense under her fingers.

"What?! How are you not in slumber?" Thylac asked, amazed. "You have the antidote she threw in the river, don't you?"

Mat frowned.

"Why do you hide behind one of your minions?" Mat asked. "Do you think I care about her? Give up or I'll kill you!"

Rapach stared at Mat, hoping she wouldn't hurt Erydis.

"Then why haven't you done it yet?" Thylac asked. "Are you aware of what will happen if you make a wrong move? Our attack on the Jerboa Clan was quite successful. I can kill all those under the influence of the miasma just by thinking about it. I can make them kill each other in seconds. Do you really want to take that risk?"

Mat blinked, perplexed, but didn't lower her bow.

"Now, give me the antidote," Thylac said menacingly. "Bring your pouches to me."

Mat, Rapach, and Nintai exchanged quick glances. Thylac had them exactly where he wanted them. One wrong move, and many would die.

Rapach unslung his pouch from his shoulder and approached Nintai, who shook her head vigorously at him.

"Give him your pouch," Thylac ordered with a booming voice.

Nintai formed a tight fist but obeyed.

Rapach walked over to Thylac with their pouches, hating himself with every step.

"Stop. Leave them on the floor and go back to the girl." Thylac pointed at Nintai.

Rapach did as he was told. He placed the pouches on the floor, still holding Erydis's device in the other hand.

"That thing you carry," Thylac said. "I know that's Erydis's experiment. I recognise that useless sceptre the Emperor used to carry with him. I remember she was quite fond of it before she threw it into the river. Too fond of it. Leave it on the floor as well."

Rapach hesitated but had no option and did as told. He stood up and walked back to Nintai.

"Go, dear Erydis." The person wearing Erydis mask started walking towards the pile Rapach had left on the floor, Thylac still holding a knife to her throat as he walked behind her.

Everyone stared as they slowly approached the pile on the floor. Rapach couldn't think what else to do other than to wait for the worst. But then something happened.

An arrow whistled through the air and pierced Thylac right in the ribs.

Rapach and Nintai looked at each other triumphantly.

"No! What have you done?!" As Thylac's powerful voice broke the silence, Rapach realised with a sinking feeling that the voice hadn't come from behind the lion mask.

Thylac's voice was coming from whom he thought was Erydis under the lost djinni mask.

It seemed Thylac had swapped his mask with hers, which meant that the person Mat had shot was...

"ERYDIS!" Rapach and Nintai ran to the figure in the lion mask, who slumped to the floor of the balcony with an arrow pierced through her ribs.

"You trickster!" Mat screamed, grabbing another arrow and shooting it at the real Thylac.

But just before the arrow struck, Thylac's dagger morphed into a round shield. The arrow broke uselessly against the shield's metallic surface.

"Coward. What sort of sorcery is this?" Mat asked.

"You would never understand the complexity of the dust," Thylac said triumphantly. "I swear to kill everyone in your clan unless you throw your bow far from you now."

Mat gritted her teeth but obeyed.

Rapach was cradling Erydis, taking the lion mask off her face.

It was really her. The exact same pale face and black hair, just a bit older. But her eyes, although staring at him, were soulless like the other Silent People, and Rapach could feel her blood dripping between his fingers.

"The lion mask!" Nintai said, picking it up.

"Stupid girl. If your intentions were to use the mask to control the ones who slumber, you won't be able to," Thylac said, pointing at Erydis's lost djinni mask. "This is now the mask that controls them."

"How dare you do this to her?" Rapach was furious. "She trusted you more than anyone else!"

"I tried to bring her back from her slumber," Thylac said in a pained voice as he took the lost djinni mask off his face. He looked lionesque, with wrinkles under silver and golden hair. His blue eyes looked pensive.

"I found a cure for the miasma to bring her back some years ago," he said. "I tried to convince her to help me, and even though she did for a time, she wouldn't listen to reason! Always telling me to change and bring everyone back. I was sure she was lying to me, trying to persuade me, so I used the miasma on her again, putting her back into a slumber, and destroyed any trace of an antidote."

Something was approaching from the elevation chamber.

Two identical djinnis appeared, walking elegantly up to Thylac. They flanked him, staring at everyone sinisterly with their red eyes.

Rapach could feel his heart pounding. He heard someone else coming from the elevator chamber. Deep inside he hoped it was Eko or Joie, but it could not be them. Instead, he felt hopeless as he saw Purple Breathers appear around them, staring silently.

Erydis's eyes were still soulless, blood from her wound pooling on the floor. Rapach passed her limp form to Nintai to hold and stood up to face Thylac. Nintai was crying as she looked down at Erydis.

"You were so close to her," Rapach said, unable to hide his anger. "If you cared so much for her, why did you swap your mask with hers? You knew you would put her in danger!"

"When you escaped Rabaska, I was sure you saw me controlling those who slumber and I knew I had to change my mask," Thylac said. He held up a flask containing a green liquid that he took from the folds of his robes. "Yes, I put her in danger, but she's not the Erydis I met a long time ago. That Erydis died when I gave her one last chance. But this new Erydis will always agree with me."

Rapach looked at Erydis, gritting his teeth.

"Please, girl. Put the lion mask back on her. I can't look at her with that stare." Thylac sounded furious and broken.

Nintai did as she was told.

"Now, Erydis, come to me." Thylac ordered.

He stared at Erydis as she stood up and walked towards him with the jarring, unnatural gait of the Silent People. She left a trail of blood on the floor behind her.

"Bring me their things," Thylac commanded, pointing at the pouch and the blue device on the floor. "It is time for the rest of you to fall into a slumber."

The Purple Breathers around them started exhaling miasma from their mouths, filling the chamber with swirling purple clouds. Mat ran to Rapach and Nintai on the balcony, looking terrified.

"What do we do?" she asked.

Rapach took something from his tunic. The last three blue flowers he had. He stared at Nintai and Mat, afraid, and gave them each a flower. The three of them chewed the flowers and hoped for the best, knowing that they would fall victim to Thylac and the Silent People once the immunity wore off.

"No," a female voice said suddenly, clear and familiar.

Erydis took off the lion mask. Her eyes were weak but awake.

Nintai patted Rapach on the shoulder, swiftly pulling an empty flask from under her tunic. She had given the antidote to Erydis.

Erydis grabbed her experiment from the floor and quickly turned the knob. The sphere on the top rotated and a large blue flame appeared, absorbing the miasma as the device vibrated in her hands.

"Erydis?! It can't be! No matter...my djinnis will tear you apart," Thylac shouted.

As the djinnis approached Erydis, the blue flame consumed their solid flesh, turning their feet into crumbling dust. They jumped backwards, trying to escape the blue flame as if they were getting burnt.

"Huh? What is happening?!" Thylac asked, bewildered.

"You forgot something very important, Thylac!" Erydis said with a smile. Her voice was the same as Rapach remembered it, but more mature. "The djinnis are made of dust! And my device absorbs all kinds of dust!!"

The djinnis howled as they tried to get away, but the blue flame continued to engulf them fiercely, until they disappeared entirely.

This was Rapach's only chance. He stood up, the blue flower in his mouth, pulled his goggles over his eyes, and sprinted towards Thylac while Erydis absorbed more of the growing cloud of miasma with her device.

Rapach jumped on Thylac.

"What are you doing?!" Thylac resisted as Rapach tried to grab the lost djinni mask from his face. Purple Breathers ran towards them and tried to pull Rapach off Thylac.

But even though they were clawing violently at him, Rapach would not give up. He pulled at the mask with all his might until its belts snapped, and it fell to the ground. Rapach quickly put the mask over his face and breathed in the earthy perfume created by the green liquid. Stop, he thought.

The Purple Breathers around him immediately obeyed his thoughts and froze even as new miasma filled the room, surrounding Thylac.

"Give it back! I can't fall into a slumber! My mask...my..." Thylac's eyes turned purple as he breathed in the miasma, his face frozen in a terrified expression.

The blue flame absorbed the rest of the miasma until every last bit it was turned into white dust, covering the floor around Erydis.

Erydis fell, sending a cloud of white dust billowing up around her.

Rapach ran to her and Benu jumped from his head to nudge her hand urgently. She was still bleeding. Rapach sat down and gently brushed her hair from her face.

"Quick…tell me how to fix this," he pleaded. "A mixture…or, or perhaps—"

"You naive dream boy," Erydis said softly. "You look exactly the way you did when I met you all those years ago."

Rapach's eyes were brimming with tears. Erydis smiled at him, a weak but genuine smile.

"What…what will I do…without…"

"Me?" she chuckled weakly. "You have time to fix this broken city and build what Thylac could never imagine. You are indeed naive but not dumb. Find someone to recreate the antidote so you can cure everyone. Take this…"

She took a piece of blue amber broken in two from her robes. Benu's ears perked up as she looked at it intently. It had been the jerboa's home once.

"I need you. I need you here," Rapach said.

"And I will be. You will always have our memories from the Vault of Echoes."

Her eyes grew weaker and weaker as her strength left her body.

"Tell Eko...he did good." She closed her eyes.

Erydis Nott left them with a smile.

Chapter XXVX

Farewell

Rapach

Everything was a blur as they stepped out onto the streets.

Rapach had ordered all the Silent People to gather in the city. As he, Nintai, and Mat reunited with Joie and Eko, they could see the hypnotised walking the streets. All the people who once lived inside the city's walls as well as members of the Vakandi and Jerboa clans. There were many victims of the miasma, but that would eventually change.

Telling Eko what had happened to Erydis was what had hurt Rapach the most, but even though the old man cried, there was a faint smile on his face. He then wrote something on a piece of paper.

"*In sorrowful times, we should never be a victim of sadness. We shall treasure each moment of contentment, and smile in memory of what she did for us all.*"

Although Eko's words warmed his heart, Rapach could not stop feeling terrible as they took Erydis to the gardens of the Dust Academy and stood silently next to where she would lie for eternity.

Rapach held on to her device as dearly as she once had, understanding that his task in Dust City was far from complete.

He took Erydis's mask and wore it to summon Herra, as Eko suggested.

Herra would surely know how to replicate the antidote to help save everyone else from the effects of the miasma.

As he approached wearing a white turban, Eko noticed that Herra hadn't aged a day. They used one of the two antidotes they had left on him, and he woke up with a dazed and confused look on his face. It wasn't easy, but they explained to him all that had happened in Dust City since he fell into his slumber, and gave him the last antidote and the blue amber pieces to try and make more.

"So Kemia created this..." Herra examined the antidote thoughtfully. "It will take some time, but I will find a way to simplify her formula and use it to help cure all these poor people. There's work to be done, and I will ask all of you to please help me." Rapach bowed his head and nodded. He had a new mission now.

Nintai and Joie took their leave, hoping to find more djinnis and members of their clan to liberate.

When they were alone, Eko asked Rapach if he could order his brother to come back to him. He wanted to see him again, even though they hadn't parted ways on the best terms. But Ferus never arrived.

Rapach felt sad, but seeing Eko try to smile in such a moment gave him hope for what was to come.

"Eko, can you take me to where she lived?" Rapach blushed, embarrassed, but he felt like he needed to see how real it all had been.

Eko did not ask why. He just nodded and led Rapach to a simple sandstone building and up an old ladder.

As Rapach entered the old room, he could sense Erydis's presence somehow. It was like she had been living there all along. Her bed was covered in clothes, and many jars lined the walls alongside pots with plants of different colours. On her desk were piles of books, a sign that she once spent days on her research and experiments.

Eko patted him on the back and walked out of the house. Rapach was alone with Benu for the first time. In silence. His heart was heavy as he imagined Erydis at that desk in front of him, writing away into the night.

Then something caught Rapach's eye. On the table was a leather-bound book, yellow with age. It was lying open to a page with some underlined words. He got closer and read the paragraph.

"Most probably, dreams are subconscious resonations of our memories. But sometimes dreams seem to reveal more than just what we've once sensed. In those instances, the dreams might take us to places we've never travelled to, and at times, they introduce us to meaningful people we would never have otherwise encountered."

Rapach saw something written in the lower corner of the page. "Rapach."

He smiled and closed the book. He placed Erydis's device on the desk. Then he lay down on her bed on top of all the dusty clothes. He stared at the ceiling until his tired eyes finally found rest once more.

Return To The Vault

Rapach opened his eyes, but he did not feel awake. He was in the Vault of Echoes again. Blue torches illuminated his surroundings as he stood on the familiar white sand. He stared at the black tree, but the clock had disappeared from its trunk. Was this a dream? Or was he really back?

He stared at his surroundings and sat down on the ground next to the tree, on a bed of blue flowers. He smiled, thinking of the time he first met Erydis Nott, when he sang that song with five notes and no words. But as he once again remembered her face, he broke into tears.

"Why the sobbing, dream boy?"

Rapach stood up and slowly turned around. There, next to a blue torch illuminating her face, was Erydis. Just like the day they met, before his life was changed forever. He froze, staring at her for a long time.

"Rapa—?" Erydis couldn't finish her sentence. Rapach sprinted towards her and hugged her tightly, lifting her off the ground.

"What the—" She seemed confused.

"Is this real? Why are you here?"

"Rapach, what happened?"

Rapach looked at her, frowning. "I don't understand. We went to the city and we stopped Thylac. But you…I saw you die."

"Oh…So you found me."

"But now you're here! This must be a dream. I'm sure I saw you—"

"Don't…say it. So that's my destiny. At least I have a long time until that happens."

"What? What do you mean?"

"Oh, you naive dream boy, you're not thinking about time. You saw me dying in your world. But in mine I was just taken by the miasma. I'm alive in my time!"

Rapach stared at her and slowly smiled.

"There's so much I need to explain," he said. "The old man was..."

"I know."

"And inside the package was..."

"I know."

"You don't have to be so annoying about it, you know?" Rapach said teasingly, scratching his head.

"I missed you as well, Rapach," Erydis said. "So you made it...I wish that I could say the same. But I was sure you would, Rapach. The moment before I was taken, I could see it all happening in front of me. I knew Eko would find my device and the antidotes. And I knew you would be the one to bring him the missing piece. And you did great. Yet I wonder what is in store for me."

She stared at the ground in fear. Rapach grabbed her shoulder.

"I know what you're thinking, and I won't let it happen, Erydis."

Erydis stared at him, hopeful.

"There must be a way to bring you back," Rapach said. "Like you once told me, to use the dust you just need to understand it. Maybe it's the same in the vault!"

Erydis looked down and chuckled as she shook her head.

"I guess I have no other choice but to assist you," she said.

"You have to...you left me with a city that needs to be fixed! Do you know how difficult that will be for a kid like me?"

"Now you're just being silly."

"So, will you help me?"

"I'm not going anywhere, Rapach..."

They smiled gently at each other and sat down with their backs against the tree, just like they had once before. They talked about everything that had happened and everything that was to come, knowing that the Vault of Echoes would bring them together once more in that impossible place.

Aknowledgement

This story first started knocking around in my head back in 2014, probably while I was waiting on renders—as CG artists often do. Between 2015 and 2017, I managed to wrangle those ideas into a manuscript, and by 2018, it was officially finished. Since then, I've spent an unreasonable amount of time bending my friends' ears about it, so this section is for all of you who've listened to me ramble on (and on) about this book.

First off, massive thanks to my beta readers: Leonardo Bonisolli, Andres Campero, Susan Gaigher, and everyone else who had the patience to read and offer feedback. You all made this book better in ways I couldn't have managed alone. A special thanks to Susan and Iman Ghosh for editing my first full novel and believing in its potential.

To Laura Cifuentes, your encouragement gave me the final push I needed to design my own cover and take the leap to publication—thank you. To my parents and sister, your unwavering support and constant presence have been my anchor through this journey.

Thank you to the Peakys for standing by me all these years, and to my friends in Mexico, Vancouver, Montreal, and around the world. Your diverse perspectives and shared stories have inspired and enriched my own storytelling. And to Eric Childs, who gamely listened to me debate the title until I finally landed on it.

Lastly, to you, dear reader: may this book give you dreams of a vault full with colors and welcoming strangers.

About the Author

Hi, I'm Roy F. Ayala. I'm a writer, and a Lighting and Compositing Artist for animated films and TV shows, who finally stopped waiting on renders long enough to write a book. Based in Canada, I draw inspiration for my stories from every corner of the world, believing that the more perspectives you understand, the easier it is to empathize with people and craft stories that feel authentic and vivid.

Some of the projects I've had the privilege to work on include Thelma the Unicorn, Paw Patrol: The Mighty Movie, Monsters at Work, Elena of Avalor, Netflix's Daredevil, The Umbrella Academy, Carnival Row, and more.

With this publication, I'm beginning my writing career and sharing the first of many stories I've long dreamed of telling. Some are still in the editing process, while others are waiting to be written. I'm thrilled to have you join me on this journey. Nice to meet you all!

www.rodrigokhervfx.com

www.ingramcontent.com/pod-product-compliance
Lightning Source LLC
LaVergne TN
LVHW091256150826
845673LV00006B/1437

* 9 7 8 1 0 6 9 1 4 0 4 0 1 *